# BANANAVILLE

# BANANAVILLE

## JAMES LILLIEFORS

ST. MARTIN'S PRESS

NEW YORK

005 539 492

A portion of this book appeared, in different form, in *Ploughshares*.

A THOMAS DUNNE BOOK.
An imprint of St. Martin's Press

Design by Ellen R. Sasahara

Library of Congress Cataloging-in-Publication Data

Lilliefors, James.
      Bananaville  /  by James Lilliefors.—1st ed.
            p.      cm.
      "A Thomas Dunne book."
      ISBN 0-312-14548-9
      I. Title
      PS3562.I4573B3        1996
      813'.54—dc20                              96-20051
                                                      CIP

First Edition: October 1996

10   9   8   7   6   5   4   3   2   1

*For my father and Liliane*

Thanks to: Neal Bascomb, for having faith in this project; Maria Cote and the folks at the Naples *Daily News;* Amy Bennett and *Gulfshore Life* magazine; and, as always, Linda and Glory.

We are a people who do not want to
keep much of the past in our heads. It is
considered unhealthy in America to remember
mistakes, neurotic to think about them,
psychotic to dwell upon them.

—LILLIAN HELLMAN

....................

Sin that pays its way can travel
freely and without a passport; whereas
Virtue, if a pauper, is stopped at
all frontiers.

—HERMAN MELVILLE

# BANANAVILLE

# Introduction

ON A WARM misty morning in December, City Councilman Rudolph Reed learned exactly how he was going to die.

For a moment, the revelation petrified him. Although Reed had thought occasionally of his own death, it was always as a clock ticking in some other room. A subject he didn't need to look at just yet.

He was forty-five, small and sturdy, with serene blue eyes; but weathered features made him seem ten years older. Often he wore the grim expression of a man who knew just where he was going—which, until that misty morning in December, Rudolph Reed thought he did.

He had arrived at Bananaville Beach minutes before sunrise for his usual three-mile run, followed by twenty minutes of meditation—dressed in the same standard-issue gray-white gym uniform he required of his middle school students.

For nearly forty minutes, the only sounds on the secluded stretch of beach were a steady scuff of surf on seashells, the occasional cries of gulls, and Reed's muffled grunts.

By the time he finished, sunlight was blazing moistly through the mangroves and the city's skyline glinted at him across the Gulf. He sat by water's edge to cool down, tasting the briny air as he gazed at his city. Mornings, it seemed to shimmer—its mirrored buildings and lush winter flowers looked as magical to Reed as they had seven years ago when he first brought his family down.

Before the sun cleared the trees, before the mist burned away, it was easy to forget the things that Rudolph Reed had learned about this too prosperous place—that he often saw with stark clarity in the bright spaces of afternoon: Something was very wrong in Bananaville.

There were things he could do about it—things he had to do.

Soon.

Rudolph Reed sat in the sand and seashells—the same place he meditated every morning—and stared agreeably at the mist, watching as the sky brightened, struck again by the illusory way the town and the enormous Bananaland amusement park seemed to merge into one, even though the two were set on separate peninsulas. After a while, he began to walk back to his old station wagon—to the things he had to do—feeling revitalized by the exercise and cool breezes. Routine and ritual had the power of anchoring a man to some force larger than the body, and he had started his mornings this way for more than six years.

Along an isolated curve of beach, where breeze rippled the sparkles of blue-green bay, he lifted his head to a sound of heron wings beating into the air, and then saw a man, stepping purposefully among the dying mangroves.

Rudolph stopped as the man came nearer, prepared for a moment to extend his hand in greeting. He had long since stopped being surprised by the sight of some wayward stranger wanting to meet him. Reed's political supporters, he had found, were liable to show up anywhere, at any time. Even as the business community derisively tagged his constituents the "Reed-jects," they had grown into the largest political faction in town.

Reed smiled faintly, seeing that the man was dressed in crusty work boots, faded jeans, and an enormous black T-shirt. In his right hand he carried a long-necked flashlight.

But then Rudolph Reed realized that something was wrong: The man's face, as he came closer, was only a blur. It didn't seem to be there at all. No matter how hard Rudolph tried to focus on the man's features, to get a fix on who he was, there was nothing there to see. The man had no face.

That was when Rudolph Reed realized exactly how he was going to die, and he stared, with unready eyes, never having imagined the campaign would end this way.

Two minutes later, it had happened—the flashlight had shattered his skull, and stopped the machinery of Rudolph Reed's thoughts. As the man in the stocking mask retreated into the mangroves, tiny waves broke against the back of Reed's head, and spilled over his shoulders. Farther out, pelicans dove into the Gulf after fish.

There was a bright familiar stillness in the air as the rest of Bananaville woke up that morning.

**1**

MARTIN GRANT CROSSED the border into Bananaville on a balmy Monday afternoon, twenty-seven days after they killed Rudolph Reed.

His decision to leave the Midwest, and the vestiges of a successful, respectable life there, had surprised many in the conservative corn-farming community of Hamlet, Iowa. For Martin, it had felt as natural as shifting gears in an automobile; the engine of his life in Hamlet had been grinding in the wrong gear for weeks.

Twelve days earlier he had answered an ad in *Editor and Publisher* magazine for a "seasoned investigative reporter."

"Have a nose for news? Willing to do what it takes to get the story? Able to write succinctly in a style that titillates? Give us a try. Daily in America's fastest-growing city has immediate opening."

Martin Grant had spent nearly half of his life working in newspapers, much of it as an enterprise reporter for metropolitan dailies—pursuing with near-obsessive diligence what his wife, Katie, chidingly called "the Big Story." His job was to solve mysteries, to ferret out truths about human hungers and motivations. Yet despite a shelf full of awards, Martin still hadn't come upon a story that was commensurate with his own ambitions or expectations; the Big Story had somehow eluded him.

Six months ago, he had turned forty, and agreed to trade in his reporter's quest to become editor and general manager of his hometown newspaper. He and Katie—willowy, perpetually free-spirited, an antiques trader—had returned to Hamlet in June, bought a small farmhouse by the grain co-op, and begun talking again about having children. In revisiting the paths of their youth, they seemed at first to reconnect to simpler, better ways of living. But the marriage, quietly fraying for years, had come apart all at once in the fall, several weeks after Martin stopped drinking. The story Katie told him, drunkenly and tearfully, was the one he had hoped he wouldn't have to hear: Katie had begun seeing Harold Mason, the hard-drinking antiques dealer she had dated as a teenager; she thought she was falling in love with him. Martin realized later—after Katie moved away, to an apartment in town—that drinking had been the glue holding them together for months, and maybe years. It had been anesthesia, their futile means of preserving something that had once breathed with promise.

THE CALL FROM Bananaville came on a snowy Wednesday evening. Peter Fudd, publisher of the *Bananaville Daily News*, had read Martin's clips, and sounded ready to hire him.

"I just have a feeling," he said, and chuckled amiably, "reading your stories, you're the one we're looking for. Of course, I've always been partial to midwesterners."

Martin chuckled, too, at the surprising resolve in the man's gentle southern twang. He stared at the thickening snow, struck by the evanescence of everything he had done and thought during fourteen years with Katie. These were his horizons—the McGinters' farmhouse, the gray outlines of their grain elevators, the distant glow from the city. Horizons that hadn't changed much since childhood and probably, he suspected, never would. Yet in the past several weeks he had felt his interior landscapes— the things he saw when he looked at himself—becoming fuzzy and unfamiliar. And maybe that was okay.

There were several "right good" stories in Bananaville, Peter Fudd explained, the connection crackling across the miles, stories crying out for a seasoned investigative reporter. "We got one in particular," he said, "that's a real peach."

"Can you tell me?"

"Do what?"

"About the story." Crackle, crackle. "I mean—is it politics? zoning? cops?"

Peter Fudd was chuckling again.

"I like your curiosity, Martin, if I can call you that. I think we're going to hit it off just fine. Always have been partial to mid-westerners. No, listen, Martin? You just come on down, and I'll tell you everything you want to know. And if you're of a mind to, I can probably put you right to work. May even be able to find you a place to stay, too. Don't worry about expenses. We cover all that."

Three days later Martin had left the snowy plains of central Iowa, enticed by the promise of warm breezes, fresh stories, and a moderate salary increase. He was only going down to have a look, he told himself—though as he traveled farther from the frozen midwest he couldn't think of many good reasons to return. He had become a genial and sober loner—a quiet, likable man with graying hair and large hazel eyes. They were eyes that drew people in, without telling them much.

Martin still believed that good things were ahead, he just didn't believe it as often as he once had. He knew too much now—and realized that if he didn't return to Hamlet, his reputation there would melt like the snow by springtime, and be changed forever, from respectable journalist to troubled wanderer. With two notable exceptions—his uncle Otis twenty-some years earlier, and his cousin Nellie five years ago—the Grants did not leave central Iowa. They stayed close—they farmed, raised families, joined civic associations, retired. There was a long, straight two-lane on the north border of Hamlet called Old Grant Road; it was named for Martin's grandfather. The forested land his family owned to the south was still called Grantsville by most of the old-timers. That was where Martin had been born—in Grantsville—the first of four children, all of whom still lived within twelve miles of one another.

Sometimes, he supposed, it was necessary to make a turn you never expected—or wanted—to take in order to get where you had to go. As he drove away from what he knew, Martin thought increasingly about his uncle Otis and Nellie—both of whom had also left in winter, headed to this same part of the country, in search of something better. Never to be heard from again.

M ARTIN  G RANT FOLLOWED the directions he had scribbled in a steno pad
Sunday night in Iowa: Take the coast
road south for eleven miles. Turn inland at Mango Drive. Go two miles,
past tomato and pepper fields and a
huge orange-shaped souvenir shop, to Riverside and turn right.
The *Daily News* would be there at the road's end.

At first glance, Bananaville seemed to Martin impossibly
lush, with thick growths of banana and bamboo, bright splashes
of winter flowers and shiny green lawns. The air was scented with
citrus and sea breeze—an exciting taste that reminded him of
childhood afternoons. As he turned onto Riverside, and his
wagon slow-rocked down the gravel road between oaks and pines,
he sensed something else, though—something mysterious and
unknowable in the horizontal flickers of sunlight. Parking in the
shade, Martin saw several people sitting on the deck of the newspaper office—an old rectangular wooden building that might
have once been a boathouse. Mounting the steps, he rose to the
eye level of a florid-faced man in a pin-striped suit, and took
pause—the man was slumped unnaturally against the wall as if
he had been shot.

An exotic-looking woman in a dark red leather miniskirt and
sleeveless ribbed top was behind him, striking a model's pose
along the old wooden rail. Martin began to introduce himself
when a man of enormous girth lifted from a rocking chair and
rushed toward him.

"Martin!?" he said, with an aggressive cheer. "Is that you?
How are you?"

The man clutched his right hand, and vigorously shook up and down, familiarly, as if he knew Martin.

Was it possible?

Martin smiled back uncertainly.

Although he hadn't seen his uncle Otis in twenty-four years, this, he imagined, was just how he would look: great-bellied and gray, with narrow, squinting eyes and a carnival barker's voice. He would probably be dressed this way, too: in a seersucker suit and straw hat.

The man finally extended his hand for a more formal—subdued—shake.

"Peter Fudd," he said, still shaking. A garden of gray hairs, Martin noticed, grew from his nostrils. "Welcome. Glad you could make it. Come on in, let me show you around."

Martin had expected Peter Fudd would be younger—that he would have a slyer, more conservative demeanor. Fudd walked with an odd bounce as he led the way through Life, Business, Real Estate, and Sports. His arms dangled like props, though his fingers moved incessantly, as if typing.

"Glad you could make it, Martin," he said, for perhaps the fifth time, as they reached the door to his office.

He opened and ushered Martin inside. The large room was unlit.

"How was the trip?"

"Fine."

"Good, good. Have a seat right here, Martin, and take a look through the paper." He added, "While I go get myself some ice."

Fudd's office was paneled in dark walnut, decorated with wicker furniture, bead curtains, potted palms. A Casablanca fan spun overhead, and the sound of ocean surf hissed softly from enormous stereo speakers behind his executive's desk. As Martin paged through the paper, impressed by its heft, its glitzy graphics and splashy use of color, he was startled to see a stuffed Bengal tiger watching from the shadows. It made him gaze more carefully around the room: There were three wildebeest skulls mounted on the walls, along with a several-hundred-pound blue marlin. Numerous framed black-and-white photos showed Pete Fudd on the docks, displaying various large game fish.

"Here we are."

He surprised Martin, coming in with a tall glass and bucket of ice. "Now, then. What do you say we get to know each other? I just have a feeling I'm going to like you, Martin."

They talked easily, and inconsequentially, mostly about newspapers, for close to an hour, Pete Fudd jotting tiny notes occasionally on a memo pad, smiling mysteriously whenever Martin began to speak. Like several small-town newspaper publishers Martin had known over the years, he seemed disarmingly eccentric, in a way that no doubt masked a keen business sense.

"Oh, and Martin," he interrupted, looking up from the notepad. "I believe I told you I'd try and find you a place to stay? Good news." At last the straw hat came off, revealing thin white hair combed back and tonicked, the lines of skin as distinct as rows in his dead father's cornfields. "I found one. Now, why don't you just take a couple of days to get comfortable in this little town. Get to know it, make sure you want to stay." Martin raised his hand, to indicate he wanted to speak, and Peter Fudd shook his head. "You don't even have to worry about filing a story for the first few days if you don't want to."

"You mentioned there was one story in particular I'd be covering—if I were to take the job."

"Yes."

His eyebrows cocked slightly as he kneaded the rim of the hat. A smile leaked uneasily into his face. Wind parted the bead curtains and Martin saw the bright green soup of afternoon mist outside, the sparkles of river water.

"But, of course, there's no hurry on that."

"Maybe," Martin prodded, "if I knew what it was, I'd just have a better idea of what the job might hold in store."

"Possibly." Frowning thoughtfully, Fudd rubbed at his eyes and then below his chin several times with the back of his left hand. Martin noticed a strange, pistachio-shaped bug crawling up the front of his desk.

11

"What it is," he said, at last, "is a story that we believe can sell us a few newspapers." His eyes seemed to twinkle distantly as he added, "It involves a crime that can't be solved."

"Ah."

The gears of Martin's journalistic instincts suddenly engaged.

"Please," he said, softly. "Tell me."

Fudd smiled, and Martin, waiting, saw that his face was a sort of medley—dark and rheumy eyes beneath bushy white brows, a broad chiseled nose, and small, dainty lips. Using pincers, Fudd transferred five ice cubes, one at a time, from the bucket to his glass. As sweat slid in fan-breeze down his face, he pulled from an inner pocket of his suit coat perhaps the largest handkerchief Martin had ever seen and delicately patted his forehead. Finally, with a protracted grunt, Pete Fudd pulled a file folder, bursting with newspaper clippings, from the top drawer of his desk.

"Rudolph Reed," he said, stroking the folder with wet fingers before he pushed it over to Martin. "Drowned here twenty-seven days ago. These are some clippings you can read if you'd like—although, as I say, there's no rush. Take them home if you want. Get yourself settled in first. Get acquainted with the town. I think you're going to like it here. It's the friendliest place in the country, we like to think. Also, the cleanest."

Martin glanced curiously at the newspaper clippings while Fudd, slumped into a nearly supine position, held up his glass of ice cubes, and moved it across the window's light stream, his eyes transfixed with childlike fascination. When he stopped talking, Fudd's breathing was raspy, like that of a man asleep.

"He was a city councilman."

"Correct. Grassroots politician. A nice fellow, actually. Who tended to get under the skin of the business community." He poured an ice cube in his mouth and chewed it loudly until there was no more to chew, then sat up and set the glass on his desk. "On the other hand," he said, "he seemed to strike a chord in the rest of the community. I didn't fully understand it, to be honest with you. But that's why I think we can sell a few newspapers. You see, there's a mystery there."

12

Martin nodded, keeping his head down. Ocean surf ebbed and then crashed. Something about Peter Fudd's concept of investigative reporting bothered him, but Martin didn't want to pass judgment so quickly; he glanced up and Fudd was smiling, as though listening to his thoughts.

"This town has attracted a lot of people, Martin. Let me tell you. I like to divide them into three groups: There's the business folks, who see this as a place to make their fortunes—and many of them have. There's the retired people, who see it as a place to spend their fortunes. And then, there's the other folks.

"Reed more or less represented the 'other folks,' and I don't think any of us really understood how many of them there were out there until he came along."

Behind his desk, Fudd stood and elaborately extended his bottom outward, toward Martin, as if mooning him. The tape of ocean surf had ended and he was inserting another into the cassette deck.

"Very relaxing," he said, seated again. "Helps me think." He stared at Martin until the new tape began to play. The sound now was not waves, but the slowly building rhythm of a locomotive train.

"The 'other folks,' " Martin prompted.

"Yes. Yes, these are the people who have maybe taken a wrong turn or two in their lives. They see this as a place to start over again—which it is. We believe very strongly in that. Now, individually, of course, the 'other folks' might be considered . . ." He paused, as if searching for the word. Martin noticed a faint tremor in his liver-spotted hand as he moved a pen set meaninglessly on the desk. "*Losers*, for lack of a better word. But Rudolph became a voice for them, and that was all they needed. In a very short time, they had become a powerful political force here. The Reedjects, we called them."

His eyes seemed suffused with humor, although the rest of his expression was placid. Thunder pealed from the stereo suddenly, followed by a violent downpour of rain.

"Rejects?"

"*Reed*-jects. That's what the business community called them, anyway. At any rate, it's a peach of a story, Martin. Once you get to understand it."

He was up again, this time standing in the huge, empty walk-in closet, hanging his jacket. The loose-fitting white dress shirt stuck to the middle of his back in a long wet stain the approximate shape of Chile.

"You said it was a drowning, though," Martin called to him. "Where does the crime come in?"

"Well—*tech*nically a drowning."

He didn't speak again until the jacket was hung, the door closed, and the glass of ice back in his hands. "But there were abrasions and lacerations and—one of them, they say, may have even fractured the skull, I don't know." He added, cryptically, "I suspect there's been very little investigative work."

The bug on the desk, Martin noticed, had changed direction and was now earnestly moving toward the floor.

"What about the police?"

Peter Fudd shrugged, smiling soberly at all that Martin didn't yet understand, and he shifted elaborately in his chair. "Of course, they're looking at it. But how closely? It remains to be seen. I don't know quite how to put this, Martin, but . . . the police here, of course, are, in a sense, sworn to protect life and limb, that goes without saying. But I like to say they're also here to protect what I call the appearance of prosperity." He drew out "appearance" with southern inflections. "The image that this town has worked very hard over the years to cultivate.

"It goes back to something my daddy used to say: It isn't what you are that counts, it's what people *think* you are. There's a very important lesson there."

Tarnished teeth emerged from behind his lips, and Fudd's down-home persona seemed to evaporate, leaving a hard-edged, unpleasant entrepreneur.

There was a long silence. Ice popped in his glass, wind stirred shadows against the wall. Another sheet of rain gusted through the stereo speakers.

"Why do you say it can't be solved, though?"

"Well: no witnesses, no evidence, no weapon recovered. But, you see, that only makes for a more interesting story, doesn't it? We're not going to solve this thing, Martin, but what we're going to do is *titi*llate. You see?" Martin smiled politely and nodded. Fudd's sense of journalism was, clearly, different from his own. Still, there was in all likelihood a story here that went far beyond the one Peter Fudd had just told.

"At any rate. We're getting ahead of ourselves, aren't we?" Fudd used the tongs to remove another cube from the bucket. He dropped the ice in his left hand and slowly rubbed it across his brow. His face contorted serenely, as sunlight glared through a sliver of bead curtain with urgent radiance. "No, don't worry about any of this yet. Take a day or two to get settled. See how you like the house. Get to know the town." He looked at the ice cube in his hand as if uncertain how it had gotten there, and set it back in the ice bucket. Then he slid down, pulled out his top drawer, and removed a document.

"The house I found for you, it's a jewel, an absolute jewel. Searched high and low for it. Pretty place, all the amenities. A tropical garden, lots of privacy." He pushed the document—a lease?—over the desk. Martin began to protest, but Fudd had his hand raised. "Don't sign this yet, Martin. Until you've spent a couple of days there. No obligation. If you decide you want it, we've got a week to wrap up the deal. You can have it for seven hundred dollars a month. And we can write it with an option to buy, if that's what you'd like."

When they shook again, standing in the doorway beside the stuffed Bengal tiger, Pete Fudd's hand was cold and damp.

**3** THE HOUSE PETER FUDD had found was old and wooden, on one of Bananaville's narrow lanes, largely hidden behind sprawling live oaks, palmetto, and wild banana trees. Like the newspaper office, it was at road's end, pleasantly secluded from the bustling city. The only other residence on the street was a salmon-colored stucco house with oval Spanish entryways and a shaded courtyard. From his bedroom window, Martin could see nets of sunshine glittering through the oaks in a small blue swimming pool around back.

He lay on the brass bed that afternoon and felt the wind as it made a steady sound like running water in the leaves outside. He smelled the fresh sheets and pillowcases and tried to really absorb, for the first time since Peter Fudd called on Wednesday, what he was doing.

And then Martin remembered his uncle Otis, and wondered what had happened to him down here. When Martin was ten, Otis had left Hamlet for this same part of the country, to open a tourist-based business that he seemed convinced couldn't fail. At first, there had been cards and letters from him every few days, dispatches in which Otis told of a place with "bluer than blue" skies, beaches "like Domino sugar," and "palms growing like dandelions." A place so fertile you could pull your breakfast right from the trees—oranges "the size of softballs," great pink grapefruits, mangoes, wild bananas, peaches, and coconuts. "It's as if I've discovered paradise itself!" he proclaimed in one of several letters addressed directly to Martin.

For a few weeks that winter, as snow froze in drifts against the side of the farmhouse, Martin harbored a secret—a notion all his own, as reassuring as the feel of the homemade quilt against his face on a windy night: when he turned sixteen, Martin, too, would travel south to the Gulf. He would take a job in his uncle's Paradise Gifts shop and pick oranges every morning with Otis.

But another summer came. The Hamlet corn grew tall, then turned brown and withered, and Uncle Otis was gone, never to be heard from again. All Martin would ever learn, after repeated questioning, was that there had been problems down there— troubles Otis had not foreseen. The shop, his father explained one late August afternoon, "was situated wrong," on a swampy rural two-lane that tourists rarely traveled. Otis, he went on, when Martin failed to be mollified, "has always had a soul like a leaky rowboat. Ever since he was a boy, he's been setting off on journeys he couldn't complete."

The words were as startling to Martin as they were incomprehensible, and he never forgot them. He recalled them again now, lying in a dusty bedroom as evening sunlight glinted in the tree branches outside.

Martin pulled on his running clothes and went out, into the green dusk, for a forty-minute run, exploring neighborhoods shaded by willows and oaks and ficus, where sprinklers clicked in the yards and air conditioners hummed. He saw people sitting in living rooms and around dinner tables, interiors sharpening like Polaroid pictures in the darkening air, and he felt something stir inside, something distantly familiar, and faintly delicious. Something he couldn't touch, couldn't yet know.

Afterward, he sat on the iron scrolled step of the old house and let the breeze dry the sweat on his skin. He stared at the near stars of lightning bugs, winking in the live oaks, and thought about frozen Iowa—about meeting Katie Thompson once in a church parking lot. For a few moments he discerned a deep emptiness out there, a sense that his life's investments had all been lost. He recalled precisely the rich burning taste of iced bourbon in his lungs, remembered Katie's intense, drunken eyes the last time he saw her, and felt temptation well up and dissi-

17

pate in another breath of tropical breeze, conscious that this air seemed to be lulling him, dimming his reporter's instincts. The wind came in regular exhalations now and Martin closed his eyes and imagined that what he was feeling was the town itself.

Breathing.

IT WAS A LONG SHOT, but Martin figured he might as well try. There was one "N. Grant" in the Bananaville telephone book, listed on Butterfly Boulevard.

Did she still call herself Grant, after three marriages? he wondered as he dialed on the 1970s-style wall phone.

The last he had heard, Nellie was working for a state attorney's office somewhere in this part of the country. But it was four or five years ago, and no one, not even Nellie's mother, had heard a word from her since. Before leaving Hamlet, Martin had called his aunt Grace to ask about Nellie, and found it was still a sore subject. "I have nothing to say about her, Martin. If you want to ask me about my daughter Jane or my son Thomas, that's different—"

"Hello?"

"Nellie Grant, please."

"Yes. Who's this?"

The voice sounded tentative and unfamiliar.

"This is Martin. Martin Grant."

"Martin Grant," she repeated.

"Yes."

*"Martin Grant?"*

"Yes."

*"Martin Grant?* Get out of here! Where the hell *are* you?"

As Martin told her, Nellie's exclamations of "I can't believe it!" became increasingly dramatic, punctuated by familiar whoops—"Ah-wooo! Ah-wooo!"—which made him smile.

Though Nellie and Martin were not close, one summer long ago—Martin wasn't yet fourteen—she had stayed at the family farmhouse for six weeks, energetically helping them shell corn and feed horses, happily eating his mother's meat pies and, late at night, sitting with Martin on a rusty swing and telling him stories, in hushed tones, about men and women she had known and the numerous sexual acts they had "performed" on one another.

By late July, as hot winds rattled through the dead cornstalks and the constellations glittered clearly with the promise of a racy new world Nellie had already seen, Martin developed an enormous, and ultimately heartbreaking, crush on her. Martin wondered now what had happened to Nellie's third marriage, wondered how she looked. And if she was happy.

"Well," she said. "We'll have to go out and catch up over dinner tonight, won't we?"

"Okay."

"I can't be*lieve* this."

"Where would you like to meet?"

"How about—meet me at the Paradise Club at seven-thirty?"

"Okay."

"And, Martin . . ."

"What?"

"Nothing. Nothing, I just can't be*lieve* it. Ah-wooo!"


Seated at the kitchen table, Martin stared for a long time into the trees, wondering if he should have a drink or two with Nellie. *If he would.* He opened the folder of Rudolph Reed clippings and glanced through several of them.

Reed had come to Bananaville seven years earlier, bringing his large family down from West Virginia and finding work as a history and PE teacher at the middle school. A staunch opponent of high-rises and, it seemed, virtually all other development, he had led petition drives and letter-writing campaigns, winning enough support four years ago to be elected to the system he had crusaded against. His term was slated to run out with the March elections.

But on December 10 Reed's body had been found on a secluded stretch of Bananaville Beach. The first week's news accounts referred to it as an "apparent drowning," although the autopsy later showed a contusion at the base of the skull. No blood was found at the scene other than Reed's, according to a police report. There was no skin under his fingernails that would indicate a struggle. A vacuum of the body, however, turned up several foreign acrylic and polypropylene fibers. In the photos he had a firm, weathered face, and steady eyes. Martin felt his own eyes glaze over and looked again at the live oaks: too much to absorb all at once. For their surface similarities, he had found, towns could be as self-contained as countries, with profound secrets the tourists and property owners whose taxes kept them running never guessed at. Only a handful of people ever know enough of the passwords necessary to enter a town's centralmost rooms.

THE PARADISE CLUB was sprawling and open, with torchlit decks fringed by European garden plants and wild shrubbery. The air smelled of steamed seafood and charbroiled steaks, and there was an elevated level of excitement in the din of voices as Martin approached the colored lights from the darkness of the parking lot. It was a casual restaurant, with well-worn wood-plank floors and rope railings, captain's wheels and giant mounted marlin on the walls—a place with many corners, and surprising perspectives: Through a side window he saw the moonlight squiggling through marshy wetland. Out back, a stone path led to the beach, where a chickee bar was bathed in red and green lights and men played volleyball with their shirts off.

He wasn't sure if he'd recognize Nellie Grant after so many years—but spotted her wild eyes almost immediately in the crush of people by the bar.

Nellie's long, thin arms were gesturing excitedly as she talked with a dour, silver-haired man, touching his arm repeatedly as if trying to spark some energy into him. She was dressed in a schoolgirl's plaid skirt and a plain, button-down white blouse.

Coming closer, hopscotching through the crowd, Martin saw that her hair had gone mostly gray, and it surprised him she wasn't touching it up.

"Hey, cuz!" she called, her eyes shimmering. The silver-haired man looked, and stepped back. Nellie had always been a flirt, favoring older, professional men. The souring of two—and now, he suspected, three—marriages hadn't changed that about her.

He received an aggressive, misplaced peck on the cheek, and then Nellie held his hands and wouldn't let go. His eyes watered with emotion.

"Well, it's great to see you," Martin said.

"I still can't be*lieve* it," she said, her voice nearly giddy. "So. I mean—what *happ*ened? With you and Katie?"

"Oh." Martin sighed. "Long story." He had forgotten this about Nellie: her embarrassing directness, insisting that painful subjects be explained in simple summaries. He had forgotten, too, the oddly conservative way she dressed, and wondered, as he had years earlier, if it reflected some inner sense of her own limits.

"Here," she said, "let's go have a seat. I got us a table outside." She signaled the bartender, grabbed Martin's wrist, and pulled him through the bar to a secluded table on a private corner of boardwalk. Nellie, he saw, as they sat, had been eating bread sticks and melba crackers and drinking vodka, by herself. Within a few moments loose plastic wrappers were sticking to her arms.

"I ordered you a Heineken—you still drink Heineken?"

"Actually." He scooted the wooden chair back, and smiled, thought of evenings that had started with Heinekens and ended on the porch with tequila sunrises as the real thing came up over the cornfields. "I was thinking a bottle of ginger ale would be fine."

"Ginger ale?" She blinked several times, before getting up to change her order.

When she returned, Nellie seemed to be studying him. "So," she said. "You're here to stay—or what?"

"Don't know." Martin stared at the wind, wondering. "I haven't really committed myself to anything. The place in Hamlet is just sitting there."

"You'll stay." She dug from her oversize tote bag a pack of Benson & Hedges. "It's a place people don't leave, believe me."

Martin waited, but, surprisingly, she didn't say more.

"How about you? How'd you end up here?"

"Oh—me? I don't know." She squinched up her face, then lit a cigarette and blew out the match along with the smoke, looking through Martin. "Remembering Uncle Otis, I guess. Those postcards he used to send?"

The waiter brought their drinks—another vodka and tonic for Nellie, ginger ale for Martin. They ordered seafood and steak and then smiled at each other over the jasmine-scented candle flame, as if they were two kids again, figuring out what to do with their lives. Nellie smoked comfortably, the cigarette hissing at her long slow inhale, and the top of the Benson & Hedges wrapper, like those from the crackers, cleaved unnoticed to her arms. In the briny wash of cool wind over the sea of wild shrubs, he remembered something else about Nellie: how she used to dot the *i* in her name with a four-leaf clover.

"Whatever happened to Uncle Otis, anyway?"

Martin shook his head, remembering Peter Fudd rushing toward him on the newspaper deck; it was one of the true mysteries of his childhood.

"Last I heard," she said, "was maybe, like, seventeen years ago? Something like that. He was living in California, working as a motel clerk." Seeing Martin's frown, she added, "My mother told me this. A few years ago. Said he'd called the house, asking to borrow money. He had a chance to invest in some sort of restaurant or coffee shop, supposedly, and was a thousand dollars short. My father wouldn't give it to him. I think by that point he'd been burned three, or maybe four, times and just didn't believe him anymore."

She added, as the cash register pinged open in the bar, "Things must've gotten rough for Otis."

"Must've."

"Yeah."

They sat in silence for several minutes, staring at each other's dark eyes. Martin imagined Otis's final wanderings, traveling with a desperate faith that the next turn might get him back on one of life's main thoroughfares.

After Nellie elaborately crushed out the cigarette, letting smoke drain slowly from her nostrils, she said, with a newfound energy, "Anyway. You've got to tell me: What happened? With you and Katie?"

6

"I STOPPED DRINKING," Martin said, "and Katie didn't."

Nellie, hunched into the light of the candle flame, looked quickly at his glass of ginger ale.

"At least that's my glib, one-sentence lead."

"Lead?"

"In the news business, we have to take complicated matters, you know, and simplify them. Turn them into headlines." Nellie stared uncertainly, her eyes retreating slightly. "But I don't know. There are dozens of reasons, I suppose. Actually, it was sort of like the cage door had been open for the last year or so, and it's just a wonder neither of us stepped out sooner."

"Huh."

She lifted the butter knife and began dressing another cracker, with a surprising intensity, a surgeon's concentration. Nothing had ever filled Nellie, and the spirit that burned in her seemed faintly more urgent now than Martin remembered.

"So, but anyway," she said, crunching on a cracker. "You're having your midlife crisis a few years early, in other words." Martin smiled: Nellie had written her own headline. "Well, you picked the spot for it. There's something about this town—very intoxicating at first and very addictive later." She cocked her head, leaned closer, and whispered, "Also, I'm sort of involved with someone."

"Oh?"

"Yeah."

"In the office?"

She nodded, once, and a fresh energy glowed in her eyes. Martin could sense what was coming.

"Is he married?"

"Mmm." She nodded almost imperceptibly, and blew out her cheeks to indicate the gravity of the situation.

Knowing Nellie, Martin suspected it was the state attorney himself she was seeing.

"Yeah, but I'll tell you about it some other time, though. Okay?" she said, looking with feigned irritation at the backs of her hands. "It's a very long story, and I'm sure you don't want to hear it your first night in town. There'll be plenty of opportunity to tell you about it later."

Her eyes looked evenly at his, the drama of her life having gained a new spectator.

Nellie's enthusiasm seemed to run down after that, as she became focused again on melba rounds and private thoughts—perhaps on the state attorney. Martin stared off into the bar area, sipping at his ginger ale. The window glass seemed to him like a television screen, the animated assortment of people all characters with drinks in their hands; the volume was turned too low, however, for him to understand what was happening.

"See that man with the Panama hat?"

It startled Martin because that was who he'd been watching: a stout gritty man, sixtyish, dressed in overalls, a tie-dyed T-shirt, and red sneakers.

"That's our mayor," she said. " 'Gator' Gorman, he calls himself. Retired auto executive from Michigan. And see who he's talking with?"

It was a cheery fat man of about forty, wearing a wrinkled white T-shirt and baggy jeans, with a fedora on his head. "That's Archie Duval. He always acts like he's my big buddy. But all he really wants is to find out what Sam Slaughter is up to. Sam's my boss. The state attorney? He's been trying for years to get a case against Archie."

"Who's the one with the bow tie?"

"Oh, that's Antonio DeRosse. He's on the City Council. A

real character. 'Your Tie to Honest Government,' his campaign ads say."

This, Martin remembered fondly, was what he and Nellie had done together that summer in Iowa: On weekends, they would catch the bus to town, sit on a Main Street bench for two or three hours, and just people-watch.

When a roguish-looking man came over to the mayor with what Martin assumed were his wife and son, waving into the crowd as if he were a celebrity, Nellie was right with him.

"That's Joey Keen," she said. "He's on the Council, too. Council president. They used to call him Hugh Heffner Jr. a few years ago. But now they're grooming him to be mayor. So he's going out of his way to act like the family man.

"Anyway," she said, abruptly, "I understand old man Fudd's made you the Rudolph Reed editor."

This surprised Martin, and his attention turned back into the realm of her dark eyes.

"Is that what they're saying?"

"It's the joke du jour, yeah." She picked among the empty wrappers for another pack of crackers, without success. "It was tragic what happened. But, you know, nothing's ever going to be proved."

"Nothing's ever going to be proved."

"No, uh-uh."

It was the second time Martin had heard this, and its matter-of-factness stirred some deep-seated instinct. As he began to insist that she explain, a congenial waiter opened a tray stand and another placed on it steaming plates of crab legs, shrimp, grilled swordfish, sirloin steak, and assorted vegetables.

7

THEIR THOUGHTS drifted as they ate, pleasant puzzle pieces that didn't quite fit, and at times Martin and Nellie seemed to become what they were: strangers. Watching her concentrate on the steak, potato, and broccoli, Martin thought of Katie's eyes, late one night just before she left, staring at him from the dark, dreamy neighborhood they once traveled to together, not understanding why he wasn't with her, why he wouldn't go there anymore. The hardest part was filling the time, finding other places to go.

"So," he said, pushing aside his nearly finished seafood platter. "Any tips you might be able to give me? I mean: about this story?"

"On Reed? I can give you all the gossip, sure. You're not going to eat this?" She stabbed Martin's baked potato, transported it to her plate. "Mmmm, let's see. Reed had been having a lot of trouble, supposedly, with his oldest daughter. I think her name's Jeannie, or Jenny. Mmm. Heavy shit, they say. Drugs and prostitution, supposedly. And, um." She took another bite, talking as she chewed. "The other thing that the gals down at the courthouse have been saying? Is that he was supposedly having a pretty hot and heavy thing with Cora Carlson."

"Who? Reed was?"

"Mmm-hmm."

Martin nodded coolly, poking at his crab imperial. It didn't sound right somehow, from what he'd read in the clippings. From the grainy pictures he had seen of the serious-eyed Reed.

"And who's Cora Carlson?"

"She owns CF and Associates. Insurance company. Folsom's her maiden name. You don't want that?" She took the crab imperial and set it by her plate. "Yeah, a very wealthy woman. A little Marilyn Monroe-ish. Reed had almost no money, you know." She took the final bite of Martin's potato. "He has seven kids and they get around by pushing each other in shopping carts they take from the Winn Dixie—can you believe it?"

"This Cora Carlson's married?"

"Mmm. Third time. Jack Carlson works for the city. Superintendent of the Transportation Department. Very weird guy. Almost as weird as her second husband."

"Weird. In what sense?"

"Just *weird.*"

"Her second husband was . . . ?"

Nellie suddenly smiled, broadly, at his interest in these details. Her face crinkled into an expression he didn't recognize.

"Still chasing that elusive Big Story, aren't you?" she said, and the voice had an edge, there was a complex look in her face that seemed to see through to his weakness, his obsession. Pelican wings beat up above the blue-lit tropical shrubbery; Martin watched their dark shapes glide above the Gulf of Mexico in the moonlight. He had to remind himself, again, that the old life was gone, it was like a person who had died.

"His little gift shop still stands, you know," Nellie said, eventually. "Out on 428. Out in the county."

"Whose?"

"Uncle Otis. It hasn't been open for, like, I don't know, fifteen years. But the building's still out there. A tiny little place. Cinder-block." A burst of laughter erupted from the bar area and Martin saw the man named Archie Duval hug the shoulder of the bow-tied councilman—Antonio DeRosse—who smiled uneasily. "That whole strip is about to be widened and redeveloped. Albert Folsom, I guess, was thirty years too early."

"Folsom."

"That was the developer who leased to Uncle Otis."

"As in Cora Folsom Carlson?"

"He was her uncle. Yeah. Mmm-hmm." Finished, Nellie languidly lit a cigarette. They were the only ones out on the deck now. Though the restaurant business had thinned, the bar area was still crowded. "He nicknamed that road the Shangri-La Expressway," Nellie said, "got it zoned commercial and leased out these cheap little wood and cinder-block buildings to people like Uncle Otis." She was cleaning her teeth now with her tongue as she smoked. "It was a boondoggle. Everyone lost money. There just weren't enough tourists yet. Nowadays, of course, they can't build condos fast enough. Everyone wants to be down here. That's okay," she said, reaching to take the check from him. "I'll take care of it."

"I've got it."

"No, I invited you."

"I insist."

"No, no."

"Here. Really. I insist."

The tug of war ended with Martin paying this one and Nellie agreeing to take the next. He was putting away his billfold, walking her back in, when Archie Duval, the big man from the bar area, stepped heavily onto the deck and tilted the brim of his hat at Martin.

"Hey, pumpkin," he said, stopping Nellie and pulling her sideways against him. His T-shirt looked to Martin as if it had been worn for several days or, perhaps, weeks, with stains under each arm. "What's you doing?"

Keeping Nellie wrapped against him, Archie Duval grinned at Martin, with a territorial, good-old-boy look.

"So what do you say?" he asked Nellie. "Keepin' 'em busy?"

"Mmm." Nellie nodded uncomfortably.

"That's my girl."

When he spoke again, the smile was gone from Archie Duval's face.

"Sam still sniffing around?"

"Huh?"

31

"You heard me."

"I don't know," she said, with irritable politeness. "I haven't seen Sam in three days. He's been on vacation."

"He needs to know anything, just have him give me a call. Number's in the book."

Nellie's smile was patronizing as he let go.

"You hear me?" He pointed a finger at her as if it were a loaded gun and walked back in.

"Jerk," she hissed.

Martin waited, looking at the sheen of moonlight above the tropical shrubbery, out over the beach and on the Gulf.

"What was that about?"

"Nothing."

"No?" He pretended to check his watch. "What'd he mean, sniffing around?"

"Oh, nothing," she said, and sighed. "He thinks Sam's trying to bring charges against him, I guess. And I'm sure Sam would if he could."

Back at the bar entrance, Nellie looked hungrily through the glass at all the people swaying drunkenly to reggae music.

"Charges. For what?"

She shook her head, staring inside. "For Rudolph Reed."

"Rudolph Reed."

The door opened and the music drowned out what she said next. A couple teetered down the boardwalk toward the sea.

"Do you think so? That he had anything to do with it?"

"No." She was smiling again, at his seriousness. But then the smile faded and she looked off with a dark earnestness. "No. Not Archie. What I really think, personally? I think Cora Carlson had some role in it, or more probably that husband of hers, who's about the weirdest guy I've ever met. But that's just speculation."

For a moment Martin wasn't sure whether to say good-bye or ask another question. Nellie stared at him as if trying to convey some secret she had learned in these years away from Iowa. As he walked down the boardwalk alone, toward a wooden bench on which the drunken couple was French-kissing, he heard his name, and stopped.

He heard it again.

Nellie was stepping rapidly back his way, her pumps in her hands.

"One other thing, cuz, I almost forgot." She stood there, half out of breath, her hair lifted by the sea wind. "For your story? Rudolph Reed's best friend. He works at your paper. His former best friend, anyway. Dale Bunch." Martin blinked at her. "He's your religion editor."

She winked and went back, plugging in to the excitement of the bar, the din of voices that grew more distant as Martin walked down the loose boards of the ramp, among the thick shrubbery and tropical trees, his nostrils flaring at the bittersweet broth of night-blooming flowers. Condo lights glittered in the Gulf up the beach, and Martin stopped several times to savor the view—vistas he was seeing for the first time, clearly, without the smudges of conventional wisdom. Seen through a clear lens, he supposed, Uncle Otis was right, it did seem like a natural wonderland. But it was also a place, he reminded himself, where a murderer was loose and no one seemed overly concerned about it.

He clicked the overhead light in his Ford wagon and on a notepad wrote the name "Cora Carlson." Underneath: "Dale Bunch, religion editor," then "Archie Duval," "Antonio DeRosse," and "Joey Keen."

At the start of a story, everything was nebulous, objects in the night. They took shape only as time passed and a familiar light settled on them. Martin didn't feel like returning to the house yet. Instead he went for a drive along the winding coast road, feeling cooler currents in the breeze as he followed the turns past oceanfront bungalows and condominium buildings, wondering what the moon looked like in Iowa tonight.

He passed a sign for Bananaville Beach, and suddenly understood why the flat, sullen face of Rudolph Reed had haunted him—it was the same humorless expression his father used to wear. "Only hard work can make you important," he often told him—a maxim Martin believed, until one day his father had died in a field, working, never having received his rewards.

Martin turned his wagon around in a beach parking lot and headed back.

**8** ALL NIGHT, WIND moaned through the moonlit oaks and rattled the screens. It was a sound Martin didn't recognize— as he hadn't that last, needy look in Nellie's eyes. He woke from sleep tasting a cooler air on his tongue, and felt far from Katie and Hamlet and the people he had known—farther still from the expectations that he had carried with him for years, like worthless currency. *Don't think,* he told himself. *Enjoy the breeze. Enjoy being here.* Vapor rose from the woodlands surrounding the old house, feeding pink and purple swamp orchids, and in the morning a softer, warmer wind tapped pleasantly on the screen windows and pushed at the fan-shaped palmetto leaves. Martin stood on the wooden floor in his Iowa pajamas and worn slippers, looking out, and it was all good again: The sky was china blue through the trees. He put on his running clothes and went out for a half hour, striding toward the western horizons, which seemed to draw him deeper into the morning, and into the town.

As he cooled down, walking past the stucco house at the end of the street, someone waved at Martin from behind a shiny white Mustang. He waved back.

"Is that Martin?" she said, coming out into the street to greet him, wearing a red Chanel-style suit and a small shoulder bag with a chain strap. Her shining black hair was pulled back.

"It is. Hi," she said, pretending to be shy. "I didn't realize we were neighbors."

"Oh, no, I hadn't either." It was, Martin realized, the woman he had seen on the newspaper porch the day before, wearing a miniskirt and sleeveless top.

She offered to shake, then saw that he was sweating, and pulled her hand away. Both smiled. She had large, engaging eyes and an alluring upward tug at one corner of her mouth, which quickly faded.

"How are you liking that old house?"

"Oh," Martin said, still panting from the run. He shrugged. "It's nice."

"Yeah? I bet Pete told you he looked high and low for it, didn't he?"

"Something like that." The woman rolled her eyes. She was China Rinaldi, the newspaper's advertising manager. Martin squinted at the house, wondering what was wrong with it.

"He's been trying to unload that thing for years. Anyway, listen," she said, and scanned the woods quickly, as if someone might be eavesdropping. "I heard something that may interest you—once you get into this Reed story? I have a little piece of information you might want to know."

"Really? What?"

"I can't say. Right now." She bit at her lower lip. "It involved someone I know, is the thing. And naturally she's worried if she says anything, it could come back at her. But possibly by the first of the week, okay?"

"Sure."

Her dark eyes looked at him brightly, reflecting the glare of sunlight on pink flowers. Martin held the stare, admiring her high cheekbones and arched brows, wondering if this was a tease of some sort, a way of joining the mystery.

"Listen," she said. "Take care."

"Oh, sure."

Her car, he noticed, as she quickly pulled out of the drive, still had a sales sticker in the window. The look in her eyes stayed with him as he returned to the house.


MARTIN SPENT SEVERAL hours exploring the town, driving its lush lanes, visiting the library, the chamber of commerce, and city hall. It was clearly a successful place, operating comfortably in the black for years, with phenomenal growth still forecast. A corner of the country where people bought homes, vacationed, and opened businesses, whose fruit-tree-lined avenues and modern architecture seemed imbued with a wispy aura of confidence he had never known before, an energy that caused Martin to feel almost physically tired by the time he returned to the paper, as if he had just run a footrace.

There was a message on his desk that "Millie Grant" had called and a number that was several digits off that of the state attorney's office. The operator box was signed "Dixie Fudd." Who, Martin wondered, looking up at the newsroom, is Dixie Fudd?

A teenage boy was walking purposefully on the balls of his feet through the dusty light of Business toward the city desk. It was only as he reached Martin's station that he noticed the cigarettes in his shirt pocket and realized that this wasn't a boy at all.

"Grant?"

Martin nodded.

"This is an addendum to the Reed file Pete gave you yesterday."

He placed a folder of clippings on Martin's desk and extended his hand. "I'm Hobart P. Lanahan. Metro editor. I guess you'll be reporting to me."

"Oh."

The grip was firm, the shake almost aggressive. Martin replied with a genial nod, though it hardly seemed possible that this man—who looked, in the dusty noontime light, barely twenty years old—ran Metro.

"Pete says you've won some national reporting awards." Martin half smiled. "The paper's won some, as well." The man grinned, and his face transformed: Deep wrinkles gouged the cheeks and circled his eyes, like rings in a puddle; his hair was flecked with white and balding toward the crown of his head. He was probably in his mid-forties, Martin guessed. "Let me know if I can help you with anything," he said, and then, turning quickly,

Hobart P. Lanahan went into his large, glass-enclosed office and closed the door.

There were two other reporters in Metro. Q. V. Robertson, an intense black woman, seemed to do nearly all of the work. Thirtyish, she wore her hair in dreadlocks and dressed like a college student, but had surprisingly sober eyes, and a mature, intelligent face that hinted, he thought, at a capability for great wit. The only other reporter was Thomas Persons, the red-faced older man he had seen sleeping on the porch the day before. Persons had worked at the paper thirty-three years and earned the title "senior writer," although the only writing he did seemed to be a rambling weekly column called "First Persons." As Martin unpacked his box of reference books and assorted keepsakes, Persons meticulously clipped his toenails over a round metal trash can.

AFTER LUNCH, a warm breeze kicked up from the west, rattling the palms outside.

Martin tapped on the door to Dale Bunch's office and waited as it seemed to come open in slow motion. A hoary, heavy man with a scraggly white beard looked up at him from behind his book-strewn desk.

As Martin introduced himself, the man watched attentively with milky blue eyes, his wide froglike mouth speaking silently in reply. It wasn't until Martin reached over to shake hands that he realized Dale Bunch could not stand.

He adjusted his wheelchair so he was facing Martin and indicated the metal folding chair beside the door. Martin sat. The walls were lined by ceiling-high bookcases, filled mostly with religious texts. Additional books were stacked haphazardly on the floor. Hanging on the wall in an ornate wooden frame was a line in script from Proverbs—"*He who keeps understanding will prosper*"—as well as several photographs.

"You," he said, "are the investigative wunderkind Pete Fudd hired." He lifted a blackboard pointer from his desk as Martin nodded, and used it to close the door. The room smelled of books and Ben-Gay and vegetable soup. The only light was the dim bulb of his reading lamp.

"My cousin tells me you were friends with Rudolph Reed. I'm doing some background on him. Getting to know the town a little bit."

Red-veined eyes regarded Martin from a sagging face, reminding him of the many lifelong alcoholics he had known. "I was, I suppose, yes, his best friend," he said, adding, "At one time. Although not so much recently. I was friends—we will say—until he went into politics." He stopped talking and closed his eyes. So much time passed that Martin wondered if he had fallen asleep. "I wasn't *not* his friend. But I was more like what we tend to think of nowadays as an aquaintance."

"I see."

He opened the moist eyes, staring with a stark, unblinking quality that made Martin look away, to the picture on the wall above his head: Several men, including Dale Bunch, were lounging on the deck of a sportfishing boat, far out at sea. In the photo, Dale Bunch was standing, grinning broadly, looking a little, Martin thought, like John Huston.

"Rudolph was very active at one time in the church, you see." He spoke slowly, at times sounding like a phonograph with a weak motor. "His foremost imperative, when he began this grass-roots business, was a spiritual one." He again closed his eyes, as if the here and now somehow interfered with his thinking, and a choking sound emanated, several times, from his throat. "It was a profound belief that if you lift your eyes to the horizon, well, by God, anything can be achieved. He was the one good politician I've known. But he wasn't very good at politics."

Bunch's features seemed to coarsen; he stared toward the ceiling. "When I first moved down here, I was, I suppose, adrift, widowed and able. Ready, at last, or so I imagined, to tackle the big issues. Rudolph moved here seven years ago, when I was sort of at the tail end of that period in my life. We were involved in a church discussion group, and became—as you say—good friends.

We traded ideas, worked on several of the essential problems. Sometimes we'd carry our conversations over to my deck. Or his back porch. And occasionally—" Straining, he placed the tip of the pointer on the framed photo behind his head "—we'd take it out to sea."

Martin studied the picture and realized that one of the other three men—the only one not smiling—was Rudolph Reed. He was holding up a can of Coke, as if toasting the photo taker.

"We shared a concern, I suppose, over what footprints we were leaving in this life, perhaps more so than other people. We wanted to discover how we could best contribute, how we could make our time here count. You see: what our options were. But what eventually happened was, he began to acquire a certain notoriety. And that's a very potent thing these days, isn't it? When that happened, Rudolph began to attract a certain fringe element. Which you'll find there's quite a bit of in this town. Some of them believed that in Reed they had found a kind of savior, the first truly noble politician. Many, though, supported him simply because it felt good to belong to something. Something opposed to the status quo."

"The Reed-jects."

He closed his eyes and then opened them, by way of response.

"Someone," Martin said, deciding to shift to more solid ground, "told me they thought Reed might've been having an affair with a married woman in those last several months."

"Oh." Dale Bunch lurched forward, his right hand clutching desperately at his shirt collar. His head pulled back eerily, his eyes shut tight; he produced a sound so loud and guttural that Martin didn't realize for several moments what it was. He stared, slightly stunned, as the same sound burst forth in frightening explosions, the stomach propelling upward, another wave replacing it—paroxysms of laughter that turned, finally, as Martin hurried out of his office, into a dangerous-sounding cough.

At the water cooler, he made quick eye contact with Hobart P. Lanahan, whose boyish face turned, disapprovingly, it seemed, into a middle-aged man's.

"THANK YOU," Dale Bunch said, when at last the coughing subsided. He lifted his pointer and again slowly closed the door. His face was mottled now, red with patches of gray. Wattles of skin shook on his neck as he sipped water, looking suddenly quite frail. His wide red lips glistened from the light of his desk lamp.

"I knew he'd become friendly with Cora. That's who you're referring to, no doubt." Martin's nod went unnoticed. Dale tried unsuccessfully several times to clear his throat. "I suppose she shared some of his political views—or said she did. And, of course, she's very wealthy. But that story about the affair." He shook his head gravely. "Twice a month, the mayor and a group of four or five business owners meet with Lodge McCloud and figure out what needs to be done in this town. That's the real city government. And that's where stories like that one got started."

"Who's Lodge McCloud?"

The mouth seemed to stretch clear across his face. "He's our Rasputin. Our wealthiest citizen. A near recluse now, who does much of his bidding through Joe Keen, the City Council president." Martin recalled Keen at the bar the night before, waving at the crowd as if he were president of the country, not just the City Council. "In recent months, these people would do whatever needed to be done, basically, to discredit Rudy."

"Short of breaking the law?"

"Short of breaking the law. Although someone did kill him." The eyes closed again, and he seemed to be thinking deeply

41

about it. "You will find, Martin, that there's a real plurality to power here. When someone gets too much, odd alliances will form in order to limit it—or eliminate it. That's what we may have here. Who benefits from this process? Never any one particular individual. What benefits is the town itself."

"I see."

Martin looked at the books on the shelves, saw the old gold-leaf Bibles, the massive Taoist and Hindu texts, tomes by Hegel and Muller and Tiele and Suzuki and William James.

"When you ask me about Rudolph—" Dale Bunch's eyes were still closed, his head raised toward the ceiling "—what I feel most sorry about is his poor wife, Lila. She withdrew completely, you know, when he got involved in politics. Lives her life in bed these days, never goes out. I was quite good friends with Lila, and have found her virtually unapproachable for at least two years."

Martin, sensing that he'd taken enough of Dale Bunch's time—though it wasn't clear what he had been doing—said, "Is there anything else you could tell me about Rudolph? That might help with this story?"

"Yes." He squinted, the eyes still closed. "The last time I spoke with him he said he was about to embark on a 'new crusade.' He did not explain what the new crusade was. But that was the term he used. You ought to talk to his children about it. They may know something. And, Martin?"

The eyes opened. He leaned forward across the desk, smiling warmly, and extended his hand. "Good luck."


THERE WAS A meeting that night of the Bananaville City Council. Although it was Q. V. Robertson's beat, Martin decided to stop by, in the hopes of learning more about the town and its leaders. But also to stay away from the empty room—the thoughts that grew more urgent as daylight disappeared, as lights brightened like temptations against the sky.

The meeting turned out to be as monotonous as any he had

ever covered. The centerpiece was a three-hour debate over the structure and billing procedures for the town's water rates. At one point, after nearly two hours of discussion, an elderly councilman named Robinson McElroy, frustrated by Joey Keen's frequent interruptions, stood and proclaimed the Council president "a shameless womanizer who likes to hear yourself talk!" then stormed out of the Council chambers.

The man sitting in front of Martin turned sideways and, catching his eye, winked. He continued to do so throughout the meeting, until it became tedious and Martin finally began to ignore him, turning his attention instead to Rudolph Reed's empty chair and to the bow-tied Antonio DeRosse, who remained hunched over, scribbling notes and smiling occasionally but never saying a word.

When the meeting adjourned, at several minutes past eleven, the man in front of Martin turned to shake his hand. Martin was surprised to see that the right side of his face, his neck, and his right arm were covered with extensive skin grafts, and that half of his right hand was missing. The wounds tugged at the man's eye socket and the corner of his mouth, and his shake, with the deformed hand, seemed deliberately quick, the muttered greeting too friendly.

THE AIR HAD filled with a dark blue mist, and for several minutes driving home, Martin felt as if he had taken a wrong turn—that he was driving without a sense of direction, on a road that wouldn't end. Back at the house, he was surprised to see the light blinking on his answering machine. He took a bottle of 7UP from the icebox, sat at the wooden table, and punched the button.

"Martin Grant, please," a nervous-sounding voice said. "This is Rudolph Reed. Please give me a call at 555-5097. It doesn't matter how late. As long as it's before twelve."

Martin stared at the answering machine and felt a shiver, sensing reality slip out of its comfortable groove for a moment.

It was 11:37. He stood by the open window, feeling wet breeze on his face, tasting the night-blooming flowers.

In seventeen years as a journalist, he had never before received a call from a dead man.

**10**

MARTIN PUSHED THE seven numbers, as moist breeze blew through the screen.

It picked up on the first ring.

"Hal-lo."

"Hello, this is Martin Grant calling."

"Mr. Grant? Hold it." A television shut off. There was a sound of shattering glass.

*"Dammit!"*

The voice returned. "Mr. Grant?"

"Martin."

"We understand you're planning on writing some stories of our dad? Sammy wants to know if you could come over to the house tomorrow. At ten o'clock. To talk with us and stuff."

"Oh. Well. Sure." Martin recognized now what had sounded peculiar about the voice: It was that of a teenager, trying to sound authoritative.

"Sammy, my sister. She'd like to talk to you about your articles and stuff. Before you write them. We put two messages in at your office earlier."

"Sure," Martin said. "I was planning on calling."

"Okay." Rudolph Reed Jr. gave Martin directions to the house and then, without saying good-bye, hung up.

Martin stared at the shimmer of faraway streetlights in the mist and the dark silver clouds floating above the phone wires and he felt something faintly familiar, some distant promise, coming back like a star's glow all these years later; the promise of things becoming known again, slowly, if he remained alert, if he was attentive enough to notice the clues.

THE REEDS LIVED on Pineapple Lane, a pleasantly overgrown residential road several blocks from the beach, in a coral-colored, thin-walled wood and stucco development called the Sea Vista. Martin, dressed in his reporter's uniform—khakis, dress shirt, Yves Saint-Laurent tie, and well-worn penny loafers—walked the winding stepping-stone paths, among buildings that seemed identical, looking for Apartment 5. The shrubbery was still moist and the cool breezes smelled of breakfast bacon and roasted coffee. He came at last to a unit with two shopping carts parked in front.

Block letters on the mailbox spelled REED.

He pushed the bell several times before the door pulled back against the security chain. A small face with sunken eyes and a poutish mouth appeared on the other side.

"Hi, there, I'm Martin Grant," he said.

The door closed.

When it opened again, a different face, higher in the crack, but with the same sullen expression, gazed out.

"Mr. Grant?"

"Martin."

"Hold on." He struggled for some time getting the chain off, finally opening it to an apartment that smelled of spicy sauces and potpourri. "I'm Rudolph Reed. Come on in," he said, without shaking hands. Wearing oversized jeans, big off-brand basketball shoes, and a loose-fitting sports jersey, he led Martin through the living room. The room was sparsely furnished and tidy, except for a Monopoly game whose pieces, play money, deeds, and cards were strewn over the floor, as if the game had ended in a disagreement. Four of the Reed children sat on the floor, their poutish faces staring at "Roseanne." The TV rested on an old hi-fi console, the likes of which Martin hadn't seen since childhood. The only other light in the room came from candles on either side of a framed studio portrait of their father on the mantel.

Rudolph Jr. didn't bother to introduce the children, leading Martin into the kitchen, where another Reed was standing barefoot before the stove, wearing a long print dress. When she turned to look at Martin, he saw the same sullen features, though her skin seemed paler than the others', with a wax-papery texture, and her hair was stringier and redder.

She had been cleaning and cutting vegetables, Martin saw—tomatoes, onions, assorted peppers and green beans—and now was picking meat from crab claws, breaking them open with a wooden mallet. A spicy sauce was stewing in a pan on the stove, and the window fan stirred the pleasant tomatoey scent of bay leaf and basil through the room.

"This is Mr. Martin Grant," Rudolph Jr. said, his right leg shaking rapidly all of a sudden. "This is Sammy, my sister." Sammy turned to face him again, and Martin briefly saw, as she nodded quickly, the lean face and sad eyes of a twenty-year-old.

"We understand you might be planning to write some articles about our dad," she said, in a tone that belied no feelings one way or the other.

"That's right."

"We'd just like to make sure, if you do," she said, "that our point of view gets into the story. And the truth about what happened."

"Of course."

"Because there's been some lies and rumors and things going around. About our dad. We want to make sure the truth is told."

Martin watched politely as she finished splitting the crab legs, pulling out slices of meat and placing them in a bowl. Through the window above her shoulder was a playground area with swings and jungle bars, and beyond it dozens of identical-looking wood and stucco buildings.

"We're doing our best to get by," she said, in a voice that seemed much older than her years. "But when we hear people call

47

it a 'drowning,' that really angers us. As I'm sure you can understand."

"Sure." To Rudolph Jr., who was standing beside the refrigerator, breathing heavily, Martin said, "Do all seven children live here?"

"Five," Rudolph Jr. said. "I have my own apartment."

"Ah."

Both of them looked at the refrigerator, which was covered with magnet-anchored supermarket coupons.

Sammy, her back to them still, gave a quick rundown on the children, leaving one out. Rudolph Jr. was the oldest boy, although Sammy herself was a year older, at nineteen. In the living room were Theresa, eleven, Benjamin Franklin, nine, Gwen, seven, and Joshua, four.

"Is there anyone else to help take care of you all?" Martin asked. "Relatives or anyone?"

In the long silence that followed, the window fan chunked and crab limbs broke beneath her wooden mallet.

"Our aunts and uncles and them?" Sammy finally said, turning slightly, rubbing at her face with a crab-stained finger. "They all come down from West Virginia and gone back. The funeral was three weeks ago."

"I see."

There was a sound next door of feet running up a stairway and a door closing. Martin had forgotten what that was like, being in such close proximity to other lives. "You want a soda or anything?" Sammy asked. She wiped her hands and turned off the stove burner. The sun had cleared the duplex across from theirs and sudden splinters of sunlight showed cracks in the window.

When Rudolph opened the refrigerator, Martin saw about a dozen half-finished pop bottles. Each was marked with the children's scribbled names on scraps of paper taped to the bottles.

He handed Martin an unopened Sprite and watched as he twisted off the top. Sammy sat at one end of the small, Formica-topped table, and Rudolph immediately sat at the other. Martin took the third chair.

"The main reason we're concerned is because of our mommy," she said, staring at him with hard, pale blue eyes that turned pinkish on the edges. She clasped her bony white fingers on the table, and a moment later Rudolph Jr. clasped his, too.

"Because. There was lots of people who didn't like our dad and stuff," Rudolph Jr. said, in a voice that was barely audible.

"It hurt Mommy to read 'apparent drowning' in the newspaper," Sammy said. "The whole first week, everyone in town was calling it a drowning." Her voice quavered slightly, and she stared with moistening eyes at the blue-checked table mat. "Our dad used to be a competitive swimmer when he was in high school, so it was sort of vicious, in a way."

"Yes." Martin looked at the wild bright rustle of hibiscus blossoms outside. "What can I do to help?"

"We're thinking about offering an award and stuff," Rudolph mumbled. He'd lifted the salt shaker from a paper doily and was fidgeting with the top, fastening and unfastening it.

"A *reward*," Sammy said. "Unfortunately, though, right now we don't really have anything to offer. Other than about fifteen dollars. Some of our father's supporters are thinking of asking people to contribute—holding a rally or a cookout or something. But we don't know how many have the money to do it."

An angle for a story, Martin thought, watching Sammy, impressed with her steadiness. He had known a brood like this once in Iowa, a family of nine children who, even as adults, kept plugging back in to the family unit because they didn't seem to fit in anywhere else. As he listened to Sammy describe her father's evolution from organizer of the Pineapple Lane Civic Association to petition drive crusader for density limits to public speaker to City Councilman, he noticed that Theresa, the eleven-year-old, was standing in a corner of the doorway, staring at him.

"My father believed in doing things straight," Sammy said. "And he was a good person, although he was forty-five, you know, and didn't have a penny." Her eyes held his, as if to convey some additional meaning in these words. There were now four children in the doorway, watching him with flat, poutish faces that were like different models of the same one.

Sammy clapped her hands abruptly. "*Git!* Back in the living room! watch television! Now. *Now!*" There was a scramble of feet, and they were gone. Sammy looked outside, through the bright glare of the window, at well-dressed children playing on the swings. Squint lines formed on the corners of her eyes.

"Anyway, whatever happened," she said, "my father saw it coming. I'm fairly certain of that."

"Saw it coming? In what sense?"

"He told me Saturday, three days before it happened, that he had just found out about something and was going to have to deal with it. I wish he'd said more. Or I'd asked more." She looked at Rudolph Jr., her eyes glistening a reflection of sunlight and hibiscus.

"I *mean* it!" she yelled. Martin heard another flurry of feet outside the kitchen doorway.

**11**

"WHAT DO YOU think?" Martin asked. "What do you think happened to your father?"

Sammy smiled sadly. The back and forth of the swing outside seemed locked to some infinite rhythm, the creak of the chain on metal, echoing, in blue air, with the clear hypnotic sounds of childhood. Martin, in the silence, traveled somewhere else, tasted the certainty he had shared with Katie in Hamlet. *Don't think so much.*

"It had something to do with shadows," Rudolph Jr. said, finally.

Sammy blinked irritably. "That's my idea about this town," she said, sighing. "That bad things happen because the shapes all blur together. The businesspeople all live in each other's shadows, so that when something happens, it's hard to ever see distinct shapes, to see who is responsible."

"Do you have any ideas?"

Rudolph made a grunting sound, playing still with the salt shaker, but deferred to Sammy.

"He fought the expansion of that amusement park— Bananaland Park—and tied it up for months. They say the opposition cost developers hundreds of thousands of dollars and was jeopardizing bank loans."

"Okay." Martin nodded. He had seen reference to it in the Reed clippings. For the first time, he flipped open his reporter's pad.

"The developer is . . . ?"

"Lodge McCloud."

"I see."

"And Joe Keen is involved, too, but we don't know how much. Dad thought he might have been a silent partner."

"Keen's the Council president."

"Yes."

Martin saw that Sammy, coated now in sunlight, had a faint sprinkling of freckles on her face and shoulders and the tops of her breasts. He watched the back and forth of the swing, the sun bouncing off the silver chain and tall clumps of grass, thinking about what she'd said.

"This thing your father had found out: It had to do with this amusement park, then, you think?"

Sammy shook her head. "Oh, no. I don't think so, no." He watched her, waiting, but her thoughts had gone somewhere else.

"But—so, anyway, he said this on Saturday. What happened the rest of the weekend?"

"Not much." Sammy stared at the table. "I hardly saw him Sunday." Rudolph Jr. nodded. "And then Monday night, he came home, around seven, with two large pizzas. We all ate pizza that night. And watched TV."

"Did he do that often?"

"What? Bring home pizza?" Rudolph Jr. was shaking his head, waiting for Sammy to give the official response.

"No," she said. "In fact, hardly ever. We tend to eat at different times, just whatever's available. Frozen dinners and McDonald's and stuff. I try to cook something at least once a week that'll last a couple days. And our dad was usually working anyway, so he wasn't home for dinner very often."

"So he got home around seven—you watched television."

"And that was it. He didn't really say much. And he went to sleep right out there on the sofa Monday night." Martin looked into the living room at the well-worn, early-American–style furniture. "He slept out there a lot of times, 'cause he didn't want to bother our mom. It folds out."

Martin looked at Rudolph, who nodded twice.

52

"It folds out and stuff," he said.

"Where is your mother?"

Rudolph cleared his throat. He stared at the refrigerator. Sammy was gazing at her nails, with a down-tilted expression like that of a middle-aged woman. "She's upstairs."

"Any chance I could talk with her? Briefly?" There was a hushed silence, during which Martin realized that the swinging had stopped. Breeze gusted in the empty play area, making a faint rattle through the abandoned swings.

"I don't know," Sammy said. Her distractedness seemed to dissolve in the sunlight and a clear, hard look came into her eyes. "I'd have to go check."

"You said only five of the children live here," Martin said to Rudolph as they waited. "And you have your own place. Who does that leave—your sister Jeannie?"

He blushed instantly, but kept his gaze narrowed on the salt shaker. The motors on the kitchen clock made a quiet grinding noise, as if time were struggling to move forward.

"Anyway," Martin eventually said. "So you're in high school, are you? Or have you graduated?"

"I haven't graduated."

"Okay."

They both stared at the fan-shaped shadows that spun circles on the worn tile floor. Another minute passed. Finally, lifted up by a thought, Martin pointed at Rudolph Jr.'s jersey.

"You're a fan of the Dolphins, are you?"

"What?"

"I say, you're a fan of the Dolphins?"

He shrugged, both hands now turning the salt shaker. "They're all right," he said, and mumbled something Martin couldn't understand.

At last, as Martin stared at the empty playground, Sammy returned.

"She'll talk to you," she said. "For five minutes."

53

MARTIN FOLLOWED Sammy up worn carpeted steps and down a dim hallway to the corner bedroom. Only Lila Reed's head and arms were visible above the quilt that covered the enormous bed. Her right hand clutched a channel changer, aimed in the darkness at a small color television. The scent of raspberry candle wax, burning on an antique dresser, mixed with smells of perspiration and soiled hair in a light breeze that stirred the tops of palms outside her window. The bureau mirror gave a yellowed, watery reflection of the room, like some window into a murkier dimension Martin had been to before.

The stubborn, downturned Reed mouth came from Lila, he saw, but everything else seemed her own. She had narrow eyes and a short, pinched nose; her skin was softly wrinkled, like fruit about to go bad. Her gray hair, weedlike, framed cheeks so thin she seemed anorexic. Lila Reed was the antithesis, it seemed, of her sturdy-looking husband.

"I haven't been well the past couple of years," she said, watching him, "and really can't tell you much. I just hope you can write about him fairly."

"I intend to do the best I can."

"Good." There was a dry sucking sound from her mouth.

Martin sat in the small wooden chair beside the bed. He explained to her who he was, how he'd been in town for just two days and was still feeling his way around, getting to know people.

"Are you going to stay?"

"In town, you mean? I don't know for sure."

"Well. You ought to decide," she said, and her gaze traveled about the room—to the window, the porcelain animals lined up on the dresser, the mirror, the television—as restless as thoughts. "You say the Midwest? Where in the Midwest?" she said, looking at Martin with suddenly damp eyes.

"Iowa. Tiny little town called Hamlet. There's Hamlet and there's West Hamlet, and then nothing else until the next county."

She nodded, sitting up slightly so that he could see her collarbones, jutting out of a nightgown above the bed quilt. "Never been anywhere but West Virginia and here. Well, North Carolina. Once." She stared at the thought, and the life seemed to drain from her face, as if some terrible memory were recurring. Several times she pressed the channel changer, leaving on a commercial for Mitsubishi. Palm fronds clicked gently behind gauzelike curtains that made the world seem out of focus.

"West Virginia's pretty in the fall," Martin said. "Drove through once in late October, when the leaves were all changing." It was with Katie, drinking vodka, reading poetry. "Very beautiful."

"Oh, yes. Nature's masterpiece," she said, looking outside. The words had a strange resonance, a familiarity he couldn't place. She nodded at the bookshelf. "A drowning," she said. "If I could, you know, I would leave."

Her eyes flickered, like mental static.

"Why can't you?"

A long gust of wind came up over the Spanish roofs. Lila Reed seemed for a moment lost in it, in the wild speckles of sunlight and shadow. When it stopped, he was surprised to see her staring at him, with imploring eyes. *"He wasn't even going to be there,"* she said, enunciating each word.

"Pardon me?"

Her gaze softened, as if the thought had gone out of her head, and she looked back at the television, pressing the changer. Martin waited, watching the screen: lions on an African plain, skinny girls dancing in a music video, "The Psychic Friends Network." She stopped on "The Andy Griffith Show," and slumped lower into the quilt. Martin saw several pairs of old slippers on the floor, misshapen to the fit of her feet.

"Did your husband give you any indication that something was going to happen? Your daughter said he told her he had just found out something he was going to have to come to terms with."

"*Sammy* said that?" Her voice was suddenly coarse. "No. No." She seemed to be looking at something he'd never know, something she hadn't fully relinquished, treading safely in memories. "I don't know. I didn't know," she muttered. "She should never have done it. But it was over, he said, there was going to be a *new crusade.*" Contemptuously, it seemed, she added, "I still can't believe she did it."

"Who? What are you saying now?"

But Lila Reed's eyes had gained distance again; they looked at him from very far away. Suddenly her face was startled, as her gaze slid uneasily to meet Martin's.

"Who *are* you?" she said, as if just seeing him for the first time. Martin stared back, unsure how to reply. Another gust of wind splashed shadows and sunlight against the walls, shaking the candle flame on the bureau.

"Mommy?"

Sammy was standing to the side of the doorway, peering in with her pale, wax-papery face and blue-pink eyes. Martin stood. He thanked Lila Reed, who was changing channels again, oblivious.

"I'm sorry," Sammy said, as they went down the creaky stairs. "She has good days and bad days. Sometimes she just gets real upset for no reason."

"She said she hasn't been well for the last two years."

"No."

Sammy blinked rapidly, standing at the base of the steps. Martin saw the backs of the four Reed children's heads, lined up in front of the television. "Well, not really," she said, her voice nearly a whisper. "She had a skin cancer operation three years ago. She tells people she has cancer. But the doctor says she's fine. It's actually just psychological."

"I see."

"Yeah."

Standing with Rudolph and Sammy on the porch step, Martin recognized what had happened, recalled his own family's experiences, on consecutive sweltering summers, when his parents had died. After the traditional outpouring of concern—neighbors bringing food, florists delivering flowers, relatives flying in—their phone had stopped ringing. They were entering that period of limbo, alone with their loss, needing somehow to get on with life by themselves.

"Any more questions or anything?" Rudolph asked, after saying good-bye for the second time.

"No," he said, and realized something. What was missing: There was no den here, no study. The extra room in their home had been made into a bedroom with bunk beds. A schoolteacher and city councilman would surely need a study area.

"Oh, he kept all his business at the office," Sammy replied. "He didn't really bring it home with him, ever."

"He worked at his office and stuff."

"An office at school, you mean?" Martin heard the chain of the swing set pull back and forth again through the morning breeze.

"No. He rented an office. The one at school he had to share with two other teachers, so he rented his own office and kept all his business there."

"I see." With a practiced casualness, Martin asked, "Any chance you could take me by to have a look?"

"I guess." Sammy looked at Rudolph Jr.

"I've got the key at my apartment and stuff," Rudolph said. "If you want to stop by."

"Okay." All six Reed children were watching him now. "I assume the police have been there?"

"Where—the office?"

"Uh-uh," Sammy said. "They came here and interviewed us all twice. Then called back. To ask some other questions. But they never asked anything about any office."

Warm winds gusted through the morning shadows of the stepping-stone path as Martin returned to the parking lot, becoming lost, briefly, in the winding, massive development of identical-looking buildings.

ORANGES HUNG PLENTIFULLY in the trees along Banana Boulevard, and palm leaves clicked and glistened in the sunlight. The air seemed to lift Martin, to fill him with good feelings the way wind fills a sail. But as he crossed the bridge into East Bananaville, the streets narrowed, the air suddenly had a closed-in smell, of car exhaust, garbage, greasy cooking.

He bought coffee at a market named Louie's and from the pay phone out front left a message for Hobart P. Lanahan, saying he would be in around noon.

The apartment was an efficiency, in an old pink masonry building that probably dated to the mid-sixties. Rudolph Jr. answered dressed in jeans, a maroon McDonald's shirt, and white socks.

"Mr. Grant!" he said, as if expecting someone else.

"Martin."

"Hold on," he said, and retreated into the room. He had been searching through a drawer, Martin saw, having dumped everything onto his single, bare mattress, which rested on the floor. The only other furniture in the room was a coffee table, on which all sorts of papers and rock 'n' roll magazines were piled haphazardly. Smashing Pumpkins played on his boom-box stereo. An electric guitar leaned against a wall. The floor was strewn with clothes and a pizza box, opened to display a dozen wedges of crust. Martin stood beside the mattress, trying to keep from imagining what his bathroom looked like.

"Here it is," Rudolph said, with a muffled tone of triumph. "Here's the key."

"Oh, good."

"Yeah." He handed it to Martin and turned with a frown, as if looking for his shoes.

"And where is the office?"

"What?"

"The office."

"Oh. It's over Captain Jack's."

"Pardon?"

"It's over Captain Jack's."

"Oh."

His right leg suddenly began to shake, as if to music. "I'm going to have to get to work and stuff," he said, and mumbled something Martin couldn't hear. "But just leave it under my door if I'm not here."

"Sure."

REED'S OFFICE WAS about a half mile away, one block west of the river on Sabal Street—a narrow, sunny residential lane. Crossing back into the city limits, Martin again noticed the subtle change: the way the breeze took on an intoxicating aroma of brine and winter flowers, the way the Bermuda grass and citrus trees shone.

The only business on Sabal Street was Captain Jack's Seafood Market and Deli. The metal shutter on the market-front was halfway up, indicating they were about to open. Martin had seen the commercials for Captain Jack's on cable television, each beginning with a friendly, snowy-haired man saying, "Hi, folks, this is the captain speaking. Have you heard about our world-famous lunch specials?"

Rudolph Reed's office had been "over" Captain Jack's.

Martin parked on a cross street and came back through the alley, passing yards that were shaded with dwarf palms, trellises of sea grapes, and banana trees. Hearing televisions and tapping silverware, and, at one point, through tall French windows, a tango.

Martin walked up the narrow wooden steps behind Captain Jack's. The lock clicked open easily and a dusty oblong of light fell onto the dirty beige carpet. Through venetian blinds across the room he saw bright slats of sky and palm tree.

Martin closed the door and locked it, studying the room: Along one wall was a file cabinet and metal desk; on another, a small bookcase and brown fold-out sofa. A barbell set and two dumbells were lined up near the center of the room.

He sat at Rudolph Reed's desk and contemplated for a moment the dead man's view over the seafood market sign—up and down Sabal Street with its lush, flower-flecked lawns, modest wood and stucco houses. On the wall to his right was a framed newspaper article from the *Daily News,* headlined REED WINS COUNCIL SEAT, and next to it one from *The Banner,* PETITION STALLS B'LAND PARK. Four years he'd been a spokesman for the "other folks," working diligently but not getting the payoff he sought, Martin sensed. Taped to the wall above his desk was an epigraph he had copied out in pen: "Try not to become a man of success but try to become a man of value. Albert Einstein." A good smell of grilled meat drifted up through the blinds, presumably from downstairs.

The books were mostly political biography, though there was also a complete Shakespeare, *The Old Man and the Sea,* several Dickens novels, volumes by Santayana, Thoreau, Emerson, Melville, Whitman, and Norman Vincent Peale.

Martin slid out the top drawer of the desk and saw tea bags, pencils and rubber bands, seven pennies. The deep drawer beside it was filled with file folders that contained minutes from City Council meetings, dating back nearly four years. The small lower drawer held a curriculum book for his history class at the middle school. He had been in the 1920s when it happened, Martin saw, teaching Harding's death and the Teapot Dome scandal.

Also in this drawer was a pocket-sized spiral notebook, in which Reed had recorded daily his exercise regimen. The entries stopped on a Sunday in December: "Morning: thirty-minute run. Aft.: Ten sets of twelve curls. Eve: Bike, 9 miles."

Martin made notes in his steno pad, pausing several times to look out the window, to soak in the view, the street Reed had stared at each day. He was something of a dreamer, Martin suspected, a man who, like his own father—and perhaps like himself—wandered often into neighborhoods of the imagination where anything seemed possible if you just kept your gaze firmly on your goals.

There was an appointment book, he noticed, on a corner of the desk. As a lulling breeze gently rattled the venetian blinds, Martin paged through it. On Monday, the day before Reed died, there were two entries: "Noon—Lunch with Art Conners." And "C.C. 6 P.M."

Cora Carlson, presumably.

There was just one appointment for Tuesday: "Keen, noon," with the name underlined, as if the meeting were of special significance. Martin paged forward, saw a notation to "Take Theresa to dentist" the following Friday, and, three weeks ahead, "Car to Newt's for oil change."

The top drawer of the file cabinet contained more City Council minutes, neatly stacked in file folders. The bottom drawer was locked, although it was a cheap cabinet, and Martin wondered if a sharp pull might jolt it open. He'd already crossed several lines, he knew—in coming here, in opening drawers and handling potential evidence—so it didn't seem to matter much if he crossed one more. He lifted the drawer and yanked—once, twice, the second time disengaging the catch in a jarring scrape of metal. Martin looked sharply at the door, as if someone might have heard. The cord knot tapped faintly on the venetian blinds.

There was a shoe box in the drawer, and beneath it a stack of papers. Martin removed the box lid and saw that it was filled with bank statements. The papers underneath were vital documents—leases, registrations, insurance policies. Mixed in with them was a laminated valentine, crayoned in a little girl's handwriting: "I love you, Daddy. Love, Ginny."

He opened the most recent bank statement, and saw that his balance was listed as $1,389.56. There were no signs of a savings account.

Martin noted the names of the people he had written checks to and then tucked everything into the envelope. He went back several statements, copying the names from the checks, searching for patterns. Each month, he saw, there was a check to Cora Carlson for $750 and one to Howard Heard for $450. At the bottom of the box was a series of check stubs, rubber-banded, from

62

D.S., Inc., in Coconut, a town to the north. They appeared to be pay stubs, with the amount of hours scribbled on each one. Martin calculated that he was being paid $6.50 an hour, although nowhere on the stubs did he see Reed's name, or anyone else's.

He stood in the center of the room and exhaled deeply several times, feeling pleasantly disoriented. The air tasted of springtime, the season of cut grass and baseball gloves, the time of year he had spent afternoons with his father in the fields, had played first base, had met Katie, had stared often into the skies beyond Grantsville and wondered what he would become. He was about to go when something else caught his attention: The telephone on Reed's desk had a built-in answering machine. Martin lifted the tape lid and hit the Reply button. The red dot blinked, twice in rapid succession. The last two phone messages Rudolph Reed had received were still on the tape.

14

MARTIN PUNCHED THE Play button, leaned forward, and listened: There was a high-pitched beep, then a tired-sounding male voice: "Uh, yeah . . . trying to reach you . . . at, uh, eight-fifteen Monday . . . I think we're going to have to make a decision by Friday and do the announcement shortly thereafter, if there's going to be one . . . But I'll talk with you."

Long beep.

A female voice, with a teasing, singsong lilt: "Officer Reed, this is Captain Carol. We haven't heard from you now for three whole days. And so, I'm afraid we have no choice but to terminate. Give me a call if you wish to appeal."

Martin felt a chill tingle slowly up his back at her inflection on the word "terminate." There was something sultry, yet unpracticed, about her tone, like voices from old movies—Mae West, with a little Marilyn Monroe mixed in.

He listened again, then pressed the Save button and went down to his car. The late-morning air was pulling noisily now through the trees and shrubbery. Martin returned with his tape recorder and set it beside the answering machine. He again felt a shiver go through him as she pronounced the word "terminate."

He sat in his car afterward, thinking about it, staring at the reference points in Rudolph Reed's life. Figuring: The first phone call was eight-fifteen Monday night. He died early Tuesday. Reed or someone else must have been in the office after that and played the recording; otherwise, the red message light would have been blinking.

*　*　*

It was 11:48 in Bananaville. Martin walked up the sidewalk to Sabal Street, stopping in front of Captain Jack's Seafood Market and Deli, where a shingle sign depicted a smiling white-haired man with a captain's hat and pipe.

It was cool inside, smelling of warm chowder and spicy seasonings. In a display case Martin saw bluefish and trout on ice, buckets of scallops and stone crab claws. A blackboard on an easel showed the day's "World Famous Lunch Special": shrimp salad and conch chowder with fried alligator bites.

The man behind the other display case, this one packed with meats and cheeses, smiled at him; a friendly, familiar face.

"You're the captain," Martin said.

"Yep." He slid a hand over his silvery hair. "That's me. What can I do you for today?"

"Well." Martin looked quickly up at the menu board. "Let me try your lunch special."

"Very good choice," Captain Jack said, showing a smile that reached nearly to his ears. "Coming right at you."

Captain Jack went to work, taking out a tub of shrimp salad and a loaf of bread, seeming to draw great pleasure from constructing the sandwich.

When Martin said, "I understand you were renting the upstairs here to Rudolph Reed," Captain Jack frowned for a moment. He pulled cooked bread slices from the toaster and stabbed a thick, dull-edged blade into the tub of shrimp salad.

"Yep," he said. "Nice man. One of the good guys. Hardest worker I've ever known. Although. I couldn't tell you for the life of me what he was doing up there half the time."

"He spent a lot of time in the office, did he?"

"Day and night, those last few weeks." He grinned like a beagle. "I drove by once, three o'clock in the morning, the light was on, and I seen Rudy's silhouette there by the window."

Chuckling, Captain Jack put the bread halves together and sliced the sandwich diagonally into twin triangles. "All the years we've rented that room, though, I must say, he had to be about the most dependable tenant."

"And how long's it been?"

Captain Jack frowned at him.

"That you've had this building."

"Oh. Seven and a half years," he said. "Well, owned it six. Lost our farm in Ohio in eighty-seven, didn't know what we was going to do. Had a few very bad months." Martin nodded. The captain looked up at him with a simple earnestness—a man with no secrets. "Finally decided to come down here, start at square one again. Rented this building with an option to buy. Only commercial-zoned property in this neighborhood. They grandfathered it in years ago.

"Of course, back in those days, my wife and I was working fifteen-, sixteen-hour days. We'd close shop, walk up those steps, sleep six, seven hours, and start it all over again. Took a while. We had a few rough patches. But then, gradually, word of mouth got around about those lunch specials. And that changed it all. This town's been good to us."

He smiled proudly. Martin, nodding politely, noticed an old-fashioned sign on the wall behind his shoulder: HOWARD AND BEVERLY HEARD, PROPRIETORS.

"My wife's the one come up with the Captain Jack idea," he said, ripping off a sheet of paper to wrap the sandwich. "We figured it'd help business to have a good nautical name. So my wife says, why don't you become Captain Jack? Just out of the blue one day. It was sort of a joke at first. Then I started doing those thirty-second commercials on the cable channel, and now everybody calls me the captain. Everywhere I go—restaurant, grocery store, bowling alley. It's like being a celebrity." He smiled at the thought. "Nobody knows me as old Howie Heard anymore. And I guess I sometimes miss that, to tell you the truth."

He leaned toward Martin and said, conspiratorially, "If you want to know the truth: I've never been to sea in my life." He looked to the ceiling, conjuring a price; $3.25, he wrote, with grease pencil, and placed the sandwich in a bag.

"Giving you ten percent off, how's that?"

Martin smiled, taking the bag. "Reed," he said, almost as an afterthought. "Had he been renting from you for a while?"

"Me? Nah, just since last summer. Last conversation I had with him was the Saturday before. Would I be willing to put a campaign sign in my window, he asked. I hated to say no, but it just doesn't help my business any to be controversial. And if he was anything, Rudy was controversial. I didn't really agree with his politics, either, I have to tell you. Like I say, this town's been real good to me. But I admired him as a hardworking fellow."

The plump, gray-haired woman doing a crossword puzzle beside the cash register smiled at Martin with a midwestern geniality. It was Beverly Heard, Captain Jack's wife.

He was eating his sandwich in the shade, on a bench out front, enjoying the breeze, when it occurred to Martin, again, for a fleeting moment, that this was a town where a murder had been committed and no one seemed to particularly care.

15

GOLDEN SUNLIGHT glared in the western windows of the newsroom with a radiance that made Martin think, for some reason, of iced bourbon. His inner weather had turned pleasantly mild in these past two days and he had begun to suspect that a storm was building somewhere.

He was typing his notes, transcribing what he had learned from Lila, Rudy, and Sammy Reed, when Martin noticed Hobart P. Lanahan coming up the corridor, through Sports, Business, and Life. There was an oddly urgent sway to his small shoulders, and his face seemed consumed with a single thought. Q. V. Robertson flashed Martin a look just as Hobart stepped into Metro.

"Had a zoning piece for you, Grant," he said, stopping at Martin's desk and looking pointedly at his watch. "Couldn't find you." The voice seemed to be trembling. "You called in and said noon, it's half past one." Martin looked quickly at the clock, then at Hobart, saw a vein pulsing wildly in his neck. "I just talked with Pete Fudd, and we're going to put the brakes on the Reed piece for a few days, shift you into general assignment. There are too many zoning issues this week for Q. V. to handle them all."

"Oh," Martin said. "Sure. No problem." This seemed like a squirt of gasoline on the fire of Hobart's anger. He returned to his office and closed the door hard, as Martin blinked at the newsroom. Q. V. Robertson stared at her terminal with an embarrassed blankness.

Hobart's door opened. He emerged, making a beeline to the water cooler. As he passed Martin, his tremulous voice pronounced, "If you're assigned to Metro, you're accountable to Metro. It's as simple as that." He drank a cup of water beside the cooler, in three long, slow sips, then poured a second cup. Martin could sense it shaking in his hand as he walked past.

Maybe, Martin decided, pretending to look through his notes, Hobart P. Lanahan had found out about his salary. Having been with the paper fourteen years, it was understandable he might have some resentment.

But, then, perhaps he was just slightly neurotic, not qualified for a position of authority. Martin had seen plenty of people like that over the years. Perhaps such episodes were commonplace with Hobart P. Lanahan.

Or was his anger justified? Martin had said noon, after all, and then come in at one-ten. He looked at the immaculate sanctuary of Hobart's massive office, saw the numerous pictures of his children and blond wife on a cabinet behind his desk, the awards and commendations on his walls. Hobart's face, tilted down into the light of his terminal, seemed green and lifeless, not unlike the face of a corpse he had once seen pulled from the Missouri River.


MARTIN DECIDED he would not make waves. He would let several days go by, helping Q. V. report on the city's efforts to draft a new comprehensive zoning code and anything else that came along. Getting to know the office, trying to know the town. It was difficult: Bananaville, he learned, had incorporated just after the war, and most of the town's development had occurred in the past ten to fifteen years. It was a place that still existed, Martin sensed, largely in the imagination of its residents.

On Saturday he cleared weeds and shrubbery from the yard on Coconut Lane, working until evening and then watching sunset through the oaks from his porch, enjoying the warm breezes that made Iowa seem very far away—not so much distant as past.

But on the news Sunday morning, he saw that there had been

six inches of snow in Iowa overnight, and it all came back: He thought of Katie, sitting in the antiques dealer's living room listening to Mahler, a warm fire of vodka glowing inside her, content, perhaps, with her new life. Marriage has two eyes, Martin used to say, and the task was keeping them focused; when he quit drinking, he had blinded theirs. He imagined Katie making the antiques dealer Italian stuffed peppers and poppy-onion pasta, fixing him her olive nut sandwich mix and spreading it on thin homemade toast before the fire as fat snowflakes fell across the farmland and ice melted in their vodka glasses.

That night he twice saw an infomercial for something called Joey Keen's "Human Potential University," with an annoying musical jingle that seemed, to Martin, just a few notes off the chorus of "Up, Up and Away."

"Remember," Keen said, with a handsome, satisfied smile, "if you think you can do it or you think you can't, you're right. *Do It. You Can.*"


RUDOLPH REED'S answering machine message still bothered Martin, though, and on his lunch break Tuesday, he took a haphazard drive along the town's wide, tree-lined boulevards, letting the Ouija board of his thoughts eventually take him back to Pineapple Lane.

Sammy Reed's eyes brightened faintly as she peered out above the burglar chain.

"I've been thinking about things," Martin said. "And had a couple questions I wanted to ask you. If you have a minute."

"Please. Come in."

Sammy was barefoot, dressed in a faded denim dress and black T-shirt. Yanni's piano music played loudly from the kitchen, and as Sammy went in to turn it down, Martin tasted wet onions and hamburger in the warm breeze. She was cooking again, making a meat loaf roll.

"The children in school?"

"Yeah, well. Joshua's upstairs taking a nap. The others are in school, yeah. Rudy was just here. I think he may still be down drying his clothes. Here, have a seat."

They sat on the old quilt-print sofa.

"So. How you making out?"

"We're okay." Sammy shrugged. "It's like my father said, I guess: Tough times never last, but tough people do."

In the awkward silence that followed, both stared at the picture of Rudolph Reed. The poutish features and steady eyes seemed for a moment to mirror Sammy's face.

"Can you do me a favor?" Martin said, and he placed his tape recorder on the coffee table. "Can you listen to these voices and tell me if either of them sounds familiar?"

She stared, expressionless, as he pressed the button. Martin watched her face: the odd, waxy texture of her skin, the mature concentration in her eyes as the tape began to roll. Sammy sat impassively as the first message played. During the second, she seemed to shudder.

"Oh, my God."

"You recognize it?"

"My God."

A flash of terror glazed her eyes. She looked away from Martin to the window and then back at the tape recorder, as if something even more horrifying might emanate from it. Martin looked, too.

"No," she said, at last. "No, I can't imagine."

"You don't recognize it, then?"

"No. No," she said. Martin sensed an uncertainty in her voice. As he lifted the tape recorder from the table, she said, "Wait. Play them one more time."

Sammy lifted her hard blue eyes to the framed portrait of Jesus on the wall, and didn't look away while the last two telephone messages to Rudolph Reed played again.

As MARTIN MADE his way along the stepping-stones back to the parking lot, he saw Rudolph Jr. with an enormous trash bag of laundry slung like Santa's sack over his shoulder.

"Mr. Grant!" he said, with a nervous breathlessness.

"Hi, Rudolph." Martin stopped. "I was just in talking with Sammy. Seeing how you're doing."

"Hold on." He dropped the bag of laundry in the grass and pulled a Walkman headset away from his ears. He was dressed, it seemed, in the same jeans, jersey, and basketball shoes.

"So. How you been?" Martin said.

His mouth shrugged, into a pout. R.E.M. played tinnily around his neck.

"Nothing much. Been getting some crank calls, though."

"Is that right?"

"Yeah. Hold on." He pushed at buttons on the Walkman, trying to turn it off. A car commercial blasted momentarily from the headset, then it went quiet. The sun felt hot above the red roofs and green palms, and the breeze tasted of cut grass. A faint film of sweat coated Rudolph's face as he squinted at Martin.

"What kind of crank calls?"

"I been getting them at my apartment—three, four nights in a row now. We used to get some here at the house and stuff. But this is the first time I've got them at my apartment."

"What do they say when they call?"

"Huh? They don't say anything."

"Hang-ups?"

"Some of them. Some of them are sound effects—like people screaming, car wrecks and stuff."

"Have you notified police?"

"Huh?"

Martin repeated the question. Rudolph's right leg shook with a nervous energy.

"Couple months ago. But they didn't do nothing."

Martin looked at his watch, saw he had ten minutes to get back to the newsroom. Sometimes he mistakenly believed that the Big Story would somehow make all the little problems in life disappear. He didn't much want to draw the ire of Hobart P. Lanahan for a second time.

"You been getting them at night, have you?"

"Usually around eight, or a little after eight. I've usually got 'Roseanne' on and stuff."

Martin smiled. "Well, keep in touch," he said, and made his way back, along the winding stepping-stones to the parking lot. The heat inside his car was so intense that for a moment Martin felt himself suffocating, felt a bubble of heat rise in his face, as he stared helplessly out at bumblebees and dragonflies, the peaceful melting pot of flowers, trees, and plants on the other side. He grabbed at the window lever and rolled, feeling himself begin to choke, and a nice breeze caught his face, with the smell of orchids and eucalyptus. The town seemed suddenly cooler, seemed to be drawing him in again, as he drove up the narrow, overgrown lane to the wider, open spaces at its center.

ON THURSDAY MORNING, as Martin was finishing a story on proposed changes in the city's berm regulations, Cora Carlson called, and his thoughts immediately jumped a groove, right back into the Reed story.

"Martin? I understand you're going to be reporting on Rudolph. I was surprised to hear Pete's so interested." Her voice sounded soft and seductive. "Anyway, why don't you stop by my house at lunchtime. I can set out a nice cold-cut spread for you. Mineral water, imported beer: whichever you prefer. We can have a leisurely lunch on my deck. How's that sound?"

Martin looked at Hobart, who was in his office talking with Peter Fudd. He felt adrenaline course through him, remembering what Nellie had said about Carlson being involved in Reed's death. His curiosity about the crime, and about the town, was such that he knew he couldn't say no. "I'll pass on the cold cuts," he said. "I had a big breakfast. But I can get away for a half hour at noon. If that's okay."

"That'd be lovely. I'll see you at noon."


THE CARLSON HOUSE was a lavish mix of Spanish Mediterranean and modern architecture, in a community known as Banana Estates. Martin drove onto the property through massive stainless steel gates and followed a winding gravel road to the porte cochere, where he parked behind a white pickup.

An alluring blonde in tennis whites was waiting.

"Martin? It's such a pleasure," she said, extending her hand as if expecting Martin to kiss it. Martin shook, taken by her perfect smile. She was tall and thick-waisted, with a mane of silver-blond hair, large, cool green eyes, and enormous breasts.

"It's so good to see you finally," she said. "Here, why don't we walk back to my deck? Where we can get comfortable."

"Sure."

Cora Carlson smiled again when Martin realized she wasn't wearing a bra. "Follow me."

As they crunched along a pathway, Martin tasted the spray from an Italian fountain and saw, down a short green hill, a huge, column-fringed swimming pool. They came to the marble deck behind the house, where Herb Albert and the Tijuana Brass were playing on stereo speakers.

"Please. Have a seat." Martin sat at one of the glass tables and watched Cora Carlson as she gazed dramatically toward the water. "There's a storm offshore, I'm told—is that right?" she said, studying the sparkles of sunlight, as if it were the Gulf of Mexico she saw and not some man-made lagoon. "We get some bad ones here occasionally. It's the only drawback to living in this town."

"It's quite a place," Martin said, with an unintentional hollowness.

"Oh, it's the greatest place in the world," she said, and flashed him a look that seemed, to Martin, briefly lustful. Her classic features had softened only slightly with age—and had been shored up, he suspected, by surgery. Martin guessed she was in her late forties.

"Drink?"

"Sure. Something lemon-lime would be good."

"Lemon-lime—like 7UP?"

"Fine."

"I'm a 7UP drinker, too," she said, behind the bar, her hair tossing in the wind. "Prefer it to Sprite, which to me is far too sweet. Of course, I've got to be in the mood for it, though."

She poured for herself a glass of Chardonnay and sat with Martin at the table, scooting her chair so it was inches from his. He smelled her flowery perfume, saw the freckles on her breasts rise and fall where her shirt was unbuttoned.

"I don't know what all you've heard, Martin," she said, her eyes moistening as if filling with emotion. "But I understand you're working on a story about Rudolph? I just wanted to make sure you hear the truth about him—before, you know, the boys get to you." She sipped, keeping her wet green eyes on his. "That's why I called you."

"Boys."

"Yes." She grinned dimly at the azure lagoon. She was a woman whose motives, Martin suddenly suspected, were complex, difficult to figure. She had an easy vulnerability in her eyes, which Martin didn't quite trust.

"What I admired about Rudolph was that he was a genuinely *honest* man. Most of the people in this town, you know, subscribe to the—what is it?—'screw the other guy before he screws you' idea. Rudolph didn't. He really didn't."

"You were good friends with him, were you?"

"We were friends," she said, and looked at her wine, running a finger absently over the rim of the glass. "Sure. We were friends."

The deck door opened and a man in jeans and an untucked work shirt poked out from the main house, locking eyes uncertainly with Martin.

"I'm going," he said, with a twang. He was skinny and unshaven, with sinewy arms and dark, unfriendly eyes. Martin guessed he was the maintenance man.

"Oh, wait. Jack!"

Cora Carlson got up showily, ran to the man, and pulled him onto the deck.

"Martin Grant. This is my husband, Jack. Martin here is with the newspaper. He's come over to ask me some questions about Rudolph Reed."

"Oh?"

"Yes. Jack is the superintendent of the Transportation Department for the city."

"What kind of questions?"

"Well—actually, she—"

76

"Don't be so suspicious, Jack," she said, in a false singsong.

Martin extended his hand, and Jack Carlson looked at it before shaking. He had a narrow, angular face covered with salt-and-pepper stubble. One of his eyeglass temples had been neatly attached, Martin noticed, with white adhesive tape.

"Well, happy hunting," he said, with a pointed sarcasm, and turned to go.

"Don't mind Jack," Cora said, gripping Martin's hand as they sat. "At any rate: What was I saying about Rudolph?"

"I don't remember." Martin saw her differently now—after the exchange with her husband—but still not clearly.

"I don't know. I mean—he just had a certain, sort of, I guess, integrity that most of the business community in this town lacks." Her eyes moistened in the breeze, and her tone became hushed. "You know, I can't stand the lies that go around—particularly at election time."

"About you and Rudolph Reed, for example."

Surprise lit her face, and then became a smile. "Well, of course, there's very little you can do about that sort of thing, though, is there?" She stared distantly at red fingernails. "I mean, I'm not about to get into a battle with phantoms, the way poor Rudy did. Because the phantoms will win. They will win and win again, and eventually if you continue to acknowledge their presence, they will kill you."

"Is that what happened?"

"What do you mean?"

"With Rudolph."

"Oh." Her eyes welled with tears as she gazed toward the water.

Martin looked where she looked: A blue heron glided just above the bank of her lawn. The sky and trees shone up from the lagoon's mirrorlike surface.

"Tell me what kind of story you're going to write," she said, fixing him with a clear-eyed, businesswoman's gaze. "I'll tell you if I can help."

"Oh, I don't really do it that way," Martin said. "Fitting the facts around a premise. I first collect all that can be collected and see what shape it takes."

Her eyes glazed coolly. "At any rate—here's a fact you might want to store in the back of your mind. For when it comes time to write your story: Rudolph had come across something, I don't know what, just in the last week before he died. Something that was really troubling him. Something—" Her eyes were starting to tear up again, her lower lip to quiver.

"I've already heard that," Martin said. "Any idea what, though?"

"You've heard that?"

"Yes."

She seemed genuinely surprised by this—but continued to look toward the lagoon, as if something were happening there. "This can't ever be tied back to me," she said, and looked at him with hardening eyes. "Because I would be forced to deny it. But what I suspect is it had something to do with Joey Keen." She looked down ruefully, and added, "Joey's a partner, you know, in this Bananaland Park expansion project. Which is a very crazy project, and something that Rudy was adamantly opposed to. It violates state growth laws, for one thing; density laws, everything else. But somehow they blithely proceed, getting variances and exceptions right and left."

There was something disingenuous in her tone, Martin sensed. He looked at his watch, wondering if Hobart would subject him to another verbal attack if he came in late.

"I understand your uncle was once my uncle's landlord," he said, trying to lighten things up. Cora Carlson stared at him as if he had just spoken in Russian.

"Excuse me?"

He explained to her about Uncle Otis and the old Shangri-La Expressway. The capricious departure from Hamlet and the dream of a better life.

"Oh, well, we're not too proud about that one," she said quickly, with a crooked smile. He saw a faint stain of lipstick on her teeth. "But it was a long time ago. The Folsoms came down here in the late forties, you know, when the town was sort of inventing itself for the very first time, and some of us did well, some of us didn't. It was a new world then, anything was possible. My father ended up making a fortune in the frozen orange juice business. His brother opened a motor court out in the county, went belly-up in six months and asphyxiated himself in his garage while my aunt slept upstairs.

"At any rate. You keep looking at your watch—am I boring you?"

"No. Not at all."

"I just wanted you to hear something positive about Rudolph Reed—before the sharks close in, Martin. That's why I called you. He was a good, decent man who cared about people, cared about families, and cared about the future."

Her eyes were filled with tears again. Martin began to wonder why she had really called him.

"It's sort of ironic, too, isn't it? He had the strength of the people, but with him gone, his supporters are all just sort of little people again."

"Little people."

"Sure."

Martin looked away from her. Across the lagoon, one-hundred-foot coconut palms tilted toward the water, which mirrored their waving green leaves and orange coconuts. Martin opened his notepad.

"One thing I'm just curious about is why Reed was writing seven-hundred-fifty-dollar checks to you every month."

"Oh." Cora Carlson smiled. "He rented from me," she whispered. "I own the duplex where the Reeds live. I own four of them, in fact. That's how I came to know them." She looked at her wine, rubbed a finger over the rim. "I feel quite bad for those Reed children, I really do. Although Sammy, bless her heart, is a little wonder."

"When did you last see Reed?"

"Me? Several days before it happened." Her gaze turned back toward Martin's. "He came by with some papers he wanted copied. That was sort of the unwritten agreement we had—I'd let him use the copy machine here when he needed it. I think that's how those rumors started—about us. He did come by, occasionally. I mean, when Jack wasn't here. But it was just to make copies."

"Not the night before?"

"Excuse me?"

"He wasn't here the night before it happened?"

She regarded him more carefully now.

"No. Why?"

"I understand he had the initials C.C. penciled in his appointment book for five-thirty the day before he died."

A poker face gazed back at him. "No," she said. "In fact, I remember, it was Saturday, because I went in Sunday morning to use the copier and I saw he'd left a sheet of paper on it."

"I see." A long gust of wind mottled the lagoon's surface again, scrambling the perfect reflection of trees and sky. "What was he copying, do you remember?"

She shrugged. "I think it's still in there by the machine, actually," she said, nodding toward the door to the house. "Here, have a look, if you want." With the urgency of a teenager, she led him into a small room just inside the entranceway. The room was dark and smelled of paper and chemicals. "Yessirree," she said, handing a sheet to Martin. "It's still right here."

"What is it?" she said, and he felt her flesh breathing against his. "I don't even know what it is. Take it if you want."

"I'll make a copy, if that's okay."

"Sure. Whatever you'd like." Her hip pressed his for a moment as he made the copy. Martin tried to avoid her eyes, which were staring.

Finally they both walked into the sunshine. It was nearly one o'clock and time to get back.

"Maybe next time," she said, as they stood in the porte cochere watching one another, "you can come over when you've got more time."

"I'd like that."

"Good."

She smiled with a provocative ease as he got in his wagon and seemed surprised when Martin rolled down the window and raised his hand.

"Oh, I almost forgot. I was just curious," he said. "Have the police questioned you at all?"

"The police? No, why would they?"

Martin left her there, with a look of deep bemusement in her eyes.

PARKED IN A Winn Dixie lot, Martin read the paper Cora Carlson had given him. It was a newspaper clipping, from 1986, about seven realtors who were under investigation in upstate New York for alleged time-share fraud. One of the seven names had been underlined: Joseph L. Keen Jr.

Martin checked his clock—1:08. Squeaky-wheeled shopping carts rattled between the rows of cars.

SIPPING COFFEE that afternoon, waiting for Hobart to leave for lunch, Martin saw China Rinaldi emerge from beneath the epiphytes of the live oaks and walk in shadow along the riverbank back to the building. She was dressed today in white jeans, a white turtleneck shirt, and white canvas Keds. On her head was a blue beret. Each day she had looked to Martin like someone different. Yesterday she'd been an executive, dressed in a burgundy suit with dainty suede pumps and carrying a small shoulder bag. But Wednesday she wore a flannel shirt and baggy green pants. And on Tuesday—if he remembered correctly—she'd had on an ankle-length flower-print dress with clunky Doc Martens and had come in to work carrying a knapsack. Always her smile seemed to dissolve unhappily after she said "Hi" to Martin, as if something were troubling her.

Shortly before two, Hobart P. Lanahan completed his drawn-out twice-daily ritual of emptying, cleaning, and drying his coffee cup, and finally left for his lunch break. Martin pulled out the newspaper clipping Cora Carlson had given him. It was rubber-stamped with the date the copy had been made: November 29. Martin got a number for the Orange County Dispatch from directory assistance and dialed, asking for the library.

After a recorded voice told him, twice, how easy it was to subscribe, a live, female voice picked up: "Have you been helped?"

"No," he said. "I ordered a clipping from you last month and I was just checking because it hasn't arrived yet."

"All copies must be prepaid," the woman said, with finality.

"Well, this would have been."

"Mmmm, hold up." The phone clunked on a desk. He heard a bag being crumpled. After a moment: "Date request was made?"

"I believe it would have been late November."

He heard the woman chew and swallow. "Save some of that for me," she said to someone, and laughed. Two minutes passed. Two and a half. "What was the date of the article? Let me try it that way."

"May twenty-first, 1986."

"Okay. And what's your name?"

"It would have been ordered by—the name would have been either Reed or Carlson, I believe."

"What?"

"Reed or Carlson."

"Hold up." Another bag crumpled. He listened to her drink a beverage. "Okay," she said. "According to our records, that was sent to Mrs. Carlson, at 1123 Flamingo Road on November twenty-ninth."

"Uh, that's our other address," Martin said. "Let me check on that first, and then get back to you."

There was silence at the other end. Martin hung up.

So.

His instincts about Cora Carlson were correct. For whatever reason, she was attempting to manipulate him, and trying to implicate Joey Keen.

THE AFTERNOON air turned breezy, creaking the old wooden newspaper building.

Martin walked along the row of empty offices, surprised to hear a light tapping sound on the window of one. Dale Bunch looked out at him, pointing at the doorknob.

"Grant," he said, gesturing for Martin to come in, and close the door. The lights in his office were all out today, even the desk lamp. The room smelled of books and Ben-Gay.

"Lose interest in the Reed story? Haven't seen anything." His sad, red-veined eyes seemed to pull down the whole face like melted wax as he waited for Martin's reply.

"No, I've been temporarily sidelined."

"Hobart?"

"Yes."

Dale Bunch closed his eyes, as if conjuring some deep and troubling thought. "Hobart, you see, is a fine fellow who will never leave the shallow waters, the way you have. He is, therefore, very protective of his accomplishments, and always looking out for the well-placed idea that might trip him. Which is not to in any way denigrate him. He's just on a different sort of journey than the one you are on." Martin eyed him uncertainly. Bunch's huge mouth widened into a mysterious smile, which Martin met halfway. "I understand you're a teetotaler," he said.

"Yes," Martin said, though he didn't think he had told anyone in town, other than Nellie. "I am."

"Are you in the program?"

It took Martin a moment to realize what he was asking. "No, I just seem to get by these days on faith."

"Ah." His loose, craggy face nodded, though the red eyes looked at him skeptically. "It's easier to fall back that way. If you're ever interested in going to a meeting, give me a holler." He added, lifting his arms and smiling unhappily, "It took this to happen to me before I came to my senses."

By "this," Martin realized, he meant the paralysis. Bunch closed his eyes and went somewhere else again. Martin found it difficult, yet somehow fascinating, to watch him—something akin to voyeurism.

"Of course, we're all disabled in some fashion, aren't we?" he said, keeping the eyes shut and tilting his head upward. "Disabled by our misguided aspirations, by our periodic inefficacies. I didn't have a higher power in those days. When you see yourself as your own authority, you can rationalize any behavior as being just. That's the problem with these city officials. And with the people who killed Rudolph."

Dale Bunch's eyes opened slowly, as if he were waking from a long sleep. A faint smile came into his mouth. "An athlete, in the course of a competition," he said, speaking in an agonizingly slow voice, "may be so unfortunate as to be seriously injured, or even killed. We have seen it in boxing, we have seen it even in football. Who do we blame when this happens? Finally, we don't blame anyone, do we?"

"No."

"No. We don't."

"Politics is like sports, you're saying? With inevitable casualties?"

"No." Dale closed his eyes. "Although, when you come to town, you do put on a uniform, in a sense, I suppose. You are now a player for the town, and at times, everyone must wear the uniform. Now, you may gain a great deal for yourself personally, financially, or any number of other ways. But you cannot forget who you are representing. To not wear the uniform and still benefit personally: That is the forbidden."

84

"And that's what you're saying Rudolph did."

Dale Bunch opened his eyes and shook his head. The breeze rustled newspapers in the newsroom. Hobart, Martin saw, had returned from lunch.

"No, what Rudolph did was to say we should forge ahead with the same philosophical fuel that our fathers and grandfathers used. He subscribed, you see, to Carlyle's epigraph, 'Work is worship.' Or Ben Franklin's: 'Diligence is the mother of good luck.' But people nowadays do not want to hear this. They are more interested in winning the lottery. As our problems worsen, you see, we want to believe in some sort of magic. That's why we keep building these theme parks everywhere—why even our shopping centers and housing developments now are done as theme parks: It numbs us. We need that."

"I see."

Hobart hurried by, for a second time, turning his head and making quick eye contact with Martin through the glass.

"There's a daughter," Martin said. "None of them seems to want to talk about her. Did you know her?"

"I met Ginny, yes." He struggled, unsuccessfully, to clear his throat. Martin glanced impatiently at his watch. "She had disassociated herself from the family—this was a couple years ago—and was trying to invent a new life. Perhaps even with a new name."

"Who were Reed's friends? Do you know?"

"Friends?" He repeated the word as if unsure of its meaning. "I think he had very little of what we would consider traditional friendships." His eyes met Martin's, seemed to sense what he was thinking. "Although he was friends, I believe, with Quentin Craig, who owns Newt's Sunoco. Chuck Craig."

"Okay."

Martin flipped open his notebook. He wrote, "Chuck Craig. Newt's Sunoco," and sensed something moving against the strip of glass behind him.

He looked and saw Hobart, standing there, stabbing his right forefinger violently into the face of his wristwatch. His neck and face were pink, as if he'd just finished shaving.

"Better go."

"Let me see what I can do about that, Martin," Dale Bunch said. His wink seemed that of a much younger man.

**18** By the time Martin closed up his briefcase, the wind was gusting wildly through the trees, blowing Spanish moss and pieces of palm fronds across the parking lot. The western sky had turned purplish gray, although to the east the air was still a perfect blue.

"Looks like a storm coming," Martin said as he approached the lobby, expecting Carol Peek, the twenty-two-year-old receptionist, to respond perkily.

Instead, a loud, cronish voice said, "Where you think you're going, boy? Ha! Ha! Ha! Ha! Ha! My brother's looking for you."

A happy old woman with badly dyed brown hair was sitting behind the receptionist's desk, working a crossword. This, he realized, must be Dixie Fudd, Pete's sister, the operator who consistently got his phone messages wrong.

"Going home," he said, trying to be cheerful.

"No, you're not."

"I'm not?"

"Nope."

She looked back to her crossword puzzle, smiling. Martin, waiting, smelled vodka as she breathed.

"Not now, you're not."

"Why not?" he said, not sure of the game.

He stepped back slightly, away from the smell.

"Pete wants to see you. Catch him before he leaves, he said. You're Martin Grant, right?"

"Right."

"Well, I guess you're in trouble then."

"Oh."

She stared down at the puzzle, barely able to contain a smile.

At the end of the hallway, Martin rapped on Pete Fudd's big oak door, expecting the worst, though not caring too much. If Hobart's undisclosed problem with him was insurmountable, so be it. There were other places to go, and a house still waiting for him in snow-covered Hamlet, Iowa.

Inside, the fans were turning. A movie projector and screen had been set up beside the Bengal tiger, and there were a half dozen eight-millimeter film canisters strewn on Fudd's desk. The sound of barking sea lions played on his stereo speakers.

"Martin! How are you?" he said, gripping Martin's shoulders and shaking him gregariously. He was dressed in white shorts and a golf shirt today, reminding Martin of the captain from "Love Boat."

"Have a seat, have a seat."

"Thank you."

Fudd himself sat heavily behind his desk. He sighed at all the paperwork in front of him, then began to sort through a sheaf of bills, seeming to forget that Martin was there. The sound of the sea lions subsided, and was replaced by what seemed to be hyenas.

"Martin," he said at last, looking up, "I just want to make something clear. I hired you because of these." He shook several sheets of paper quickly in the air; it wasn't clear what they were. Then he pushed the chair back from his desk so he could slump down more comfortably. "This is the most successful town in the nation right now, Martin. Fastest-growing, cleanest, most prosperous. And I frankly don't think we're selling newspapers in the kind of numbers we should be. You want to know why? Because what we print isn't indispensable. What we print, they can get on TV, radio. They can get it in the *Banner*.

"I want you to give me investigative stories. Stuff they can't get anywhere else. I want you to climb right back on this Reed story, go after it from every angle you can think of." His slow, southern accent seemed to have disappeared. "Give me a story a day, if you can. Make it hard-hitting, even a little sensationalistic. I want the town talking."

"Does Hobart know this?"

Fudd smiled, showing his overbite.

"I just talked to him. Hobart means well, but he sometimes has a short fuse. From now on, you answer to me, not Hobart. I want us to do everything we can to keep this story out there. I want the town talking."

WIND SHOOK THE old house on Coconut Lane that evening and heat lightning illuminated the trees and thick growths of tropical shrubbery. The rain Martin had expected, though, never came, and when he woke early—4:31—there was a surreal quiet in the silver mist, as if the storm had passed by. The moon-soaked oak leaves stirred only faintly, and the air was cool and jasmine-scented. Martin stood at the bedroom window and saw that a light was on in China Rinaldi's house. Several times he had seen that glow, late at night. He tried to sleep again, but couldn't, picturing the pinkish edges of terror in Sammy Reed's eyes, the way they had turned to his, seeking some answer he couldn't give. For her, Martin wanted to figure this crime.

AT THE OFFICE, Hobart's door was closed and his back turned disconsolately to the newsroom. He didn't acknowledge Martin.

There was an envelope in a corner of Martin's desk pad, marked with his name.

He opened it: *"You owe me one. D.B."*

Dale Bunch.

Most everywhere Martin had worked he'd found this—a secret army of helping hands, quietly assisting one another—just as he had found the loners like Hobart P. Lanahan, people who insisted for whatever reason that their accomplishments be largely unassisted.

Martin spent the morning typing out everything he knew so

far about Rudolph Reed, the names he had recorded from the canceled checks, the asnwering machine messages, and the impressions he had gathered from those people he'd talked with: Nellie, Cora Carlson, Dale Bunch, Sammy, Lila, and Rudolph Reed. By noon, he decided the person he most wanted to see was Joey Keen.

19 CHECKING IN THE phone book, Martin found half a column of Keen listings. Five private residences, six Keen Real Estate offices, two listings for Keen Enterprises, two for Keen Human Potential University, and one for Keen Real Estate School.

Martin began with the offices.

Keen, one receptionist said, would be unavailable until February, but he could leave a message with his secretary.

At another office, Keen was expected to be in meetings all day. When Martin asked if he could leave a message, a Muzak version of "I Just Called to Say I Love You" began to play.

He decided to try the residences, but got recordings at all five numbers listed.

Stumped, Martin stared at his terminal, listening to the light breeze in the palms outside. Sometimes the Big Story seemed perpetually beyond his reach, like the sound of wind, like smells that conjured delicious memories of things he could never taste again.

Q. V., her hair braided today in cornrows and tipped with bright-colored beads, came around her desk several minutes later. Without smiling, she dropped a folded scrap of paper on Martin's desk.

"You trying to reach Keen?"

Martin nodded, feeling a little stupid.

"All you had to do was ask me," she said, and winked. "This'll get you inside his house. After that, you're on your own." Martin watched her, as she went back to her terminal, the beads in her hair rattling. He liked Q. V., her coolness and competence.

Her membership in the secret army of helping hands.

Martin dialed this new number, and he waited.

"Hello?" a voice said after the fourth ring.

It was an abrupt, harsh sound.

"Joey?"

"Archie, what took you so long?"

"Hello?"

"Is this Archie?"

"Martin Grant."

There was a quick intake of breath on the other end. "Who?"

"I'm a reporter with the *Daily News*."

"Hold on." Muzak began to play in his ear: "Baby, you can drive my car . . ."

A moment later, a woman's voice said, "May I help you?"

"I was calling for Joey Keen."

"I'm sorry, Mr. Keen's out of town until next week. May I help you with something?"

"Is this Mrs. Keen?"

"No, it isn't."

"No message, then."

Martin looked at Q. V., who just shrugged and went back to the story on her screen. Martin sighed.

So: The seemingly ubiquitous Joey Keen could not, in real life, be found anywhere.

ON THAT LONG-AGO summer in Iowa, when the warm winds sounded like freight trains over the darkened prairie and constellations sparkled with unspoken promises deep into the night, Nellie Grant had left Martin, saying that if he ever at any time felt "stuck," he should give her a call.

He remembered it today, after being told by Police Chief "Tuffy" Cole that no one in the department was authorized to say anything whatsoever about the Rudolph Reed case, so long as it was an open homicide investigation.

Martin dialed the state attorney's office for Coconut County and asked to speak with Nellie Grant.

"I'm sure glad you called," she said, nearly breathless.

"You are?"

"Sure. Listen. There's a gal in the county clerk's office. Her name is Jocelyn. I think you ought to meet her."

"Oh? How come?"

"Well, I mean: We're talking perfect match here, Martin. She's big on art and books, metaphysics and that kind of stuff you like."

"Is that what you think I like—metaphysics?"

"Cuz—I'm telling you."

Nellie's energy was still mildly contagious. Yet as subtly as he could, Martin nudged the conversation to police sources. And Nellie followed.

"Oh. I mean, yeah. Sure, I know someone real well. Rick Howard—he's one of the detectives. I'm sure he'd talk to you off the record. Let me see if I can get ahold of him."

Five minutes later, Martin's phone buzzed.

"Hey, cuz," she said. "He'll meet you at four. Not the head investigator or anything, okay? But he's involved in the case. He said there's only so much he can say. So it's a matter of asking the right questions."

Martin felt himself smiling inside. "How'd you manage this?"

"Oh, never mind," she said mischievously. And added, "I went out with him for a couple weeks last winter. No biggie. There's something sort of—I don't know—brutish about him, though."

She lowered her voice to a whisper: "His back is all covered with hair." Martin surprised himself by laughing out loud, looking up to catch Thomas Persons's startled, bloodshot eyes, then Q. V.'s.

"Ask him what evidence they've got," she added. "Sam says they found some shards of glass on the body that might have come from eyeglasses. Oh, and the 911 call? I understand it was female. Anonymous."

"Gotcha." Martin was jotting notes.

"Cuz?"

"Let me take a rain check on Jocelyn. Just for now."

Nellie sighed deeply.



DETECTIVE RICK HOWARD'S biceps were huge, straining the sleeves of his police uniform. His lantern-jawed face had a dark, dull-eyed steadiness and the first traces of five-o'clock shadow. He was surprisingly short—probably five foot three—and spoke with a soft, distinctly midwestern accent.

"You're Nellie's cousin," he said, as if it were something Martin might not know.

"Yes."

"Good girl. Come on back." His black eyes stared for a moment into Martin's. "How's she been?"

"Nellie? Oh. Good."

"Good." He held a Styrofoam coffee cup in one hand and a folder of police reports in the other. He led Martin down a bright tiled hallway to the conference room. There was a pleasant fragrance of fresh coffee in the corridors, a sound of computer keyboards and easy conversations.

"So what's this about, anyway?"

"No big deal. I just wanted to ask a couple of questions."

"I told Nellie I'd talk to you," Rick Howard said, ushering Martin in. "But there's not much I can say."

"Sure." He closed the door. It was a small dusty room with a long wooden table and six metal card chairs. A fan spun at one end of the table.

"It's an active case. So there's really nothing I can say. Other than we're actively investigating it as a homicide. But have a seat if you'd like."

Martin did. He flipped up his notepad. A cooling breeze rattled gently on the screen window.

"Just a couple of things, then," Martin said, frowning at his notes. Rick Howard sat, too, across the table from Martin, gripping his coffee cup. "Let's see—I understand the 911 caller was female, is that correct?"

In the room lit only by daylight, Rick Howard's face went quickly blank, like a television that is turned off and on again.

"Where'd you hear that?"

Martin tilted his head and waited. The fan swept the room, a cool uneven slicing sound.

"Off the record? I don't know. We have indications that it was a female, that's correct. The voice sounded—to members of this division—as if it had been disguised."

"I see." Martin looked back at his notes, feigning confusion. "Disguised in what sense? Muffled?"

"We're not in a position to further comment on it at this time," he said, and coughed unnecessarily. The thick fingers of his left hand tapped nervously on the coffee cup. His nails had all been bitten down.

Martin nodded, turning pages.

"Okay, and let's see. I understand police found glass fragments on the body—which may have come from a pair of eyeglasses."

Again, his face flickered with surprise.

"No. Off the record?"

"Off the record."

"That's sort of right."

"Okay."

He stared vacantly at Martin as the fan sliced the air. Finally, as if in their silence some agreement had been reached, he said, "It wasn't eyeglasses, though. Unless it was clear glass."

"I see."

"Yeah."

Rick Howard glanced at the wall clock.

"One more thing," Martin said. "I understand the Reeds had been getting some crank calls for a number of weeks. Repeated hang-ups and that kind of thing. Now Rudolph Jr.'s getting them. He claims it's been reported but that police have never followed up on it."

"Categorically false," the detective said, his voice thickening surprisingly. *"One hundred percent incorrect.* No . . ." He at last opened the Reed file, looking through it intently for several minutes, as Martin watched. "Okay. Here we go—on November twenty-second. We traced four hang-up calls reported by Reed, all to the same two pay phones."

"Uh-huh." Martin squinted to see the report, but the detective had it shielded from his view.

"Each time Reed complained, we checked it out. Each time. In some instances, it proved to be a flagrant waste of police time and manpower. For example: Rudolph came in here one time—this is the father we're talking about now—and said he thought the chairman of the Planning and Zoning Commission had stolen his daughter's coin collection. Just to give you one of the more embarrassing examples. City police investigated that one for two weeks. Two weeks. Questioned the chairman of the Planning and Zoning Commission—who happens to collect coins.

And found after two weeks that Reed's daughter had actually left her collection—Indian-head pennies, primarily—on the school bus."

"I see."

The intercom squawked: "Detective Howard, pick up the local, please. Detective Howard."

Sausage-shaped fingers closed the file, and Rick Howard set his coffee cup on top. "Excuse me," he said, giving Martin a sharp look. The telephone was on the hallway wall, outside the conference room.

Martin, waiting, stared at the lengthening shadows on the green lawn, the glimmer of sunlight in the pear-shaped fruit of an avocado tree. He thought of Rudolph Reed trying to elude the phantoms that surrounded his life, trying to stay ahead of them, and then he thought of his own phantoms. It took less than two minutes before the urge to remove the coffee cup got the better of him. He went through the Reed file quickly, scanning autopsy results, incident reports, photos of the crime scene, transcripts of interviews, the telephone tap release and report. There were three pictures of Rudolph Reed in the file, lying on the beach, his blue eyes open as if staring into space, at his life's reward.

From this cursory look, it didn't seem to Martin as if the police knew much more than he did. He jotted down the two telephone numbers where the calls had been traced, figuring he could find their locations in the cross-reference book back at the paper.

Howard, in the hallway, said, "What?" and "What for?" repeatedly, as if he were being joshed by someone. When he hung up, Martin set the coffee cup back on the folder and stared outside, at the stop and go of tourist traffic in the afternoon shadows.

"That was your cousin," he said, showing an odd, crooked grin. "I'm not sure exactly what she wanted."

Martin nodded, and tried not to smile. "So, anyhow." He closed his notepad. "How do you like it here, anyway?" The question seemed to confuse Rick Howard, but also to jar him from any suspicions he had about the phone call.

"Here?"

Martin nodded.

"You mean this town? Or the police department?"

"Town."

"Oh—it's the best. It's clean. Great. A great place to raise kids, bring up a family." A comfortableness came into his face for the first time. "We moved here from Minnesota three years ago. My wife, three daughters. Believe me, I don't miss those Minnesota winters even a little bit."

He showed a nice set of white teeth. His biceps seemed to involuntarily flex.

"I know what you mean," Martin said. "How do you feel about this case, by the way? Off the record. Any chance of breaking it?"

"Off the record?" He shook his head surreptitiously. "Right now, we don't have the evidence. No weapon, no witnesses. We keep interviewing people. But we're not developing anything new."

"I see. So nothing'll happen?"

"Well, eventually it'll fade away. Everything does, doesn't it?"

"Yep."

"Sad, when you think about it."

LONG STREAKS OF sunshine slanted through the newsroom when Martin returned. There was a hushed, busy sound of clicking keyboards as reporters and editors worked toward unseen deadlines. Martin could taste the fish that Thomas Persons was cooking in the parking lot, on an aluminum grill, and watched, feeling relieved of life's deadlines, much as Thomas Persons seemed to be, though for different reasons. He was a ruddy, portly man who dressed in three-piece suits nearly every day, whose curly white hair was receding haphazardly. Periodically he took nips, as he watched the fish, from a canteen that Martin suspected contained vodka. Senior writer.

A woman with wild dark hair, wearing a black crepe jump-suit with gold chains and backless black platform shoes, surprised Martin, coming up the corridor toward his desk. It was China Rinaldi.

She had barely spoken to him since he'd arrived in Bananaville, but came over now as though they were friends. Martin studied her face as she stood beside his desk: deep brown eyes and long lashes, high cheekbones, a European nose, and the unhappy mouth. A model's face.

"Q. V. said you were trying to get up with Joey Keen," she said. "I'm going over to his house in about fifteen minutes, if you care to come along. I have to drop off a proof of his ad."

"Oh, sure. Sure," Martin said, and looked up: Hobart P. Lanahan was blinking in at them as if he had just put on a new pair of eyeglasses.


CHINA RINALDI'S MUSTANG was white, a new-model convertible, which she drove at remarkable speeds, her long black hair whipping wildly in the wind, as she negotiated her way through slower traffic like the front-runner in an auto race. She smelled fresh, of mineral bath salts and herbal soaps, and Martin realized that everything about China Rinaldi seemed that way: the house, the car, the way she looked each day. She had the skin of a woman in her mid-twenties, though he suspected she was at least ten years older than that.

"Tom Persons cracks me up," she said at a traffic light, looking at him for only a moment.

"Tom Persons does?"

"He's a friend of mine. A very smart man. But he cracks me up. You know, he says he sleeps with a bottle of vodka and a bottle of water next to his bed each night. Last night, he was telling me, he reached for the water bottle, right? It turned out to be the vodka."

She zoomed ahead of the car beside them.

When they were stopped again, Martin asked, "What do you think of Keen, anyway?"

"Keen? Condescending and chauvinistic." She added, "But he's got bucks. And he's gonna be our next fricking mayor. So I play along with him."

"He's being groomed to be mayor, is he?"

She couldn't hear in all the wind—the whoosh of passing coconut palms and houses and parked cars. Martin repeated himself, shouting, but she waited until the next traffic signal to respond.

"Oh, big-time. Total remake. Used to go out playing 'hide the salami' every night, now he's Mr. Family Man. That's what politics is, though, and he's very good at it." She watched the traffic lights, tilting at different angles in the wind. Then she looked at Martin, giving him a big grin. He couldn't imagine what she was thinking.

"So," she said. "How are you and Hobart making out?"

"Oh." Martin groaned.

A car pulled up next to theirs, thumping with rap music.

"He can't stand the idea of an investigative reporter being placed right under his nose, can he? But you know what? I don't think he should be in that fricking position in the first place. I don't think he has the temperament for it. He's actually a pretty nice guy. Best father in the world."

"Is that right?" Martin watched as she sped through the entrance to Banana Estates and along a narrow, winding road, skidding several times as it twisted.

A tunnel separated Joey Keen's gargantuan Spanish-style villa from his six-car garage.

"Just watch," China said, parking. "Watch how he acts around me. You're going to get a kick out of this." She led Martin familiarly through the bright concrete tunnel, coming out into a vaulted ceiling foyer—with marble floor, walnut-paneled walls, and Venetian footstools. There seemed, to Martin, peering in at the house, far more of it than was necessary—skylights stretched across the dining and family rooms, cantilevered mahogany and brass stairways rose from the living room to places he couldn't see. Through tall Palladian windows he spied an interior courtyard with a huge European fountain.

"I'd hate to pay the electric bills," Martin muttered.

"Oh. He can afford it."

At just that moment, Keen seemed to step from a closet, materializing as a blur of geniality in a white Armani suit. "Hey, doll!" he said, giving China a sloppy hug. "How you been, what you got for me?"

He was probably forty-five years old, Martin figured, watching, with thick dyed black hair, blue eyes, a rugged grin, and faint cleft in his chin. Without acknowledging Martin, he led them into the living room—an enormous open space with crystal chandeliers, French doors, and an Italian mural. In the huge Palladian window across the room, Martin saw a terra-cotta statue of Orpheus.

"Here, let's take a look," Keen said. He spread the ad on a narrow gilt table, and the two stared, as if it were ancient art they were studying.

Martin moved closer to have a look. Most of the ad was Keen's smiling face; below it, in twenty-four-point type, were three decks of words:

> He Was the Right Man Then
> He's the Right Man Now
> Reelect Joey Keen

Humorlessly, and with a deepening frown, Keen said, "I don't know. It isn't centered properly, is it? I thought we were going to center it."

"It isn't?"

He meant the picture, Martin realized, not the type.

China frowned now, too.

"Mmm. You may be right," she said. "Let me see what I can do with it. The typeface is all right?"

"Typeface?" He looked again, as if he hadn't noticed. "It's better than what we had before, anyhow." A flush of lechery momentarily filled his eyes as he took a quick inventory of China's legs and rear. "And this can go full page? half, quarter?"

"Whatever you want."

" 'Kay."

The three of them stared down at the picture of Keen's grinning face for more than a minute, as if waiting for it to move.

"Oh, Joe," she said. "Joe, I'm sorry. This is Martin Grant here. Our new special assignment reporter. At the paper? I was giving him a lift home and he wondered if he could talk with you—just for five minutes, before we go?"

Keen looked with feigned irritation at his Rolex. "You know what? I'm kind of pressed right now, darling." He smiled at Martin affably, though the eyes seemed far away. "But how about if we make a point of getting together sometime next week." A different, more facile, smile appeared. "How you doing? How you liking the town?"

"Great."

"Isn't it great? Greatest town in the world."

Martin looked at China, then at his own watch, bought at Wal-Mart in Iowa City. "How about if I take just two minutes?" he asked. "One quick question, two-minute time limit."

"Oh." This time Keen's smile was delayed, and he seemed to shrug. "I don't care. 'Kay, why don't you have a seat in there, I'll be in in a second."

His study was a startling departure from the classical tone of the living room: The walls were white, and the desk and chairs were of an ornate Chinese design. Against one wall was a velvet-upholstered love seat, with tassels and silk-embroidered Oriental pillows. Against another, on the bare, basket-weave parquet floor, was a grandfather clock and life-sized bronze Buddha. Through the oval windows Martin saw a bright garden of flowers, a Japanese torii gate, and what looked like a Shinto shrine.

Hearing Keen banter energetically with China, Martin walked behind his desk to look at the photos and plaques on the wall: There was one of Keen with the governor; another with

Donald Trump, who was eagerly gripping his hand while Marla Maples looked on. He saw an appointment book on the credenza and flipped back quickly to the Tuesday Rudolph Reed had died. There was only one notation for that day: "Call J.C." Martin closed the book.

*Jack Carlson?*

"So what can I do for you?" Keen startled him, standing in the arched doorway. "Have a seat, Martin. Relax." The easy smile crossed his face as both men sat, Martin in an ornate, uncomfortable wooden chair. "How you enjoying the town?"

"Fine."

"Glad to hear it."

"What I wanted to ask, though: I'm doing some background on Rudolph Reed—"

"Well." He nodded with an ambiguous grin. "I certainly had nothing against Rudy. Didn't always agree with him, of course. But he was a hard worker, and his hard work paid off, didn't it? Won him a lot of friends and supporters." Keen leaned back in the chair as if to contemplate what he'd just said. He had several smiles that he rotated, Martin noticed, the mouth managing his facial expression and, it seemed, his personality.

"I try to be philosophical about it. In a sense, it was the same thing anyone's after: prosperity. That's what this town's all about. Now, that word means different things to different people, of course. Prosperity of family. Of ideas. Of the spirit. Maybe it's financial prosperity you're after. Whatever it is, it's available in this town if you're willing to roll up your sleeves and do the work. And that's what I admired about Rudy."

There was a well-oiled quality to Joey Keen that made Martin sense that if he didn't speak up, the man would go on about prosperity for five or ten minutes.

"My question is a simple one," he said. "I understand you had an appointment with Reed at noon on the day he died."

"I did?" The eyes, rather than register surprise, seemed amused.

"That's what his appointment book indicates."

"Whose?"

"Reed's."

"That *I* did?"

Martin nodded.

Keen's face filled with a wide, ingratiating smile, a new one. "Then I guess I must have," he said, letting the smile fade very slowly. "No, actually. I think what that one was—we were just going to get together, talk over our campaign goals, swap stories about our kids, that sort of thing. Before it got too crazy. Just a courtesy lunch. I don't know that we'd actually set a date for it or anything, but we were talking about it. That all you need?" As if on cue, his phone buzzed. Keen pressed a button. "Right," he said. " 'Kay, honey, I'll be right there."

Shaking hands with Martin, Joey Keen seemed to smile more slyly, at something beyond the room—his own success, perhaps. It was, in some ways, an ingenious smile, Martin decided, as he walked back, through the living room and foyer, down the bright, chalk-smelling tunnel to the massive garage, where China was waiting with the engine running.

"I told you," she said, pulling from the garage onto the winding road to Joey Keen's gate.

"How well do you know him?"

"Joey? As well as I want to." The Mustang picked up speed as she passed out of the Keen property. "He's got too much ambition, though," she said.

"Why do you say that?"

"I just don't think he really knows what he fricking wants."

"Yeah?"

"I always say, it's how you end up that matters, not what you accumulate along the way."

"But how did he accumulate what he's got?"

"Simple. He plugged in to the right person, that's all. Lodge McCloud."

"The developer."

"Yeah, the developer. McCloud decided several years ago that he didn't want to deal with the little people anymore. So

Keen does all his bidding for him now, and look what it's gotten him. Keen's slick. He calls himself a fricking HPM, not a Realtor."

"What's that?"

"Human potential motivator." She downshifted, rounding a curve marked by poplars, which tilted against the wind. "Humongous piles of manure, I call it."

"But you know," she said, speeding past the gated estates, "if they get this Bananaland Park expansion approved—it's going to transform the city. They say it could make this one of the leading tourist attractions in the country.

"I want to show you something," she added, slowing again. She turned onto a narrow road, which was shrouded by palmettos and oaks and Australian pines. Martin saw her smile tug down sadly for a moment, as if some haunting beautiful music were playing that he couldn't hear.

"There was something you were going to tell me about Reed," he said, as the road turned to gravel.

"I was?"

"Don't you remember?"

"Oh. Well, yeah." She seemed suddenly guarded, slowing at the crest of the forested hillside. "I probably shouldn't have said anything."

"Did you know him?"

"Not closely. His youngest son was the same age as mine, they were in day care together. I know there were family problems, particularly with the oldest daughter." Nervous, she added, "I'll tell you who knows about the daughter is fricking Tony DeRosse."

"The councilman."

"Yeah. The councilman."

The road twisted downhill into a long slant of brilliant sunshine, which seemed to split the purple clouds, as if light and darkness were waging some final battle in the afternoon sky; then it leveled off and China pulled to the shoulder and stopped. They both looked out across the green lagoon at a Gothic stone castle with turrets, jutting gables, a winding terraced escarpment, situated between two moats. It was the largest, most elaborate residence Martin Grant had ever seen.

"That's it," China said.

"That . . . ?"

"Lodge McCloud's house."

As they sat there among the thick growths of trees and shrubs, looking, Martin felt something sad and desolate blow up through the sunlit woods, from some faraway place—though it drifted off just as quickly, and the warm currents of winter air again felt numbing.

A large, rotund, white-haired man was walking on the lawn behind the mansion, head down, hands thrust in pockets, as though he were lost in thought. Martin watched as the man stopped on the stone walkway by the water's edge and gazed across the bay at the skyline of downtown Bananaville—the office buildings, and beyond it the amusement park. He was dressed, it seemed, in a black boxer's robe and combat boots.

"He's not happy," China said. "You can tell just by looking at him."

"Wait—you mean, that's him?"

"Yep."

As Martin watched, the man turned uncertainly toward the house, and then up toward the hillside where Martin and China were watching.

When he looked back to the city, Lodge McCloud appeared to be talking—and gesturing angrily at someone with his right fist, although there was no one else in sight. And then Martin realized what Lodge McCloud was doing: shadowboxing. He was jabbing and hooking punches at the air with a mounting fervor, his large body beginning to jiggle with an easy rhythm as he outdanced and outpunched some invisible foe in the late-afternoon shadows while the bay waters turned blue one final time before sunset.

21

HOBART P. LANAHAN nodded grudgingly from his office as Martin came in but quickly looked away. The lights were out in Entertainment, Sports, and Business. On Martin's desk were two messages, both taken by Dixie Fudd:

"Nilly: Did it work?"

He smiled.

Also: "Toni DeMoso (?) 8:30 555-7696."

A young woman's voice answered.

"Mario's?"

"Is Tony there, please?"

"Hold on."

After about a minute, a deep, gruff-sounding voice said, "Dis is Antonio DeRosse. How may I help you?"

The tie to honest government.

"Oh, hi. This is Martin Grant. I had a message you'd called."

"Martin? Yeah, let me turn dis thing down here. Hold it. We're doing inventory here—Martin?" The blaring rock music stopped. "How you doin'? I just hadn't had d'chance to sit and properly talk wit' you yet, you follow? It's been so crazy here lately."

"Right." This streetwise voice didn't seem to match the image Martin had of DeRosse, scribbling nervously at the City Council meeting.

"I see you covering d'city government there, and I just thought: Why don't you and I get together. Have some lunch, or whatever. My treat."

"We could," Martin said, although he wasn't big on lunching with politicians during an election season.

"Or if you don't want lunch, you come on by for a Coke or a beer. How's tomorrow sound? I'm gonna say—twelve? twelve thirty? Only if it's convenient, of course."

"Sure," Martin said. "I'm not a big lunch eater. But I'd be glad to stop by for a Coke."

"I'd like that," Antonio DeRosse said.


BEFORE LEAVING, Martin checked the pay phone numbers in the newspaper's cross-reference book, and then spread a city map on his desk. The two phones, he saw, were on the eastern edge of town, about four blocks apart—equally distant from the city's transportation annex, where the municipal buses were stored. Startled by Hobart's neighing laugh as he talked on the telephone, Martin gazed up, saw the dusky air among the mangroves, above the dark river, and remembered something: Jack Carlson worked for the city's Transportation Department.

As Martin stepped back outside, the warm air watered his eyes, and he stood on the porch for a while and watched the darkening currents of the river, the distant orange glows of streetlights.

*Jack Carlson.*

J.C.


IN MARTIN'S MAILBOX that evening was an envelope from Katie Grant, with a rural route return address he did not recognize.

He creased open the blank card—a George Caleb Bingham river scene—which smelled of fresh hopes, birthdays, long-ago best wishes. At the kitchen table Martin read the words Katie had written, in her slanted scrawl that still seemed to him like that of a schoolgirl:

"Everything about the same here. Snow again last Saturday. Sold the old French daybed finally: $400! I'm going ahead and filing the divorce action. I think it'll be best for both of us. Smile at the waves for me."

Breeze gusted in through the screen; the air was cooler and damp now with the coming of nighttime. Martin stared through the oaks at brightening moonlight, at a sky that stretched all the way to snowy Iowa, clear back to the day he had met Katie, it seemed. He was still staring hours later, turning over the pillow on his bed so the cool side touched his face, remembering through a filter of nostalgia the haphazard way he had met Katie Thompson, in a feed store on a Thursday afternoon, a meeting that shouldn't have happened at all.

They were twenty-five and filled with premature certainties, moving too quickly through life. He had been taken by her shrewd smile, that was all; but they quickly went to far-flung places together. Martin watched the night breeze through his bedroom window, remembering the horrible caprices of the marriage in those final weeks, feeling anxious until just before dawn, when he fell finally into a series of dreams. When he woke, a wet glaze of morning light glittered in the trees, on the lawn, the iron railings of the porch. The whole town, it seemed, had been washed clean again.


THE NEWS THAT divorce papers were coming had a numbing effect, though as he ran through the narrow lanes, looking up at ranges of white clouds in the western sky, Martin sensed that a door was opening for him somewhere, allowing the future in, and that was good. He would sell the house and look for something else down here—find new paths, new friends.

Martin sat at his desk in Metro all morning thinking about it, looking out at the slanting light that glowed in Thomas Persons's aftershave as if it were a bottle of Jim Beam. A phone message, he noticed at 11:27, was wedged between Q. V.'s desk and the trash can. Martin walked over to pick it up, and saw it was for him: "Rud-a (?) Reed" had called at eight-thirty, shortly before he arrived. The operator was Dixie.

Martin flipped up his notepad and pressed the seven numbers.

"Hal-lo."

"Hi, Rudy. This is Martin Grant."

"Mr. Grant."

"Martin."

"Do you have a pencil?"

"Fire away."

Rudolph Jr. cleared his throat, as if he were about to give a dramatic reading. Stone Temple Pilots played in the background.

"I wanted to tell you that I am going to announce tomorrow of my intention to seek a City Council chair that had previously been held by my father."

"Oh." Grimacing, Martin watched pelicans gliding effortlessly above the river. Loss can take people on some strange flights, he thought—although in a sense he also sort of understood: This was Rudolph's attempt to strike back at the thing that had taken away his father. The phantoms.

"Have you talked this over with Sammy and your mother and other family members?"

There was a long pause.

"I've already decided. So I'm not going to change my mind," he said, his voice trembling with uncertainty.

"It just seems like a sudden thing."

"I'm holding a press conference at Newt's Sunoco, ten o'clock in the morning. Tomorrow morning. Just in case you wanted to cover it."

"Newt's." Martin was writing it down: Newt's 10 A.M.

"Yes. It's at 1125 North Banana Boulevard. By the waterfront."

"Okay."

He added, "Newt's father, Mr. Craig, has offered to be my campaign chairman. And the gas station will be my campaign headquarters and stuff."

"I see."

Martin sighed. At least he had his Reed story for the next day.

**22**

IN FRONT OF Mario's Family Restaurant was a sidewalk café with red and white checkered cloth tabletops, candles in empty Chianti bottles, trellises, and Italian lights. Inside, though, Mario's had the sparse appearance of a pizza parlor.

Antonio DeRosse was at a back booth with the *Daily News* opened to the horse race spreads. He'd taken off his bow tie and his face had a harder set than Martin remembered.

"Martin Grant? Please, have a seat." His enormous body rose only slightly, and sat again. He was olive-skinned and flabby, with an ingratiating, boyish smile that didn't fit with the tough-guy patter. "I had breakfast yesterday morning wit' Peter Fudd. Says he's very pleased wit' d'work you doing, Martin. Investigating a very tragic event. Please, have a seat." Martin sat opposite him, facing a poster on the wall for the International Citrus Festival. "Orange You Excited?" it asked. A ceiling fan stirred the warm, garlic-scented air. "Said you moved here from d'West?"

"Midwest, actually."

"Well, I'm from Jersey. Atlantic City, originally. Lived in Trenton a couple of years. Spent some time down in Sea Bright, Long Branch, Asbury Park, in there."

"It's a long ways for me, too," Martin said. "Iowa."

"Is that right? I had a cousin lived there. What was it—Six Falls? Six Flags?"

"Sioux Falls?"

"Something like that. Or—no, I'm thinking of *Boise*." He

pulled a toothpick from the plastic holder beside the sugar packs, and rolled it between his fingers.

"Idaho."

"Okay, I'm thinking Idaho. You say you're from Iowa."

"Right."

The jingle of a cowbell sounded, and a cloud seemed to cross DeRosse's eyes. Martin turned to look, just as DeRosse stood.

"I'm sorry, gals," he said. "No bare feet."

The cowbell rang again as the girls pushed out, giggling.

The palm of his right hand shrugged at Martin as he settled back in the booth. "You got a policy, you got to enforce it. Otherwise, they take advantage. Anyway. Martin? Have anything you want to on this menu. The seafood section, you can see, we just added that. You want seafood, try the lobster enchilada." Martin nodded.

"Up in Jersey, I started with one little pizza stand. Out in a little strip mall. Down here, I take over an existing place, prime location on d'highway, you follow? put in the sidewalk tables, name it Mario's Family Restaurant. Now I'm getting ready to open up a second store. You know what dat is? I'll tell you very succinctly: It's opportunity. D'opportunity here is tenfold what it was in Jersey. *Tenfold.*" He pulled off a second toothpick and stuck it in a corner of his mouth, watching the front of the restaurant. Journalism, Martin had found, put him in life's audience. There was never any telling what he'd see.

A petite waitress with huge gray hair was standing now beside DeRosse, who didn't notice. Martin traded a smile with her.

"Oh, I'm sorry, sweetheart. Lorraine, this is Martin Grant. Martin, this is my wife, Lorraine." The two nodded hello. "You say you don't want lunch, that's not a problem. What I'm going to do, can you just bring us out some samples. Don't eat anything you don't want," he cautioned Martin. "Okay, honey? Can you bring us a couple chef salads, then wait ten minutes, bring us a big plate of dose, uh, lobster enchiladas. Throw a couple appetizers in wit' dat. Give us fifteen more minutes, bring out a half Sicilian wit' d'works." He smiled at Martin. "How's that sound?"

"Fine."

"Ice tea okay? Bring us a pitcher of ice tea wit' dat, too, honey."

Martin watched as Lorraine lifted the hinged piece of counter and went back into the kitchen.

Wanting to take the wheel of the conversation, he said, "I'm working on a story about Rudolph Reed. Getting to know him posthumously, so to speak. I wonder if there's anything you might be able to tell me. You served with him, what, almost four years? And you were about to run against him again."

"Not against him." He held up a finger, to point out this particularly tricky distinction. "We just happened to be running in d'same race. You follow?"

"Okay."

"What did I think of Rudy? Well, you know. What's d'quote? Every man's death diminishes my own. Or—what's d'quote? Anyway, Rudy, he was a good man. Or could be." He cleared his throat, struggling, it seemed, to summon a municipal persona to replace that of the restaurant owner.

"He had his enemies, though, evidently," Martin said.

DeRosse's face hardened. "In what sense?"

"I mean, he didn't seem very popular in certain circles. The whole business community, for example."

"Well. Now." He looked at the bright noon sunshine on the front windows. His face was sweating. "Dis town—it's a funny place, Martin. And I can't speak for somebody, someone, who isn't here to defend theirselves, you follow? But, I mean, Rudolph? As a member of the community—and an indentured public servant, if you will. Had certain—" He clenched his hand, grasping for a word. All of a sudden his left eye began to twitch. "Rights to uphold, if you will. And some people, let's say, uphold those rights more rigorously—or, what's d'word?—vigorously than others. And in any city there are certain votes that are clearly for the good of the town and others that are not for the good of the town, you follow? And Rudy, God bless him, tended to fall on d'wrong side of d'fence in dat regard. That's all." He forced a smile. "As did his group of supporters."

"I understand the business community called his group the Reed-jects."

Martin was surprised to see no change in DeRosse's expression. "Did they? I hadn't heard that."

The salads arrived first, then the enchiladas, along with a steaming medley of seafood appetizers, and finally the half Sicilian pizza. DeRosse ate heartily, talking about opportunity and success, while Martin sipped iced tea and poked at his salad. By appropriately inserting periodic "uh-huh"s, head nods, and smiles, he was able to keep the monologue rolling. It seemed to surprise DeRosse profoundly when he asked a question.

"Any idea what might have happened? To Rudolph?"

"Pardon?"

"Who might've been responsible."

"I wouldn't have a clue," he said definitively, but then glanced around the restaurant as if the guilty party might be within earshot. He ate several bites of enchilada, using his fingers. "Although, off d'record? I'll tell you one thing. And dis is something you take to d'box wit' you, you follow?" He winked ominously. "Archie Duval has not liked Reed since the day Reed came to town. You know Archie Duval?" Martin shook his head, picturing the cheery bully in the white T-shirt and fedora. "Fisherman, active in d'fire company, good old boy. His uncle was mayor."

"Okay."

"Okay? Now, I'm not saying dat means anything, d'fact he didn't like him. But I'm saying that is a *fact*." He overemphasized this last word, spitting in Martin's direction, then leaned forward and spoke in a low voice. "But, again off the record? D'problem there? They can't get Archie. He's like fuckin' what's his name. Don Gotti. *John* Gotti. Man's always got an alibi."

His eyes were looking off again. He tossed an arm on the booth back and poked absently at his teeth with the toothpick.

"You know anything about his daughter Ginny?" Martin asked, and DeRosse looked at him sharply.

"Yeah, I know something about his daughter Ginny." He

114

leaned on the table, whispered, "Pro," holding the shape of an O on his lips, then leaned back again, quickly holding up two fingers.

"Two-bill-a-day habit to support, I'm told."

"Is that right?"

"I'm told." He tilted his head slightly, looking over Martin's shoulder. "I happen to be in charge of d'task force looking into some of d'problems over in east side, some of which they say may be spilling over into the city. That's what we're trying to—what's d'word?—eradicate this sort of thing from d'town."

"What do you know about his daughter?"

"What do I know about his daughter? Well, I understand she got involved in d'skin trade out on the Coast for a while. Changed her name. I understand she just moved back here a couple months ago."

"Any idea who Captain Carol might be?"

"Huh?"

"Captain Carol? Doesn't ring a bell?"

"Who?"

Martin waved the question away. "There's prostitution, you say, in East Bananaville? And drugs?"

"I'm told, yes. And naturally, we're not pleased about it—if it's true." He aimed his toothpick at Martin. "If dis city were a face, we're talking—I mean, we're talking Marilyn Monroe, right? Sharon Stone, Sophia Loren, and Raquel Welch rolled into one. It's a beautiful place. East side, dat'd be d'only blemish." Martin nodded uncertainly. "Even though it's not technically even on d'face, you follow?"

"It's unincorporated, you mean."

"That's correct. How you liking dis town, anyway, Martin?" His demeanor changed, glossing with a practiced politeness. He sat up and pushed the plates away. "I'll tell you, I come down here—I was just scraping by up in Jersey, like I say. Trying to stay out of trouble. My wife and me, tree kids. Dis place has been a godspeed for us—or a godsend. It's taken care of us. No place in Jersey ever did dat. You couldn't pay me to go back. It's like Joey

Keen says—he happens to be d'landlord owns dis building, incidentally. And a man I have a lot of respect for. It's like Joey Keen says: Success is spending your life the way you want to. That's what dis town lets you do."

As Martin typed his story about Rudolph Jr. running for City Council, he looked up at the green slope of grass and saw China Rinaldi through the Spanish moss, dressed today in a black leather miniskirt, a tight fucshia sleeveless top, and sandals.

He watched her come back across the parking lot to the building—singing—and felt uneasy that this was his neighbor and he didn't know her. Or perhaps it was her remark about having something to say about Rudolph Reed that bothered him.

Martin stared at the intercom list taped to the side of his phone—21 was her number. He watched the white clouds move like floating islands through the blue sky, the pelicans soaring and gliding above the mangroves and live oaks. Finally he pressed the two numbers.

"China."

"Yes. Hello," he said. "With a name like yours, I bet you could give me some advice on where to find the best Chinese food in the area."

There was no response on the other end. *I'm going to need a little practice at this*, Martin thought.

"Hello?"

"Yes—who is this?"

"Martin Grant—your neighbor. I was planning to pick up some Chinese for dinner tonight. I just thought, maybe, you'd care to join me."

"Oh. Uh-uh, the munchkins have rehearsal tonight," she said quickly. Now Martin was silent, not understanding what she had said, and not sure how to slip out of the conversation gracefully.

"Why? What time were you thinking of?"

"Seven-thirty? Or—whatever time's convenient."

"Okay. Okay. Seven-thirty. That'll be okay."

She seemed to sigh deeply.

"Good. And where—"

But China Rinaldi had hung up. And when he punched her number again, there was no answer.

As Martin emerged from the Chinese restaurant, the sky was a roiling veil of purple and black, and sudden veins of lightning lit the street. He stood in the blinking violet neon of the restaurant's overhang and watched the wind whip the tall palms above the streetlights. The smell of the food and the cooling air felt good, and for a moment, in a flash as quick as heat lightning, Martin thought he understood the town's seductiveness, its charms and its secrets. Down in the next block, he saw a silver Coors Light sign glowing across the sidewalk and he thought of picking up a twelve-pack to go with the food.

All the way back to Coconut Lane, on a road littered with leaves and pieces of palm fronds that had broken off in the wind, Martin tasted old temptations, saw the full moon glowing above the trees, and wondered how it looked right now in Iowa, shining across the frozen, glittery fields of snow behind the farmhouse where Katie Grant was living with her antiques dealer.

"Welcome," China said, raising her wineglass in the gesture of a toast. The smell was warm and spicy as he came in through a dark, plush-carpeted hallway. Candlelight cast jumping shadows on the living room and kitchen, on the wicker furniture and new white sofa set, on several paintings of European landscapes. He was surprised to see China barefoot, dressed in cutoff jeans and a black halter. A gold chain and small cross hung between her breasts.

"Very nice," Martin said, not sure exactly what he meant. Across the room, he saw, in the darkness by the patio door, was an old black upright piano.

"Wine?"

"No, thanks." He conjured up his number, like a lucky talisman in his pocket: seventy-four days.

"The munchkins," Jody and Jamie, came out for a moment and watched Martin curiously, their eyes still glazed with TV images. They were twins, young and cute, more souls than bodies, it seemed, wearing matching Mickey Mouse pajamas.

Sitting on the sofa, Martin felt an odd freedom, as if he were entering rooms of his life he hadn't been to in years, and was struck once again by the evanescence of everything.

"All I usually have is one fricking glass in the evening," China said, sitting at the other end of the sofa and tucking up her legs. Outside, green lights quivered beneath the surface of her swimming pool, sending soft strobes of shadows into the trees. A telescope was aimed at the sky. "Which they say is good for you. I like to sit on the porch, watch the trees. Make a wish."

"You play piano, do you?"

"I play piano." She turned to look at it, and her smile tugged down sadly. Her eyes returned to Martin's. Softly she said, "It's my favorite thing, really. I've been trying to get these Bach variations down, it's fricking murder. What I usually do is make my own music. From what's out there. You know what I mean?"

Martin wasn't sure, but as they exchanged a long, easy look, he imagined that he did and smiled with her. China took her wineglass to the piano. She sat with a rigid posture and stared at the keys, her hands at her sides. After a long time, she began to play, quietly—a piece he recognized as *The Pachelbel Canon*, although it soon became something else—going off on a slow, beautiful melodic tangent, then incorporating blues runs, old jazz progressions, vivid and dark instrumental colors. Martin watched, transfixed, as it became *The Pachelbel Canon* again. The serene look on her face as she finished seemed, to Martin, as lovely as the music.

*  *  *

THEY TALKED OVER the Chinese dinner with a Ping-Pong of politeness, Martin imagining, from the enthusiastic way she spoke of her co-workers, that China Rinaldi enjoyed being advertising director at the *Bananaville Daily News*. But when he suggested this, after they were finished and back on the sofa, China laughed.

"Are you kidding? No, I think I'm about ready to quit, actually." A faint mustache of 7UP shone below her nose. She was beautiful, yet when he focused on her brown eyes she seemed sadly vulnerable, as if the most private part of her soul were showing. "I already quit once before. Six months ago. Fricking Elmer didn't know what to do. He says, 'Listen, China, what would you want to go and do that for?' " The corners of her mouth curled at the memory. "And I said, 'I have to look out for the munchkins.' Which is true. He says, 'Let me see what I can do.'

"He eventually makes me an offer. And I say, 'That's almost what they're offering me at this other job'—of course, he thinks it's the other newspaper, the *Banner*, although I claim I'm not at liberty to divulge just where it is. And sure enough, he comes back the next day, wearing one of his Hawaiian shirts, and offers me what I want. Asks if I want to be ad manager."

Martin chuckled politely, assuming "Elmer" must be Peter Fudd.

"The thing is, I really didn't. But I knew I could do it. That's my whole problem. I'm good at it."

He held her stare until she looked away. She was graceful but shy, and Martin suspected that her palling around with Thomas Persons at the office was some sort of security blanket.

"So," she said, "I understand you're going through a divorce."

He nodded.

China's face seemed to darken in some new shadow the moon cast across her patio. "I was married to a very abusive man," she said, "and didn't know it for a long time.

120

"I came down here to make a fresh start. With the piano. And to raise the munchkins away from their father." She looked off and her eyes widened, then glazed: It was as if you could see her thinking. "But somehow I drifted back into advertising, which I don't enjoy but I'm good at. And with commission, the bucks are good." He saw the reflection of the candles in the sliding glass door and burning absently in her eyes. She was thinking, Martin sensed, of illusions she had spent.

"You know the thing I was going to tell you? About Rudolph Reed?" she said, surprising him. "I probably shouldn't have brought it up. I mean, if it were ever even mentioned."

Martin waited, sensing she very much wanted to tell him something—maybe everything—as most people eventually need to share their deepest secrets.

She looked at his eyes and a current of sensuality flowed briefly back and forth. Outside, wind shook the banana trees and the wrought-iron balustrades.

"I maybe was being indiscreet. But the thing is—" She closed her eyes and seemed to be concentrating, as if preparing for a dive off the high board. "All I'll say is this: The woman who called the 911 in?"

"Yes?"

"I know her."

Martin's eyes grew larger, and China responded with a flat and knowing nod. A question and answer in body language.

**24**

MARTIN'S SOFT-SPOKEN manner had, over the years, exposed him to all types of people and had taught him a simple rule of human behavior: Nearly everyone likes to talk about himself. Most have a hard time keeping secrets. China's was now dancing on the edges of her eyes.

"It's kind of a tricky thing, though," she said, looking away. "I'm sure I'm the only one she's told. This lady—I think I'm sort of her best friend. I mean, there's no way she's going to talk to the police. And I really can't see her talking to a fricking newspaper reporter, either." Martin nodded. "But I just have a feeling she needs to come to terms with it. I don't know. I don't know why I said anything."

"That wouldn't be fair to the Reed family, though, would it?" Martin leaned forward on the sofa, watching her. "Not saying anything."

China's eyes glistened. Her face filled for a moment with indignation. "Look," she said. "The fricking police are only going to invest so much in this, believe me. I've lived here for six years. They're going to low-key it and see if it'll die away. Most of the business people are still calling it a drowning, you know."

"I've heard."

"Yeah."

They both stared out: The wind grew louder.

"The thing is." She blinked herself back to the earlier channel of conversation. "This friend of mine—she walked her dog down by that beach every morning. She's a very timid lady. About the kindest woman you ever saw, though." She added,

"She weighs close to three hundred fifty pounds." Martin frowned appropriately. "Anyway, I could ask her, but I don't think so. How many times have witnesses been 'gotten to' before a case goes to trial?"

"You're saying she witnessed something?"

"I'm not saying anything. Excuse me."

Martin realized, as she left the room to put the munchkins to bed, that China was edgier and far more complicated than he had thought.

While she was gone, Martin walked out front, into the warm misty night air, and heard China's voice through a window, admonishing her children in Italian: *"Diavolino! Basta!"* A door slammed. The full moon, bright above the swaying palms, seemed for a moment cartoonishly large to Martin, as if it were man-made, and the town owned the rights to it. Wind pulled through the sabal palms, tearing at the fronds. Martin looked north, toward Iowa, felt something shaking loose in himself, also.

He returned with his tape player, thinking that it might even the playing field they were on, sharing his own secret.

CHINA'S EYES WIDENED knowingly as "Captain Carol" pronounced the word "terminate."

"You know what that is, don't you?" she said, with a surprising certainty. "Captain Carol? And Officer Reed?" She made an imaginary whip crack in the air, twice. "S and M."

"You think so?"

"Mmm-hmm." Her eyes glazed with thought, her lips pursed. "I never would have imagined Rudolph Reed being into that, though—would you?" She met his eyes for just a second. "Although when you really think about it, maybe it's not so surprising. As weird as his fricking wife has gotten? Maybe it's not surprising at all that he needed a little fantasy life on the side. Most of us do in one way or another." He watched as she thought it through. "There's several sex businesses over in east side, you know. Supposedly his oldest daughter has worked there. Massage parlors, a couple of strip clubs. A triple X bookstore where they, like, give hand jobs in the back."

The kids were calling her again. "Mo-om!"

"They've been trying to shut them down, but it's outside of the city limits and the county boys don't seem to see it as any big priority."

"The first voice on the tape. That isn't Jack Carlson, is it?"

"Are you kidding? Have you met him? He's fricking nuttier than her second husband, Wayne. As a matter of fact— Wayne . . . You know what Wayne's doing now? He works in east side, at one of those strip places."

"Really?"

"Yeah, hold on."

China's long slender legs moved with an athlete's grace as she hurried off to check on the munchkins. Martin felt a warm, anxious rush of anticipation. He went to the back door and slid it open, sensing himself enter another room of this story: a dark place of aberrant appetites. The wind, fresh-scented with chlorine and sea mist, made a rushing sound through the banana trees. Moonlit hibiscus dripped over the patio walls. Pool lights beneath the rippled water strobed in the trees.

Martin paced halfway around the pool and stopped, wondering about it: Had Reed somehow gotten involved in pornography? Or prostitution? It didn't fit with any of the impressions Martin had formed about him. But what was D.S., Inc.—an unlisted business that used only a P.O. box in a town called Coconut? What was going to be "terminated"? Was there an underbelly to this place that Reed had somehow stumbled onto?

China, in the doorway, stared at Martin as if he were modern art.

"What are you doing?"

Martin shrugged.

"You're funny. Let's sit out here," she said, and pushed two wicker chairs together on the brick patio.

She hugged her arms against herself as the wind kicked up, though the air was warm. "Look," she said. "I'll talk to my friend about it, again. Maybe she'll want to say something to you. Off the record. Maybe she won't."

"I'm sorry I pushed it."

"It's all right." They sat there for several minutes, just feeling the breezes. Martin liked this; it was the most relaxed he had felt with another person in months. Smiling dimly, China said, "You've probably heard some of the things said about me at the office by now."

This surprised him. "No. What things?"

She looked at his face, her brown eyes widening, as if flooding with pools of hidden energy. Martin smiled back and the moist breeze lifted her hair against his arm. He looked out at the distant lights of the city above the stucco walls, and the Big Story he had been pursuing all these years seemed suddenly unimportant—it seemed to dissolve in all that air, the wet breath of night, the musky perfume she wore, the liquid motion of the pool lights; it became just some fanciful long-ago notion of his father's, as chimerical as the old man's own futile goal, borrowed from Eisenhower: "Live to score a hole in one."

Using the same tone with which she might have asked, "Do you want another 7UP?" China said, "Do you feel like kissing?"

He felt her fingers taking his and her warm breath in the damp air as she leaned against him. Her lips were sticky at first, then she pulled away and looked at him, trying different angles as the wind came up through the banana trees. They kissed for a long time and then China pushed away comfortably and straightened her clothes. "I don't really feel like doing anything else tonight," she said. "Is that all right? If we just kiss?"

**2 5**

MARTIN STARED AT the moon through his bedroom window, the stars and shifting leaves, the halo-rimmed streetlights, filled with a sensual yearning that kept him awake for more than an hour. He felt returned to an old path—the good trail he'd strayed off of years earlier, in some dark patch of the imagination. After sleep came, the wind gusted harder, more coldly, and he tasted raindrops in his dreams through the window screen.

The morning light, the stillness in the trees, surprised him. There was a message on his answering machine, perhaps from the evening before. Martin made coffee, browned a coconut muffin, and then pressed the button. A scratchy sound, like that of an old phonograph record, was followed by a long, loud screeching of automobile brakes and a collision.

He stared into the yard—a glaze of sunlit dew covered the weeds and wild shrubbery that stretched to China Rinaldi's house. Her car was gone. There were portentous streaks of gray in the sky. Martin wanted—suddenly and passionately—to find out what was really going on in this town.

HE WAS THOROUGHLY unprepared for the sight of several hundred people at Newt's Sunoco that morning, milling about festively in the street and in the small park next to it. He wondered, at first, if there were a fair or concert scheduled that he hadn't heard about. But the banners festooned above the garage bays, the signs and buttons—LET REED LEAD—everywhere made it clear: This crowd had gathered for the kick-off of Rudolph Reed Jr.'s City Council campaign.

Wearing old jeans, a tight blue blazer, and a brown necktie with a huge, mistied knot, Rudolph Jr. stood in the bed of an old Ford pickup and mumbled a prepared statement into a feeble PA system as television crews and newspaper photographers took aim. He mispronounced enough of the words to make it clear to Martin that someone else had written the speech. Three Reeds sat in chairs behind Rudolph in the truck bed, their expressions uneasy, as if they were suffering from toothaches. Sammy and Joshua, Martin noticed, did not seem to be present.

It was only when he finished reading and the crowd roared its approval that Rudolph Jr. looked up, and his lips quivered, briefly, into a facsimile of a smile.

Afterward, Reed supporters sang under the magnolias, many raising clenched fists to a guitar-kazoo-washboard rendition of "The Times They Are A-changin'." The mood became that of a village fair. There were unicyclists and jugglers and Frisbee players. Picnic lunches. Senior citizens played with children on the seesaws and monkey bars.

These were life's odd birds, Martin thought, watching with amusement as the band struck up a folksy version of "Blowin' in the Wind," with Rudolph Jr. adding warbly, out-of-tune acid-rock electric lead. These were people who had found a voice, a connection, in this town impatient with the undisciplined, yet which drew misfits in large numbers through some mysterious polarity of spirit. He wondered, as he walked away from the frivolity toward his station wagon beneath royal palms that glowed dully in the sun, what was going to happen to them now.

THOUGHTS OF CHINA Rinaldi blazed like sudden fires in his thoughts as he tried to focus on the story about Reed's rally. He looked up and saw sunlight coursing in brown currents along the river, noticed how the red mangroves on the east bank all grew together—the compacted peat preventing deep roots so the trees formed massive clumps, too tall to step over, too dense to break through. Towns do that too, Martin thought.

He pulled the pay stub for D.S., Inc., from his desk, scrutinizing the small print, and saw a P.O. box address. Box 74, Coconut. Was Reed moonlighting? Or were the stubs something else?

He was startled to see Hobart P. Lanahan, standing behind him with an odd, thirsty look in his eyes. The two hadn't spoken in several days.

"Anything new?"

"Not really, no." He put the pay stub in his shirt pocket. "Still doing background, basically. The turnout this morning surprised me."

"Oh, Rudy had his following, all right."

"Say," Martin said, thinking of something. "What do you know of Cora Carlson—and her husband? Do you know them at all?"

"Jack?" He sat on the edge of Martin's desk, probably not liking the tension between them any more than Martin did. Hobart trying to be friendly, though, made Martin a little uneasy. "I've known Jack for twelve years. Used to bowl with him. Still a little shell-shocked, I think, from Vietnam. Not very sociable. But a really good man when you get to know him. Not saying it's easy to do. Used to be an engineer, then worked for years in the building inspector's office, before he took over as transportation supervisor."

The youthful face became years older as he smiled, and there were crumbs, Martin saw, on his lips. "Cora's a good lady, I suppose, smarter than she seems. Although I don't think she's been the same since her first husband died. And then, of course, the fire. I don't think Wayne's ever fully recovered from that, either. They're both walking wounded, in a way."

Wayne Vaughn. "What fire, now? What happened? I'm not familiar with that."

"Oh." Hobart let out a long exhalation of breath as if he wasn't sure where to begin. "The Satellite Hotel. This was six years ago. They say it was an arson, but it's one of those things. One of those cases that's never been solved and probably never will be. People still say the town did it," he said, with a trace of sarcasm, "the town was venting its anger."

"Over what?"

"Oh, the man that died in it—he and his wife both, actually—was Coleman Clark, who at the time owned most of that whole block that burned down. Very arrogant man, who didn't feel that he had to comply with the building codes like everyone else, was always being cited—by Jack Carlson, incidentally. Just a bit of a wealthy deadbeat. Didn't think he needed to abide by the rules."

"So how did Wayne Vaughn get in the picture?"

"Oh. Wayne was managing the hotel on weekends. Working for Joe Keen's property management company during the week. Before Keen fired him. He was tending the desk there and supposedly had fallen asleep when the fire started."

"I see."

"Got pretty badly scarred on his face and arm from it. One of his hands."

Martin felt a joggle of recognition: Wayne Vaughn was the man sitting in front of him at the City Council meeting the week before.

"And—what? They got divorced because of what happened, or—"

"Well, no." Hobart sighed again. "They were more or less separated at the time. Wayne's a story in himself. A very checkered past. He'd been in jail in Ohio a couple times for drug distribution and for check-kiting, and the last time he supposedly went through this major conversion. Started a prison ministry, and then came down here and went into the schools, talked to kids about drugs, was active in the church. Cora, for whatever reason, took him under her wing—very strange, emotional lady. And then it later turned out Wayne wasn't quite as pure as he made out to be. Even before the fire." He added, "Although, of course, I guess Cora wasn't, either."

Hobart smiled at some distant scenario Martin couldn't see. "What do you mean?"

"Well, there was just a lot of gossip going around about Cora at the time." Martin saw the pictures of the Lanahan family in Hobart's office, and thought it strange somehow that he would have traveled places where gossip circulated. "They say she had a fling with Joey Keen, is it in a nutshell. And then Keen cut it off, and she became bitter. I don't know. It's all hearsay." He got off Martin's desk. "That was right before she met Jack. I think in some ways she's still trying to prove herself as a Folsom."

With the determined stride of a racewalker, Dixie Fudd came into Metro, wearing a silk paisley blouse, untucked in back, brown stretch pants, and white deck shoes. Her hair was a different color today, yellowish brown.

"What are you doing, boy?" the voice cackled. "Ha! Ha! Ha! Ha! Ha! Ha!"

She placed a telephone message on Martin's desk, and stood with hands on hips, looking from Hobart's face to Martin's, waiting to be invited into the conversation. At last she said, "You two look like you just got back from a funeral. Ha! Ha! Ha! Ha! Ha!"

The smell of alcohol lingered as she walked off, with the same purposeful stride. Hobart rolled his eyes and Martin nodded.

"Yep."

"What can you do?"

The note said "Nillie Glen (?)" had called for him, and listed a telephone number that was within a few digits of that for the state attorney's office.

"Excuse me," Martin said.

"Oh, hey. Don't mind me." Hobart backed away, raising his arms as if he were being robbed. He closed his office door with a thunk. Martin had enjoyed the chat and wondered if this meant he was angry.

**26** MARTIN TOOK Interstate 75 north toward Coconut, past haphazard tract housing developments, strip shopping centers, trailer parks, and long scrubby stretches of wild palmetto and saw grass, where brackish-smelling wetlands glittered with sun sequins through dead trees. Coconut, he found, was a shadier, older town than Bananaville, with large ficus and banyan trees in the chain-linked lawns. Moss swung from the oaks, casting patterns of light across Main Street Extended.

Approaching downtown, the road wound alongside a narrow stream shrouded by oaks and buttonwoods, and at one point Martin saw two elderly black men sitting in shade on the bank, cane-fishing. There was, on Main Street, a fire station and city hall, a line of brick stores and office buildings, and, finally, an old wooden post office, with a sign above the door identifying its location: COCONUT.

Martin parked in a space diagonal to the curb and went in, recognizing the smells of old wood and varnish, the sound of creaky floorboards.

Seventy-four was one of the medium-sized boxes, with a glass half front. Martin got down on his hands and knees, turned his head sideways, and pressed up against the glass to look in. Several elderly men, their life-worn bodies dressed in Bermuda shorts and flowery shirts, stopped to watch, as if he were some sort of new, quirky Florida entertainment. There were three or four letters in the box, Martin saw, but only part of an address was visible. He could make out the first six letters: "Dragoo."

Nodding at the men who were watching him, Martin walked back out. There was a phone booth on the corner and he found inside it the slim phone book for Coconut, which had a pastoral picture on front of two black men cane-fishing—the same two he had just seen. In the business listings under *D* was Dragoon Security Corporation. Martin wrote down the street address.

IT WAS A WHITE frame building, on a side street of jerry-built, shacklike houses and overgrown shrubbery. An accounting firm occupied the street level. Dragoon was upstairs.

A banyan tree root, Martin saw, climbing the steps, was flush against the building's crooked roof, and he suspected it would crack through the wood in another few months. The rail was loose and splintery.

Inside, a man with large ears and sunburned nose—his hair was cut military style—stared across the room at Martin from behind a metal desk. He was wearing some sort of uniform, with a brass badge and a star on each of the epaulets. There was nothing in the room but his desk and chair, and another chair by the door. The air, dust-speckled with the light of a single window, smelled of disinfectant and roach spray.

"May I help you?"

"I hope so, yes." Martin closed the door. He explained that he was a journalist, gathering information for a story on Rudolph Reed. The tilt of the man's head seemed to indicate he knew Reed, although Martin wasn't sure: The dusty sunlight made him hard to see; it was as if a tiny meteor shower were moving across his face.

"I'm not authorized to give out any information of that nature," he said, once Martin stopped talking.

"Is there anyone who is?"

"What's this regarding?"

"Well. Like I say." Martin explained again what he was doing, watching the sky that framed the banyan roots outside, thinking

132

again, with a desperate urgency, of China Rinaldi's patio, the musky smell of her perfume as she leaned toward him. The man stared up, blinking slowly, as if it were Martin's turn to speak and not his. The pale blue eyes were a surprising contrast to his dark skin and black hair. "As I say," Martin added, "I'm with the *Daily News.*"

"Okay."

The man looked at his desk, preparing to choose from among several options. There was nothing on the desk but a blotter, a telephone, and his hat. A sheet of paper, thumbtacked to the wall behind him, read, "For your interview, please bring a black pen!" The word *black* had been underlined twice.

"Colonel West," he said into the phone, "this is Sergeant Lake. I have a gentleman here who has some questions regarding Rudolph Reed. One of our guards? He says he's with a newspaper." The man listened, his eyes on Martin's. "Uh-huh," he said, "uh-huh." He looked abruptly at the desktop. "I don't know, he wouldn't say. No."

Martin smiled inwardly at his mistake: The security company gave its guards titles, as if they were military personnel. Rudolph was Officer Reed. The person at the other end of the line was Colonel West. The woman with the come-hither voice on Reed's answering machine was Captain Carol. Reed was moonlighting here to help pay his bills, that was all.

"You can go back through this door," Sergeant Lake said. "Colonel West will see you. It's the last office on the right."

"Thanks."

Martin walked down a dim wooden corridor that sagged and creaked, the carpet worn through in spots so the floorboards showed. In an office on the left, empty except for a desk, chair, and wall calendar, a severe-looking, bald-headed man, dressed in the same white uniform shirt, was smoking, staring at a wall. Next to this was a large space full of hanging security guard uniforms, piles of hats, and billy clubs. Martin walked to the last door on the right and peered in. Colonel West was hunched over a *People* magazine, dressed as the others but with three stars on each of her epaulets. She was a very hefty black woman, probably in her late twenties or early thirties.

"Can I help you?" she said with a deep and convincing voice. Her lips were painted dark red, and she had nice curls in her hair, which might have been a wig.

Martin explained again what he wanted. Colonel West pointed at the other chair in the room.

"I was not his immediate supervisor, although I am the company commander. His immediate supervisor was Captain Marjorie Carroll. But information about our employees is strictly confidential. I'm not sure I understand the nature of your request."

Martin, clearing his throat, sensed something uncertain in her tone, something slightly off. She had Reed's file opened in front of her, he saw; there was nothing in it but his completed application.

He said, "You are aware that Rudolph Reed was killed five weeks ago?" Her face at first was expressionless, then seemed to be seeking an appropriate response. She coughed softly several times and looked some more at the application. It was possible, he supposed, that residents of a town thirty-five miles away had missed the news. Or, more likely, that she had heard about the killing of a city councilman but didn't realize he had also been one of her employees.

"You hadn't heard."

"No." She gazed down at the paper clip she was pulling apart. Songbirds sang in the elm outside. Martin knew she'd say more if he waited. "I hadn't. I know he'd missed two nights in a row. Without notifying us. We felt we had no choice but to terminate him."

Martin winced again at this word choice. "You didn't hear about the city councilman who was killed on the beach down in Bananaville?"

Her eyes glazed. "I heard about *that*," she said.

"I see, but you didn't realize the Rudolph Reed who had worked for you was a councilman, then."

134

"No. He said he was a schoolteacher," she said, looking at his application. "In fact, we verified it." Martin watched as it became apparent to her that a schoolteacher could also be a councilman. He heard the wind outside in the leaves, the caw caw of blackbirds. This job had been a secret compartment in Reed's life, which he'd kept hidden even from his family. Like the places he and Katie had gone to in those final months rather than confront the fact that their marriage was losing its focus.

"How long had Reed been working here?"

"Reed?" She blinked rapidly. "About three months. He guarded the Coconut Professional Center, always worked grave-yard, eleven P.M. to seven A.M. Nicest man you could know." She was smiling in a distant, numb sort of way. Reed was, clearly, a man people had liked, despite his unpopularity in the business community. "He kept his uniform locked in the cleaning closet over there and dressed in the men's room after he arrived."

"Was that unusual?"

"Oh, yeah. Most of the security officers wear their uniforms to work. He said he couldn't do that, because he had a long drive and it would get wrinkled. Very good guard. We were just about to promote him to a sergeant."

"Can you remember anything else unusual about him? Anything odd ever happening?"

"Reed? No." She shook her head, blinking long black lashes. "Well." Something came back to her, as she stared out the window, at a white butterfly that rose angel-like into the blue sky and disappeared. "I periodically tour the posts, okay? As just kind of a check-and-balance procedure. And the only time I ever saw anything unusual: This would've been a couple months ago. In the parking lot down there at the Professional Center. He was dressed for duty and all, but arguing with a young woman, who wasn't—I don't know any other way of putting it—wasn't wearing very many clothes. You know, short-shorts and sort of a bikini top. And his voice—I don't know how to explain this, either, but it was almost like it wasn't his voice. It was almost like a different voice."

"I see."

Her eyes flickered at Martin, dissatisfied with her explanation. "Do you know what they were arguing about?"

"Oh, no. Because, when I got out of my car, he walked away from her very quickly. But he had said something like, 'You can't do that anymore.' Or 'We're not living that way anymore.' Something that sounded very personal, and made me think it was somebody else. So I had to look again. But it was Reed. It was just the weirdest thing. I never said anything about it. Never thought too much about it."

She looked at Martin with steady eyes and an uneasy smile, waiting for him to ask another question.

Martin left a newspaper business card and she walked him back out, the squeak of her shiny black shoes seeming to echo the creak of the floorboards. He said good-bye to Sergeant Lake, who sat silently in the giant beam of dust and light, without any reading material, no television. Nothing but a clean desk.

So Reed had been moonlighting, too proud probably to tell his own family. But a young woman, who "wasn't wearing very many clothes," in the words of Colonel West, had known him, had argued with him one evening in a Coconut parking lot shortly before he was killed. The daughter? Or someone else? Someone who worked with Wayne Vaughn, perhaps?

Martin walked up the shady cracked stone sidewalk to his car, thinking about it, feeling the pleasant breeze on his face as it caught in the oaks, the dangling Spanish moss. This seemed a place more suited for Rudolph Reed than the manicured boulevards of Bananaville. A place that maybe was coming apart in some ways, but seemed nevertheless more genuine than Bananaville. He wondered, driving back along Main Street, where the dust was white in the sun and several old men sat on benches watching him, if Reed could have moved here and been happy, instead of fighting the way things were in Bananaville and losing his life.

What he decided to do next was find Reed's oldest daughter. Ginny.

**27**

CROSSING THE BORDER into Bananaville, Martin recognized again that the city had a taste: a fragrant blend of food and flowers, citrus and sea breeze, which made him feel for a moment as if he were entering a theme park. Downtown was bustling, with well-heeled men and women returning from lunches, buoyed, it seemed, by the same promise, the same heightened sense of possibilities.

At Mario's Family Restaurant, a teenage waitress shrugged when Martin asked if Antonio was in; she nodded vaguely toward the back.

"D'door's unlocked," Martin heard, after knocking on a cheap hollow-wood door marked OFFICE.

Antonio DeRosse's eyes looked up, over pince-nez bifocals.

"Hey!" he said, startled. "How you doin'? Martin, right?"

"Right."

"Enjoyed talking wit' ya yesterday. How you been?" With some effort, he rolled the chair back from the desk and stood. He was wearing a New York Giants sweat suit. "Come on in. Have a seat right dere. In dat chair. How you been?"

"Just fine."

"Good. Have a seat dere."

"Thank you."

Martin sat in the worn-out one-armed easy chair and glanced quickly at the office: There were framed pictures on the walls of DeRosse with Sugar Ray Leonard, Joe Pesci, Danny De Vito, and other people Martin didn't recognize—mostly sitting around Italian restaurant tables—and several framed pictures of New

York Giants players. A Giants helmet was on the bookcase, beside it a Giants jersey.

Both hands shrugged as Martin's eyes returned to his.

"I get a kick out of collecting stuff, what can I say? I still got a certain amount of Jersey in me, I guess. But how you doing, anyway, Martin?—is it Martin or Marvin?"

"Martin."

"Good to see you again, Martin." His eyes seemed to narrow. He leaned forward, elbows on the desk, as if about to share something very confidential. "Listen, Martin, everything dat was said dere yesterday. Strictly between you and me, am I right?"

"Right."

"Good. Good." He scooted back again and seemed to relax. "I wanted to make sure we were square on dat. I get to talkin' sometimes, you follow? Get myself in trouble. Ninety-nine point nine times out of a hundred you're better off for keeping your mouth closed, you know dat?"

Martin smiled with him, sensing that DeRosse was genuinely concerned about having said too much.

"So what can I do for you? Dis afternoon?"

"Oh, I was driving by," Martin said. "And figured I'd stop in and see if you were here. I just had a thought, something I wanted to ask you."

"Sure. Whatever you want." He clasped his hands impatiently on the desk.

"You indicated yesterday that you thought Rudolph Reed's daughter worked over in east side somewhere. And that she had a drug habit?"

The eyes shaded slightly. "Did I say that?"

Martin nodded.

"Well. I probably shouldn't have, then, you follow?" He smiled as if he'd told a joke. "Dat whole business about d'daughter. It's just one of d'rumors goin' round. I've heard it, dats all. Dat she had a big fight wit' d'old man or something and then she saw to it that d'deal was done. You follow? I don't believe it."

Martin saw DeRosse's eyelids drop, trying to make a point.

"That she had him killed?"

"I'm not suggesting dat's what's happened, no. Or even remotely hintin' at it. Dat's just one of the things I hear goin' round. The other one is, uh, d'wife had it done, you follow? I guess stress and strain, being cooped up in the house. But I don't pay much stock in dat one, either. You're always going to have stuff floating around. What can I get for you, iced tea?"

Martin shook his head. He hadn't heard either of these rumors, and suspected, for some reason, that DeRosse had just made them up. But why? To steer him from Archie Duval—or Jack Carlson?

"You were talking about Ginny. I'm just curious: What can you tell me about her, off the record? Where she works, for instance."

"Ginny?"

His telephone buzzed. DeRosse picked up the receiver, keeping his eyes on Martin. He made several muffled sounds of disapproval, then averted his gaze and said in a low voice, "No, it's in d'right-hand drawer. *Right*-hand. Are you looking in d'*right*-hand? Yeah, yeah. Okay. Hold on, I'll be up in tree minutes."

"My wife," he said, shaking his head. "Anyway. What were you saying?"

"Ginny Reed. Do you know her?"

"Know who she is, dat's all. I've heard the rumors about her. Understand she went away four, five years ago, and stayed away for a while. And I'll be honest wit' you—I don't know why, don't know what it was all about. She's a hot number, though," he said, and winked. "I'm told she later got involved in d'pornography business, out dere in California. But you're going to have to check that one on your own."

He stood elaborately, tucking in his sweatshirt, then pulling it out, ducking slightly to look into the alley, where a van was unloading a crate of tomatoes. "If you can excuse me for just a moment, I'll be right back. My wife, God bless her, has lost the keys to one of the fuckin' cash registers."

Martin summoned his genial smile. When the door closed, he

stood and made a closer inspection of the room: The Keen and Associates calendar on his wall had several notations for November and December, mostly City Council meetings, and one reading "Lorraine to N.Y." Nothing else. He tipped the trash can, saw numerous Reese's Nutrageous bar wrappers. He looked at the shelves, where dozens of videotapes were lined up like books, marked neatly with the names and dates of football games and prizefights. Beneath the football helmet on the bookshelf was an envelope with the word "Jersey" written on it in Magic Marker, and a stack of professional football game programs.

When the door opened again, Martin was sitting in the broken easy chair, staring at sunlight in the alley.

"I don't know what's d'matter with 'em," DeRosse said, sitting back behind the desk, shaking his head. Without explaining, he looked at Martin and said, "So. What can I do you for today?"

"Ginny Reed," Martin said. "You say she works as a 'pro'? Can you give me any idea where?"

DeRosse studied him for a moment.

"Dis conversation isn't happening, right?"

"Right."

"I like you, Martin, and it's d'only reason I'm gonna even, uh, breach this subject, you follow?" He leaned back and pushed away from the desk, pausing for effect. It's not unusual for elected officials to trade information for favorable coverage, and Martin supposed this was some variation of the idea. "D'Treasure Chest," he said. "Over in east side. Strip joint. She been working dere." His hands shrugged. "Two months? I'm *told*. Ever since she come back d'last time. Okay? Is what I've *heard*, anyway. Strictly on the Q.T."

"Is that the club where Wayne Vaughn works, by any chance?"

DeRosse's eyes did something funny when he said that. But then his face quickly cocked into a comfortable pose and he seemed to be staring Martin down.

"I wouldn't know anything about dat," he said.

140

**28** DARK CLOUDS DRIFTED across the afternoon sky and a throbbing line of silver light rimmed the horizon. Palm trees rustled. An offshore tropical storm, Martin heard, had changed direction in the Gulf of Mexico and was headed now toward the Bananaville coast, with sixty-mile-an-hour winds, threatening to reach land by as early as the following evening.

He finished his story and sidebar about Rudolph Jr., and tried to read through the national news wire. Mostly, though, he just stared at the same sentences, over and over, thinking about China, the naked look in her eyes, wondering how the pieces of this story—DeRosse, Vaughn, Cora Carlson, Ginny Reed, Jack Carlson, Joey Keen, Antonio DeRosse—might all fit together. Wondering why Cora Carlson hadn't returned his last three phone calls.

He glanced at Q. V., tapping out her story about the storm, admiring her quiet intensity, the fact that she wrote most of the local news copy while Thomas Persons, the "senior writer," contributed nearly nothing, other than his rambling "First Persons" column. Right now he was on his hands and knees, in his three-piece suit, looking through a box of old *Field & Streams*, mumbling to himself. His face seemed dangerously purple.

Martin looked up and saw a white car whipping far too fast into the parking lot, swinging in a wild arc toward the building. He was certain for a moment that it was out of control—that it would jump the concrete space-end and crash through the window, right about at the spot where Martin's desk was. His heart clutched in that instant, though immediately afterward the car came to a perfect stop, beside Martin's station wagon.

China Rinaldi got out and walked confidently toward the building, wearing faded jeans, a black silk shirt, and hiking boots. As she came up the newsroom corridor moments later, through Business and Life, the clank of her bracelets became steadily louder as if a volume knob were being turned up. Although he had no idea what was fueling her, the fact that China was coming with such urgency to see him made Martin feel very happy.

"Come here," she whispered desperately, grabbing his arm and tugging.

Martin saw Hobart P. Lanahan straighten, and blink rapidly. On the front porch, China nearly burst with her news. "She'll do it!" she said, breathing heavily. "But we've got to go over there right now!"

Martin nodded, from a distance. "What're you talking about?"

"Joyce Jasper. But we've got to go right now. Get your fricking notepad and let's vamoose."

Martin hurried back into the newsroom. He was halfway out again, cutting through Sports, when he realized Joyce Jasper must be China's friend who had placed the 911 call. It was all he could figure. He sensed the secret army of helping hands mobilizing again.

JOYCE JASPER, China explained, stopped at an intersection of Banana Boulevard where the bas-relief likeness of Joey Keen smiled at traffic, grew up in Wyoming. She moved to Bananaville five years ago and still lived off the inheritance from her parents, who died in an automobile accident in 1975, when Joyce was sixteen.

"She's extremely sensitive about her weight," China said, "so you've got to be very careful what you say."

China drove rapidly into a quaint neighborhood Martin hadn't seen before, of old, newly painted houses trimmed with gingerbread men, and bright, candy-colored picket fences.

"They wanted to call this Storybook Lane," China said. "It was going to be the centerpiece for a 'make-believe village' sort of community. But the fricking developer ran out of bucks. It was sort of a stupid idea, if you ask me. Weird guy." She added, "He ended up going to jail."

"The developer did?"

"Yeah."

"Over this?"

"Huh? Uh-uh. Molesting a twelve-year-old boy."

She parked on the edge of the road, by a candy-cane-striped telephone pole. China opened the gate of the miniature pink picket fence, and a path of stones—shaped as elephant foot-prints—led them through the weeping willow branches around a sandlewood tree, to the back of Joyce Jasper's cottage-style apartment house.

China knocked three times and opened the door.

"Hey, honey!" she sang.

The apartment smelled of banana bread. It was sparsely furnished—Navajo rugs, a sofa, two wooden chairs—but full of stuffed cats and bears, hanging wreaths, several huge, elaborate dollhouses. The predominant motif quickly became apparent: a dozen or more mobiles of shih tzu faces and bodies hung from the ceiling. Paintings and photos of shih tzus were framed on every wall. A shrine of shih tzu figures filled most of one corner, and a large lithograph of six shih tzus in Christmas coats and Santa hats hung from a wall. As Martin took it all in, the real thing—a small white and black shih tzu—energetically wagged its way out of the bedroom and pranced toward him.

Joyce Jasper followed timidly—she was an enormous woman, with pageboy haircut, dressed in a flannel nightgown and fuzzy slippers. One side of her face was red, as if she'd just woken up. She looked at Martin, briefly, and the other side turned red, too.

"This is Martin, honey."

"Hi," she said shyly, looking at the floor. All of a sudden the dog grew cautious, too, sniffing at Martin warily as he reached down to pat it. "Let me get us some banana bread first," she said, speaking in a baby voice. China smiled, and followed Joyce Jasper into the kitchen.

"I FEEL VERY, very bad about what happened," Joyce Jasper said, once they had all settled, cross-legged, on the wooden floor with their banana bread served on plates depicting colorful scenes of Winnie the Pooh.

Martin made an agreeable sound as he bit into the bread, and China nodded.

"Isn't it good?" China said.

"Excellent," Martin said.

Without looking up, Joyce Jasper's face reddened again. The shih tzu, lying on its stomach, kept its tilted gaze on Martin.

"Anyhow," he said once they finished. "Whatever you're comfortable saying, Joyce—I mean, nothing will be used in the paper or anything like that. This is just for my own edification, just to see if it could be of any bearing on the story. Or the eventual story, as it were." Martin, smiling at himself, didn't really know what he was saying. Joyce Jasper, though, nodded attentively, like a child receiving instructions. China sat to the side as if a chaperone, her eyes moving from one to the other.

"Well." She cleared her throat. "I walk . . ." She carefully set her plate on the floor, and stared at China. "Every morning I walk down there—or, I mean, used to walk—down there where the mangroves are, that part of the beach. By that little point?"

"Okay."

"Cleopatra likes the fresh air, and when she's in the mood she also chases the seagulls?"

Martin nodded, though she wouldn't look at him. Cleopatra's eyes were watching Martin's.

"I had seen Mr. Reed one or two times before. He jogs on the beach there. Jogged, I mean."

"Uh-huh."

China was tilting her head as if this were her third child, reciting lines from the school play.

"In the same spot every morning. It's sort of secluded, with the trees? And the dune?"

"Okay."

"So—and we were walking, Cleopatra and I. And then I looked up and I saw Mr. Reed off in the distance. At first, I didn't know if it was him, but then I thought it might be. And I thought I saw another man, too. On the beach with Mr. Reed."

There was a long, long pause.

When Martin said, "And what happened then?" her eyes glinted reproachfully, as if he were about to strike her.

"Tell him what they were doing, honey," China said, in an endearing tone used to address pets. "You thought they were talking at first, didn't you? But then you thought they might have been fighting, too, isn't that right?"

She nodded, looking at the dark, shiny, narrow floorboards.

"Like . . . ?" Martin spoke more to China than Joyce. "Fist-fighting?"

A warm red glow filled Joyce Jasper's cheeks. "I couldn't see because it was so far away. But I thought for a minute that the other man—I think he may have had something in his hand." She stared at China. "At first I thought maybe they were just playing or something. But then the other man did something very bad." Her eyes shifted to the floorboards, and like a sudden unexpected rain shower, tears filled them and overflowed down her face.

China's eyes blazed briefly at Martin. She hugged Joyce's shoulders for several minutes, rocking her back and forth until the sobbing stopped.

"Tell him, honey," she said, at last. "It's okay. Tell him what you thought he did. Let's just get it over with."

"I didn't really see anything," she said, to China. "But. It was a very bad sound." Her eyes welled up in the round face, and she looked right at Martin, her mouth opening and closing in frightened fishlike motions. Suddenly the moist darkness of her eyes seemed to open up, pulling him in, down deeper than he wanted to go, the sobs starting to sound almost hysterical again. Martin stared back, wanting somehow to help, wanting to pull the little child stuck in this great big body to safety, but not knowing how.

"It's okay," China said, wrapping her arms over Joyce's shoulders again. "It's okay. Just relax. It's okay." She comforted her for several minutes, before saying, soothingly, "Tell him, honey, tell him: What was the sound?"

"A crack?" She looked at Martin quickly, her face all shiny now. "And then—so I picked up Cleopatra, because I didn't want anything to happen to her. And we started back. I wasn't even sure what had happened. Before I got across the road I saw this vehicle coming, out of the next parking area."

"A vehicle."

"Yes." She lowered her damp eyes. "Because—and usually there aren't ever any other cars there that early in the morning. And it looked like it might have been. I mean—the same man."

The wall clock struck the hour with an excited sound of barks, startling Martin.

"What happened then?" China asked.

"I walked back up the road very quickly. Carrying Cleopatra. I was too scared at first to know what to do. But finally I stopped at a pay phone and I called the police: 911."

Martin remembered what Detective Rick Howard had said about the voice sounding disguised. The tears were drying in crooked lines on her face.

"You didn't wait for the police?"

"No." She looked to China, and began sobbing all over again.

"She was too upset," China said impatiently. Martin nodded, waiting. He understood sensitivity; withholding information about a murder was something else.

"What about the vehicle?" he asked. "What sort of vehicle was it?"

"I think. It was a white pickup truck?"

"Had you ever seen the man before?"

"No, I don't think so. But I was too far away to really see him."

"Can you describe him?"

She stared right at him now and her frightened eyes locked on his. "I can't remember. Except—I don't think he was large. He might have been small."

SHE SERVED A second helping of banana bread along with cherry Kool-Aid and then, in a small-child's voice, read aloud two stories she had written the week before. Both were about a frog family called the Weatherbys, who had become friends with Cleopatra the shih tzu. After the second story, Martin tapped his watch, and reminded China that he had an appointment at five o'clock.

"What appointment do you have at five?" she asked, as they sped away from the house.

Martin didn't say.

"They could almost make her one of the attractions at Disney World, couldn't they?" Martin said.

"Not nice."

"No, I'm kidding," he said, wondering if Joyce Jasper had actually seen more. He added, "How did you meet her?"

"Just out with the kids one day. About four years ago. She's not at all shy around children or pets, only around adults. I think she really wanted to get this off her fricking chest."

"Seemed like it."

"Yeah."

There was an odd distance between them all of a sudden, a thick silence as China sped along the wide, well-kept boulevards. In town, the east sides of buildings were in shadow, the air was breezy and gray. He looked up and saw sunlight gleaming on an airplane that was moving like a stainless steel toy above the clouds.

"It doesn't help much, though, does it?" China said, stopped at a traffic light.

"What?"

"What she said."

"Maybe, maybe not."

Not seeing a smile, she punched him playfully in the arm, as if he were an old record that had gotten stuck. Martin smiled back.

"Come on, you're never going to figure this thing out."

"I don't know," he said. "Who drives a white pickup?"

But he didn't have to think about it. The answer came to him as soon as he posed the question.

Jack Carlson.

INSTAING OF RETURNING home, Martin drove to the neighborhood where Jack Carlson worked. He parked his wagon beneath the crimson leaves of a royal poinciana, and tried to sort out what he had learned that day, hearing the crepuscular sound of insects in the front yards, watching the sun drop. What he now knew: Jack Carlson worked within two blocks of pay telephones that had been used to harass the Reeds. Jack Carlson's glasses had been broken, and there was broken glass found on Reed's body. Jack Carlson was a small man, who drove a white pickup. If Cora Carlson had, indeed, been having an affair with Reed, or if Jack Carlson believed she had been, there was a motive.

On the near horizon, above the roof of the transportation center, he watched strawberry-colored streaks turn blood-red in slow motion; then, as sunlight's afterglow disappeared, the street seemed to blur, filling with a breezy mist that tasted of sea salt. It was possible, Martin thought, that the person making the hang-up calls was still using the same two pay phones—although hardly likely. Still, he waited, here and then a block away from the other pay phone, on a street where night had already arrived. He tried to enjoy the breeze, the blowing mist, and not think too much. Streetlights glowed orange down the empty lane, and the yellow slashes of kitchens and living rooms brightened across lawns.

At 7:37 a figure emerged from out of an alleyway and began to walk along the sidewalk toward the phone booth. He stopped, looked down the street toward Martin, and stepped inside the booth. Trees rustled wildly. Martin thought he saw the receiver go down and lift again. The man came out. He began to walk back up the street quickly into the mist, past the lawns of dimly outlined tropical plants, heading, it seemed, directly toward Martin's wagon. Martin ducked down below the steering wheel, watching, and as the man came to within a car's length, Martin saw him eerily transform in his imagination from Jack Carlson into someone else—a man with a deformity on his face, on his right hand, someone Martin had seen very closely once before: Wayne Vaughn, Cora Carlson's second husband.

The man's left hand seemed to tap the back fender of Martin's car, and then he was gone, a shape in the mist.

CHINA'S WINDOW SHADE burned like a soft, buttery hope through the trees on Coconut Lane, as Martin sat at his kitchen table thinking about what he'd seen. What do you do now? he wondered. How do you take what you've learned and find the Big Story?

He dialed Rudolph Reed Jr. and waited.

"Hal-lo."

"Rudy? Martin Grant."

"Mr. Grant."

"Did you get a hang-up call twenty-five minutes ago?"

There was a long silence, during which Martin heard him breathing, heard Kurt Cobain wailing in the background.

"Was that you?"

"No," he said. "No, but I think I'm starting to figure this thing out." He was staring, still, at the glow of China's light on the shade, forgetting for a moment, as he tasted night-blooming cereus in the breeze, who he was talking to. "No, Rudy. Let me call you tomorrow and I'll try to fill you in. Okay?"

He lay in bed, unable to sleep, and sensed something as obvious yet elusive as the wind: Somewhere, his questioning had poked closer than he knew to a nerve, some raw truth. Where?

At 12:22 China's light disappeared, and it seemed to Martin

as if the moon had gone out. Forty minutes later, his phone rang. Martin listened as the machine downstairs picked up, and he heard the same fuzzy sound—like a scratchy record—growing louder, replaced by a screech of brakes and a crash of metal. The phone clicked off.

He lay, waiting for what came next, but all that happened was the morning, surprising him again with its soft warm currents and sparkling air. The storm, he heard, driving across town, had stalled overnight in the Gulf of Mexico.

INSTEAD OF GOING directly to the office, Martin drove south, past gleaming tomato and pepper fields, to Banana Estates, pulling off where China had pulled off, staring at Lodge McCloud's castle. There was no sign, this morning, of the man himself.

Martin proceeded to Jack and Cora Carlson's house, still wondering why Cora Carlson wouldn't return his calls. The southern drawl of Jack Carlson—a man Martin had been certain, just twelve hours earlier, had killed Rudolph Reed—greeted him at the front-gate intercom.

"She's not here," he said, when Martin identified himself.

"No—but could I talk to you? For just a couple of minutes?"

"Talk to me?"

"Just for a few minutes."

"What would you want to do that for?"

"I just want to ask you a couple of questions. I think you can help me figure out what happened with Rudolph."

"Oh?"

Jack Carlson said nothing else. After a long wait, the gate swung open.

MARTIN STEERED ALONG the gravel drive to the Carlsons' house, parking again behind the white pickup truck in the porte cochere. Carlson was standing there waiting, unshaven, dressed in jeans, sneakers, and a work shirt.

"What can I help you with?" he said, looking at Martin with the same unfriendly squint.

"Just a couple things I wanted to run by you."

"I don't have anything to tell you." His features seemed costive, tightening as he stared into Martin's eyes. "What—are you interviewing everybody in town now?"

Martin shrugged. "Just people who might know something."

"Yeah?" Carlson shook out a Camel, and he lit it, looking at the lawn, the flower gardens that stretched brightly behind the house, the columned pool that glimmered with webs of morning sunlight. He seemed made of pieces that didn't quite fit, a conservative man whose personality was dressed in some leftover defiance. Clearly he wasn't going to invite Martin inside.

"Did you know Rudolph Reed well?"

Jack Carlson grunted, continuing to stare at his lawn.

"Did you know him at all?"

He squinted at Martin. "I didn't have any beef with Reed."

"Okay." Martin nodded, and pretended to be taking in the property. "I understand you used to work in the building inspector's office. When that fire happened down at the Satellite a few years back."

Jack Carlson looked toward the sun as he smoked.

"Did you have to cite the property?"

"Numerous times."

"I've heard some speculation," Martin said. "About what might've caused that fire. That maybe there was some connection between that and what happened to Reed."

"The fire?"

"Yes."

"Where'd you hear that?"

Martin shrugged; he hadn't actually heard it anywhere. Carlson, though, was staring at him.

"Okay, buddy," he said, and took a long drag from his cigarette. "Maybe I do have something to say to you. Why don't we go have a seat back here. Talk for a minute. Then I got some chores to do."

"Sure."

He led Martin along an oyster-shell trail across the lawn, stopping by the water beneath a sprawling live oak.

"Have a seat," he said, pointing with his cigarette at a stone bench nestled in the shade. Both men sat. "I'm going to tell you exactly what was responsible for that fire, okay? Just so there's no confusion on your part." He was watching Martin, with small, dark eyes. "Guy by the name of Wayne Vaughn was responsible. Ever heard of him?"

Martin tried not to seem surprised.

"But he was burned in the fire, wasn't he?"

Carlson stared at his cigarette; slowly, he smoked.

"Okay? I can speculate on what happened. Maybe he rigged up some sort of explosive and it went off too soon. Maybe he was intoxicated and fell asleep. But that's what happened. The man fucked up."

"Why would he have set the fire, though?"

Carlson shook his head, almost imperceptibly. He took a long, final drag of the cigarette and crushed it out in the dirt, letting smoke drain from his nostrils into the afternoon air. He was in his late forties, Martin guessed, but, with the white stubble, looked considerably older. "All I'm going to say is that the person who owns the property today plans to use it for one of the largest amusement parks in the country."

"Lodge McCloud."

He squinted at the lagoon for a long while. "What Wayne did, see, was fool people into thinking he was some kind of true-hearted do-gooder. All bullshit. And Cora can be gullible. She's a vulnerable lady, who gets hurt easily and then toughs it out. It breaks my heart sometimes, believe me.

"She was hurt by some of the questions you were asking her the other day," he said. "I told her, don't talk to him anymore, if it upsets you. That's why she hasn't returned your calls."

"I see. So you think Wayne Vaughn was responsible—"

"I don't think, son, I know. Okay? I'm not saying how I know. But I know. And I'll tell you one more thing before I get back to work. I'll tell you how I found out about Wayne Vaughn, if you got a minute." Martin nodded, as Carlson tapped out another Camel. "I'd gotten friendly with the lady, met her when I was doing a site inspection right here on this property. Back when they wanted to add the deck. And Wayne, he was just starting to come around again, like her ol' puppy dog. 'Cause he'd lived in this house, too," he said, nodding behind him at the mansion. He lit up the Camel and shook out the match. "And, of course, it was a far cry from where he's living now. Now, Wayne Vaughn didn't know me from Adam back then, and I was out here one day planting some bulbs for Cora. Wayne does a lot of talking, and I'm listening. And we're walking along, right out here by the lagoon, he's saying a lot of things about a lot of things, and then he happens to mention that he had served in 'Nam. Well. I played twenty questions with him, and he didn't pass." He stared at Martin with a rough, simmering anger.

"Where'd he flunk?"

"He had himself in Cambodia in the fall of Seventy. Well, it so happened our campaign ended there in July. I lost two buddies in it. I never had nothing to do with Wayne Vaughn after that day, and neither has Cora."

"Would he have had any motive to kill Reed, though?"

Carlson seemed strangely uninterested in the question.

"You ought to forget about that one, son," he said. "That one's like the fire, Martin. You're just going to have to accept it. It happened. Shit happens."

WAYNE VAUGHN'S ADDRESS was listed as 2121 Sharktooth Lane, just a half block, Martin saw on the city map, from the transportation annex where Jack Carlson worked. And just two blocks from the pay phone he had used to call Rudolph Jr. the night before.

There was only one photo of Wayne Vaughn in the newspaper's files—a blurry shot of him with Mayor "Gator" Gorman on a restaurant deck that seemed to be the Paradise Club. Martin wanted to take it over to show Joyce Jasper, to see if she could identify him. The sign-out board showed that China was on the road all day, though, and he didn't know how Joyce would feel about Martin coming over by himself. And Joyce's number, he saw, was unlisted. After filing his story—about the Reeds receiving harassing phone calls—Martin got in his wagon and headed north, into the wind, into neighborhoods he didn't know, feeling safer, almost, being lost, and yet ending up beside the now familiar candy-cane telephone pole and pink picket fence.

Elephant tracks led him back to Joyce Jasper's apartment, where he rapped several times on the door, standing in a breezy shower of sunlight and shade.

There was no answer.

He peered in the window, saw the hanging plants and ferns, the dollhouses, shih tzu statues and mobiles, the shiny floorboards and Navajo rugs. Just visible above the living room's largest chair was the top of Joyce Jasper's head; below it, he saw her left arm and shoulder, slumped against the floor.

Martin tapped on the glass.

"Joyce? It's Martin Grant."

Cleopatra ran alertly toward the door, then stopped and tilted her head, looking anxiously at his eyes. Martin saw Joyce's head slide lower behind the chairback, so that it was no longer visible.

He followed the elephant prints to the street and looked up into the western sky, which seemed purple and bruised now, though tinged with a silvery aura. The storm, he heard on the news, had regained momentum and was aimed again for their coast, with winds approaching hurricane strength.

**31** CHINA RINALDI WAS standing barefoot in the long, late shadows of her lawn, reaching into the orange tree as Martin drove down Coconut Lane. Seeing his car, she waved excitedly for him to stop.

"Got a whole bag full of shrimp!" she said, leaning in the window with a musky aroma of perfume. "Come on over?"

Put that way, it was hard to resist, though he had been thinking only of phantoms since leaving Joyce Jasper's street—had sensed them closing around him like webs of darkness in the twilight sky. The same phantoms that had chased Reed and caught him were now chasing Martin.

On China's patio, they ate shrimp and watched sunset—the smoky trails of red light on the horizon—as lightning bugs blinked in the live oaks. He felt the hot sauce pleasantly in his sinuses, and forgot about Wayne Vaughn for a while, forgot about the look in Sammy Reed's eyes. "Moonlight Sonata" played in the cooling air; warblers and sapsuckers sang. He told the munchkins a story about the time it had snowed six feet in central Iowa—and he'd had to go out in his father's pickup with his brother to deliver newspapers all over town. The details seemed to fill their faces with wonderment, as if Martin were talking about a trip he had taken to Mars.

After China put the children to bed, she came back outside with two bottles of ginger ale, wearing a sad smile.

"You know what I did today?"

"What?"

"Nothing." Her eyes looked searchingly at his. "It was nice. I dropped the munchkins at day care, came home, and played the piano." She added, "I'm going to quit the job, I think."

"Why?"

"I told you," she said, her expression shifting into thinking mode. "In fact, I think I'm ready to leave this fricking town."

Her eyes glistened adventurously, at new horizons, at the prospect of getting out; for a moment, it pleased Martin ineffably.

"It used to be I thought everyone who lived here was sort of like a stockholder, you know what I mean? We were all entitled to get something back. But it isn't that way at all. The town's sustenance is the people. I want the munchkins to see what else is out there."

The air had turned breezier, stirring the leaves. They sat for more than an hour on the cool brick patio, listening to sonatas, watching the stars above the stucco wall and the occasional western lightning, holding hands comfortably. What had happened between them two nights earlier wasn't mentioned, yet it sat there like a shared secret, a bridge to unseen places where, maybe, life was forever more satisfying.

Hearing his own voice—a question rising from his thoughts—surprised Martin.

"Say," he said. "Do you know this guy Wayne Vaughn?"

The dreaminess closed down in China's face and she stared, her lips slightly pursed.

"Yeah. I know who he is." Moonlight squiggled with the breeze over the darkened pool surface. "Why?"

"Well. Between you and me? I think he's the one who killed Rudolph Reed."

"Wayne *Vaughn?*"

"I just can't figure out why."

She looked up abruptly, as if seeing a flying saucer. "Oh. No, I don't know. That doesn't sound right somehow."

"It doesn't?"

"*Wayne?*" She crossed her arms and hugged them against herself. "No, it just doesn't seem—I mean, I know there's kind of a bad buzz going around about him right now, like maybe he's gotten into drugs again. And he's managing that club."

"The strip club?"

"Yeah. Treasure Chest. And from what I've heard, they say he doesn't have any friends anymore, except for maybe some of those people over at the club. But I mean—I don't think he'd *kill* anyone. Although I don't know him," she quickly added.

"What do *you* think?" Martin asked.

"What do I think?"

"I mean—about who was responsible."

She shrugged. "I don't know. I used to have a funny feeling about Jack Carlson. Just because he's so weird. And I always suspect Lodge McCloud has some role in everything that happens. But I don't know—I really don't know."

Martin looked up at the clouds floating across the moon, felt China's fingers closing around his. The air filled with a soft urgent flapping of wings and he saw four pelicans, soaring together over China's patio toward the sea. That's all any of us really wants, isn't it? Martin thought: to belong to something that soars.

When he got up to leave, to return to life beyond these stucco walls, China held him, and they swayed silently for several minutes beside the swimming pool, not wanting to let go, the hug becoming a slow dance in the wind, to subtle, soundless music. It seemed to Martin a kind of recharging, a shared confirmation, a wish.


MARTIN TURNED OFF his telephone that night, locked his doors and windows, and went to bed. He tried to watch television, but his attention strayed. He stared through the trees at her glowing yellow window until the light went out and the whole world seemed suddenly dark again. In the morning he turned on his phone and went for a run, enjoying the warm currents of winter air.

When he returned, China's car was gone. The telephone was

ringing. Martin counted the rings, as he fixed himself a glass of ice water.

"Hello?"

"Martin?" a male voice said. "You sound out of breath. Listen, I know you've been working overtime on this Rudy Reed thing. Well, I thought you'd like to know, you can take a rest on it," Hobart P. Lanahan said, and there was a trace of something unpleasant—triumphant?—in his voice. "The police have just taken in Archie Duval."

"*What?* He's been charged?"

"Yep. They found the weapon right in the back of his truck. A flashlight. They believe there may be traces of Reed's blood on it."

"Jesus."

"Yep. Just thought you'd want to know."

Martin hung up and stared through the screen window at the bright sunlit lawn. The night had lifted, and with it another potential Big Story had just kind of evaporated into the air of a new day.

3 2

THE NEWSROOM SEEMED bathed in a psychic glow that morning, emanating from Hobart P. Lanahan's office. The Metro editor stepped in and out of it all morning, striding back and forth past Martin's desk without ever looking him in the eyes.

Martin went to the newspaper's library, and checked out the file of clippings on Archie Duval. They didn't add much to the image he had of him from the Paradise Club—a large, sloppily dressed man. He was a real estate agent and a charter fishing mate who lived at the commercial harbor on a converted lobster boat. His uncle, Leslie "Bullfrog" Duval, had been the town's eleventh mayor.

Five years ago, Archie was named to something called the Beach Mediation Board. Another clipping, though, dated six months later, indicated he was being replaced because he hadn't attended any meetings.

Then, just three months ago, he became a member of the "East Side Liaison Drug Task Force," which was chaired by Councilman Antonio DeRosse.

There was just one picture of him, wearing the fedora hat and a leather jacket, standing with Mayor "Gator" Gorman and a group of Realtors at a VFW hall function.

What Martin couldn't glean from these files was this: Why would he kill Rudolph Reed?

\* \* \*

He WENT DOWN the hall to see Dale Bunch, who seemed to have some mysterious pipeline to the secret motivations of the town. Bunch was dressed today in an oversized black turtleneck sweater and jeans, typing his "On Religion" column as Martin knocked.

"Come in," he said, indicating that Martin should close the door and have a seat. "Good piece you wrote this morning on the Reed case, Martin. About the phone calls?"

"Thanks. I understand they got something of an unexpected break in the case today."

"Oh?" Bunch turned away from his terminal. Uncombed strands of white hair glowed with the green light of the text behind him—the room's only illumination. "But, of course, not a real one."

"No?"

"Not a real one, no." The great, red sagging eyes closed. "But then so much of what we talk about—so much of the discourse of our entire lives—turns out later to be in some way false, doesn't it? To be based on wrong assumptions, or misinformation. Or, perhaps, a lack of information. It makes you wonder, how much of our time here is wasted on the wrong activities, how much of our life is lived incorrectly." The eyes came open again, slowly, and he nodded, as if to say hello. "I've been thinking about that quite a bit lately, Martin. Life, lived correctly, must be this: a continual process of learning what things are worth."

"Things?"

"Time, friendship, relaxation. Those kinds of things."

Martin cleared his throat.

"So—but the police don't have a strong case, you're saying?"

Bunch's face took on a wide, uncomfortable-looking smile. "It doesn't seem likely, no. But what have we learned, Martin? what lessons can we use as reference points?" He shut his eyes, mulling over, Martin suspected, some ideas he'd been writing about in his column. "All the great myths teach us the same thing: that the world is circular. From that we can extrapolate a good deal. Now:

cle where what happened to Rudolph will begin to make sense. But we will."

"It was surprising, though—to me—that they brought in Archie Duval."

Dale Bunch was watching him soberly. "Well, they aren't going to bring charges, though," he said. "Not based on planted evidence."

Martin felt a flush of anger rise in his neck. "Wait, I thought Hobart said he'd been charged already."

"No, they just brought him in for questioning. He'll probably be released by noon. They did find the murder weapon in his old truck, though—it was a large black flashlight. Police went there on an anonymous tip this morning. But there are no prints, nothing linking it to Archie. And Archie will almost certainly have some sort of alibi. These are the things one learns."

FOR THE FIRST time since arriving in Bananaville, Martin felt himself losing his grip. Six minutes later he was in Hobart P. Lanahan's office.

"You told me Archie Duval had been charged. He hasn't been."

"Charges pending, Grant." He looked at his page layouts, as if Martin had disappeared.

"You said he was charged."

"They found the murder weapon right in the back of his truck."

He looked up and smiled, without meeting Martin's stare.

Martin turned, and walked back to his desk. For several minutes he watched the cursor on his computer screen, feeling warm gusts of air tugging him back to complacency, but remembering, too, the taste of straight bourbon in his lungs, wanting to feel it again, to let it soak his spirit one more time. Q. V. was solemnly typing, Thomas Persons was playing solitaire.

He wished he hadn't let Hobart P. Lanahan get to him.

163

                    *   *   *

SHORTLY BEFORE NOON, as a hard wind rattled palm fronds on the edges of the parking lot, the call came in: Archie Duval had been released. Martin got in his wagon and he drove to Pineapple Lane, wanting to filter some of what he'd learned through Sammy Reed's lens.

There was just one shopping cart out front today, and among the other children, only Joshua seemed to be home. He was seated on the floor staring at "I Dream of Jeannie," across the room from the still-burning shrine to Rudolph Reed Sr.

"Come on back," said Sammy, who was again barefoot, wearing a flower-print dress that scraped the floor and a white T-shirt that seemed a size too small. Her hair was stringier than before and there seemed to be smudges of dirt on her face. The house, as he followed her to the kitchen, had a comfortably familiar smell of potpourri and Italian spices.

"I'm making a vegetable stew," she said cheerily. "Throwing a little of everything in it. Drink?"

"Sure. Anything cold would be good."

Sammy took down a "Jurassic Park" cup, filled it with ice, and poured in tap water. A cassette of George Winston was playing on a cheap tape recorder beside the stove.

"So," she said, handing it to him. "You're here to ask me about Rudy?"

"Yeah." Martin sat. Sammy lifted a wooden spoon and dipped it into the stew pot. "Did that surprise you?"

"Well. He feels obligated to be the family leader, I guess. And all my father's supporters were egging him on. They want the party to continue. Mommy's not happy at all about it."

As she stirred the stew, a warm sharp spicy smell watered Martin's eyes.

"I don't mean to sound judgmental," he said. "But Rudy just seems a little out of his element running for political office."

"Oh, of course." She looked at him with hard blue eyes—too jaded for someone only nineteen. "All he cares about is that

                           164

crappy music. But I guess they convinced him he'd be carrying on the tradition or something. I never even wanted Daddy to get into politics, and neither did Mommy."

"It can be demanding."

"It can be mean."

Martin listened to the bubble of the stew, as Sammy's thin, hairless arms pulled and pushed the wooden spoon through it. One strap of her dress, he noticed, was attached by a safety pin.

"I'm curious," he said, "about your older sister, Ginny. Someone told me she went away about four years ago. Wasn't that about when your mother got sick?"

Her eyes began to blink rapidly.

"Not really. And anyway, that doesn't have anything to do with anything," she said, with an odd finality, and Martin could sense in her silence that there was an unspoken secret the adults of the family shared—something they had never really talked about.

"Where did she go when she 'went away'?"

"Oh. All over the place," she said quickly. "I don't know."

Martin stared at the swings shifting in the wind outside, the sunlight waving brightly in the hibiscus.

"Was she pregnant?" he guessed, and Sammy made a noise, a sound like "mmm" or "hmmm." But then she surprised him, turning with strong, steady eyes to meet his question. "I appreciate your interest," she said, "but we don't talk about that between ourselves. I could never talk about it with a stranger. And, I mean, she's still my sister. I'm not going to cut her off the way Rudy has, pretend she doesn't exist." Her eyes glittered with suppressed tears. She looked outside. There was nothing more he could ask.

From the living room Martin heard a burst of television laughter, and saw the flat face of Joshua, the youngest Reed, staring without expression.

He was struck again by the darkness in this house, the fact that, as with Dale Bunch's office, no lights were on. The brightness of the sunlight startled his eyes when he stepped back out again, and walked with Sammy along the housefronts through cool black shadows.

"Oh, I meant to ask you," Martin said, as if remembering something. "If there is any chance I could get Ginny's address— or phone number?"

Sammy blinked at him warily. "I don't know, I don't even know it. I've never been to her place. She just moved back here a couple months ago."

"I see."

"I mean—"

A Hispanic woman came out of an adjacent unit, slamming the door. She smiled quickly at Sammy, swatting at the tops of her children's heads as they walked down to the parking lot.

"I do have a phone number, though. If you want to hold on."

"Sure."

She walked purposefuly back to the house and returned with a number scribbled on a torn corner of newspaper, and handed it to Martin, squinting pensively into his face.

"Don't tell her you got it from me, though."

"I won't."

The shadows of palms blew wildly across the boulevards as he drove back. The storm, he heard on his radio, was raging toward their coast.

HOBART P. LANAHAN's door was closed, and he was hunkered in front of his computer. He did not acknowledge Martin's return. Q. V. was gone, covering a story. Thomas Persons was sleeping like a schoolboy, his face down on the desk.

Martin dialed the number Sammy had written for him, and on the third ring, a husky female voice said, "Hello."

Ginny Reed.

Martin explained who he was and that he was writing a story about her father. "Uh-huh, uh-huh," she repeated impatiently. Afterward—cool, detached—she said, "Thanks, but I don't do interviews."

166

"Off the record."

"Right. Off the record, on the record, I don't do interviews." In a rougher tone, she added, "It's a sad story, isn't it?" and hung up.

The words echoed ominously in his head as he sat there staring at the newsroom. Q. V. came rushing in, letting her knapsack fall to the floor as she flipped through her notebook with an urgency he'd once had. It was a difference in ages, perhaps: the idea that if you do something with a lot of energy, you do it better.

He wondered: Why had Ginny Reed gone away and what had made her come back?

Martin sorted through his notes for several minutes, trying to find leads he hadn't followed, people he still needed to talk with. Finally he decided to try Quentin Craig, Reed's friend and Rudolph Jr.'s campaign manager. A frond, torn from a tall coconut palm, thunked against the newsroom window, causing everyone to look up.

"Yes?" Quentin Craig said.

There was dead silence after Martin explained who he was and why he was calling. "I just wonder if I could ask you a few questions about Rudolph."

"Uh. Questions?" The voice was gruff, and somehow familiar.

"Yes."

"I don't know. I'm having lunch now. This is, uh, a little intrusive, isn't it?"

It was, clearly, the other voice on Rudolph Reed's answering machine tape—the person who needed something settled by Friday. A gate opened and Martin felt himself entering another neighborhood of the story, although nothing was discernible yet, the shapes were all nebulous. *An announcement.* Did Quentin Craig know the thing he "had to come to terms with"?

"Let me call you back," he said, and abruptly hung up.

Martin was surprised to see, several minutes later, China walking alongside the river, lost in thought, wind blowing her long black dress tight against her body. He hurried out, and for several minutes walked beside her, under the live oaks, into the wind. He wanted to touch her, to feel the anchor tug, but for some reason China wouldn't look at him. They held hands awkwardly, until China said, "I've got to get back," and let go.

"What's wrong?"

"Nothing. Nothing," she echoed, turning to look at the newspaper office, as if gazing into another country. "Nothing. I'll talk to you tonight."

Martin walked back up the riverbank in the breezy glare of sunlight, feeling mildly drugged. Picking for his key from the key ring, he heard someone behind him, feet scraping twice on the asphalt.

"Martin Grant?" a low voice he recognized said.

MARTIN LOOKED INTO the glare of sunlight and couldn't see anyone. He turned slightly and realized there was a man standing directly behind him, as if hiding in the sun's aura. The man seemed to have something in his hand, and now raised it slightly—in a short, slow stabbing motion. The face wore an enormous, fixed grin, like that of a clown.

The moment passed.

"I'm Chuck Craig," the man said, extending his hand again, and stepping forward so that he blocked the sun. Everything slipped back into focus. Martin recognized him as the washboard player at Rudolph Jr.'s campaign kick-off. Quentin Craig, a short, kindly, bowlegged man with thick white hair. Newt's father. "I'd like to apologize for being so brusque with you on the phone. You have a minute? They told me at the desk you'd just left and might still be out in the parking lot. I didn't see you at first. I'm parked on the street out front. You want to take my car and go get a cup of coffee?"

"Sure." Martin looked at the car, though, and felt an inexplicable apprehension. "Actually. Why don't I follow you? I'm on my way home."

"Oh. Okay."

Martin wondered, as he drove up the narrow, windy lane, why he had said that—if the sounds of screeching brakes and crunching metal on his answering machine were rattling him more than he realized.

The two of them sat on the bench outside Captain Jack's and drank coffee from Styrofoam cups, watching the trees shake.

"I called Rudy after we hung up, and he said you were doing a story on the family. Marvelous thing," he said, his smile almost too friendly. "I've been getting some unusual calls lately. I prefer to talk with people in person these days, you know. Ever since Rudy was murdered. I was having a late lunch today and I just didn't know who you were."

"Sure." Martin raised his hand, indicating the explanation wasn't necessary. "You were a good friend of Rudolph."

"Oh, I adored the man. Salt of the earth. Not an evil bone in his body. Almost something saintly about him. Like he was here to be an example for the rest of us. He seemed to know things the rest of us didn't."

The door creaked open and Captain Jack stepped out, grinning. He stared into the palm tops and frowned. "She's blowing, isn't she?"

"Sure is."

"Mmm-mmm." All three looked for a while at the breezy sky. Finally Captain Jack went back inside.

"Any theories?" Martin asked. "About what might've happened?"

"The truth of the matter? I think Rudy Reed could have won the election next month. *Won* it. First place. And that would have affected this town enormously, in ways you can't imagine. He had a tremendous momentum, you know, and that infuriated the business community. Infuriated them.

"He didn't plan to run again, though—did you know that? Didn't think his family could take it for another four years. But he had a lot of supporters and he felt an obligation to them."

"Wait a minute. He wasn't going to run again?"

"Nope."

A furious gust of wind shook the trees. The newspaper rack on the corner blew over, a trash can lid careened wildly down the street.

"What do you mean? I thought he was."

"No, Rudy had told me, in a series of very personal conversations. That he was going to withdraw from politics and try to pull his family together. It was going to be his 'new crusade,' he called it. He thought in the long run he could do more good that way.

"He had asked me if I would run in his place, on his platform. He would endorse me. Said he thought he could get my campaign signs around town for me."

Chuck Craig sipped coffee, a smiling, unassuming old man who seemed to Martin as unlikely a political candidate as Rudolph Jr. "I don't say I have the same abilities he had, or the same experience, although I used to do a bit of public speaking—this was thirty, thirty-five years ago. But I did share a lot of his ideas."

So that's what Lila Reed had meant—"He wasn't even going to be there." Captain Jack, standing behind the screen door, nodded and smiled when Martin caught his eye.

"So that's the thing he was trying to come to terms with."

"No." Craig surprised him, shaking his head. "No, that's just it. It wasn't something he was trying to come to terms with at all. He'd already made up his mind, he was definitely getting out of politics. But then in those last few days, something else happened. He found out about something, I don't know what, and it just overwhelmed him."

Martin sensed the streets of the story narrowing.

"If it was all set, why didn't you get into the race, then, after he was killed?"

"Well, because I knew Rudy Jr. was thinking about it. We had a long talk, and Rudy indicated he really wanted to take a crack at it. I wouldn't do anything to hurt him. I'm fully behind him. In fact, I'm going out door-to-door tonight, and we're planning another rally for him this weekend. He's a good kid. I think he's going to win."


MARTIN RAN FIVE miles that evening to clear his head, most of it into the wind.

The phone was ringing again as he came into the old kitchen, sweating profusely.

"What are you doing?" China Rinaldi said. "I've got something to tell you. Can you come over?"

**34** MARTIN DRESSED IN clean-pressed jeans and a brand-new dress shirt. He splashed on some Jovan and walked up the lane, gravel crunching beneath his feet.

China was waiting at the door, dressed in a halter and cutoff jeans. "Come on out back," she said. "I just got the munchkins to bed."

They stood on the patio in the wind, leaning against the stucco wall as tree branches beat wildly overhead.

"What I wanted to tell you: I'm quitting. I gave notice this afternoon. I just want to play piano again. Raise my children."

It was okay, Martin thought—quitting, starting over, reinventing yourself. It was becoming the American way.

"Why now?"

"I don't know. It's like I said before. There's something insidious about this place. And I just can't explain to myself why I'm not playing piano somewhere. Why I'm still selling advertising."

"Except that you're good at it."

"That isn't enough."

There was something he felt then, watching her eyes—a shared hunger, an affinity. They held each other, dancing faintly to the wind, until she stopped and wordlessly, with the surprise of a perfect jazz riff, led Martin in, to the bedroom, where she pulled him easily onto a thick, clean-smelling quilt. Her hair was damp and had a raspberry scent. They held each other, kissing, fitting together as pieces of moonlight glinted through the upper window and the shadows of magnolia and jacaranda jockeyed on the walls. She was slender and sinewy, a striking contrast to Katie's softness, wearing the same musky perfume.

They undressed with the ease of conversation and began to kiss again, kissing for a long time, slowly, as the curtain on the lower window filled with the warm damp breath of outdoors. She put him inside her and as she sat up he saw her dark eyes watching without smiling, telling him to follow, to go where she was going. She flattened herself on top of him, touched her hands to his face, and moved slowly, her breath warm and steady. They turned over and he saw her eyes watching, seeing he was with her, until she closed them and her face filled for a moment with a private pleasure as she breathed roughly against his ear.

When he looked at her afterward she was staring at him comfortably, her eyes smiling now. It was the first time, he realized, as they lay there silently, breathing the wind, that he had broken his vow.

**35**

IN THE MORNING, shiny fan-shaped palmetto leaves dripped against the screen windows at Martin's house. Lying there, he heard China's bracelets rattle, her heels on the sidewalk, just before the Mustang started up.

DIXIE FUDD WAS working a crossword puzzle at the front desk when he came in and didn't notice Martin, although the door banging closed jarred her attention.

In Metro, Q. V. strolled around her desk and over to Martin's. She was dressed today in well-worn blue jeans, boots, a blue dress shirt, and wide black necktie. The cornrows were gone and her hair was pulled back in a long, thick ponytail.

"In case you hadn't heard," she said, "Jack Messersmith plans to file for City Council today." Martin shook his head. "He's president of the Realtors' association."

"I see."

"Yeah."

Martin stared into her dark, deft eyes. "The idea being what—Rudy Jr. is vulnerable?"

"Very. I'd say Messersmith's a shoe-in for the third seat."

"One and two will be . . . ?"

"You know Keen'll be the front-runner, no question there. And DeRosse, because he's got the experience—although all he's done is spend four years staying out of trouble, barely speaking. But I think he'll probably edge out Messersmith."

"Interesting."

She shrugged, pushing off his desk. "Not really," she said, and went back to her own station, to the story she'd been writing, with a concentration Martin admired and recognized. Yet what was it, he wondered—feeling a pang of sadness and regret at all the false certainties he and Katie had lived with—she was moving toward so quickly? What had been his own frenzied destination all those years?

He looked out, saw green mist rising from the river into the sun-dappled oak branches, bright brown water coursing past—he could hear it rippling on rocks and broken branches—and wanted to be out there, in the puzzle of city streets, getting closer to this mystery, this story, finding out what had really happened to Rudolph Reed.

First, he decided, he needed to know more about Wayne Vaughn.


ON HIS WAY to 2121 Sharktooth Lane, Martin detoured down a narrow weed-lined oyster-shell road to the commercial fishing harbor. Seagulls dipped and screeched above black shrimp boats, oyster sloops, and massive metal clammers, the vessels all shifting incongruously with the wind. The road was horseshoe-shaped, on an inlet that connected to the Gulf of Mexico.

Martin parked at the horseshoe's bend and walked out into the briny, bracing air of the docks, where tie-ropes creaked against the dock posts. The only activity was on the deck of a white, pine-wood oyster ship, whose catch was being shoveled into metal buckets, which were swung on pulleys to the dock. The rusty sound of the pulley seemed a discordant cry of some out-of-tune instrument, playing against the wails of the gulls, the low creak of the ropes, and the refrain of wind.

He watched for a while, then walked farther along the wood-plank horseshoe, until he came to an old lobster boat with the name ARCHIE D. painted on its stern. In the grass across the shell-covered road an old Ford truck rested on cinder blocks: the vehicle where police had found the murder weapon. He walked down the finger dock beside *Archie D.* and stared into the empty boat, then up at the horizon of boat masts and blue sky—taking in the scenery of Archie's life, as huge brown pelicans floated in the harbor water, waiting for fish.

A small Hispanic man appeared on the deck of the next boat over, an extension cord wrapped around his elbow.

Martin cupped his left ear.

"Not there," the man barked. "He's only there at night."

Martin nodded. The pulley screeched across the deck of the oyster boat; wind gusted on the water. The man watched him walk away, and was still watching, standing on a wood-plank engine cover, as Martin drove back up the crunching lane, between tall shade trees, back toward one of the town's major boulevards.

Who, Martin wanted to know, put the flashlight in Archie's truck?

**36**

WAYNE VAUGHN'S HOUSE was directly across the street from a Publix supermarket. Martin parked in the crowded lot, rolled down his window, and waited, soaking in the ambience of the neighborhood—scrubby chain-fenced yards, modest stucco houses crowded together on tiny lots. Above the roofs rose an imposing white hull of the city's transportation annex—although directly behind the houses, still-wooded lots were being cleared for more homes. Unlike other parts of town, this neighborhood seemed haphazard, an unplanned hodgepodge of business and residential development.

After about thirty-five minutes, the front door of 2121 opened.

Wayne Vaughn came out, wearing dull green shorts, a blue and white striped T-shirt, and deck shoes. The scarred face was lowered in thought as he climbed into his white Chevy Blazer.

Martin waited as the Blazer disappeared around the corner—chased behind a chain-link fence by two anxious dobermans. He walked through the parking lot and down the sidewalk past the modest lane of houses, seeing in the opened garages tools and trash cans, lawn mowers, bicycles, auto parts, aluminum grills. This neighborhood seemed less kept up, less hopeful somehow, than those elsewhere in town—as if the earthy disharmony of East Bananaville had encroached into the city limits.

He walked south, to a cul-de-sac where woods were being cleared for new houses. The morning wind was pungent with a smell of freshly turned earth and standing water. Martin stepped through the woods, jumped a mucky stream, and came out in

Wayne's backyard. He was about to cross, he realized briefly, another line—propelled by instinct more than common sense.

The two rear windows were locked. But in the heavy growth of weeds along the side yard he loosened the catches of a screen, removed it, and felt the window lift, opening into a laundry room. His heart racing, Martin pulled himself up with his elbows and squiggled inside the room, landing beside the dryer. Standing, he smelled eggnog, grilled meat, cooking oil. At one end of the worn hall rug was a grandfather clock, in the living room a mix of old furniture. A barbell set—not unlike Rudolph Reed's—was on the floor. Hanging on the wall was a large framed and matted picture of Wayne Vaughn shaking hands with Mayor "Gator" Gorman. He saw a disheveled bed through the partially opened bedroom door—socks and pants strewn beside it.

The study, though, was as neat as Rudolph Reed's, with a full-sized file cabinet, desk, and a small safe. On the wall was a raunchy calendar featuring a naked blonde mounting a motorcycle, wearing only black panties and a shoulder holster. Beside the desk was a campaign poster for Antonio DeRosse, who was grinning broadly in the picture, dressed in his City Council bow tie, with the slogan "Your Tie to Honest Government" underneath.

Martin pulled open the top drawer, saw a neat stack of white typing paper, perfectly sharpened yellow No. 2 pencils, a pocket dictionary, a box of paper clips, and several discount coupons from Arby's, Pizza Hut, Domino's. In another drawer was a stack of simple, generic business contracts, with Wayne Vaughn's name on the top, a package of photographs, several credit card receipts paper-clipped together, and a checkbook. The credit card payments, Martin saw, were to G&W Gun Shop for $96.78, Riverwalk Fish House for $46.98, Disney World for $81.62.

The photographs, taken at Disney World, showed Wayne and a stringy-haired, plain-looking woman about half his age and three or four inches taller. There were four other pictures of her, nude on a motel bed, fondling herself in a way that was supposed to be seductive. Martin noted a pattern of modest withdrawals and deposits in the checkbook. Then on Friday, December 6—the Friday before Reed died—Vaughn had deposited $6,000 into his checking account, bringing the balance to $11,321.73. If he was dealing drugs, Martin figured, it might be drug money.

Or, more likely, it was the payment for Rudolph Reed.

In another drawer was a pile of newspaper clippings about City Council business; in the bottom drawer, numerous odds and ends: yo-yos, Elvis Presley playing cards, a pack of batteries, cassette tapes of C & W artists he'd never heard of, pennies, nickels, fishing hooks and sinkers, a couple of old tape players, one without batteries. Martin pressed the Play button on the other one and heard a scratching sound, like an old phonograph record, and then a hiss of silence. He rewound all the way, heard the same scratching sound, followed this time by a screeching of automobile brakes and a violent collision.

*Bingo.* Martin set the tape player back in the drawer, feeling a rush of adrenaline. He had come, perhaps, into the central clearing of a Big Story, and needed now to find his way back out, so the story could be told.

He walked back up the hall, glancing in the kitchen: Plastic dishes filled the sink; newspapers were piled on the table; a .22-caliber handgun rested on the counter. He peered into the bathroom, saw green and red towels and washcloths lined up, and smelled the fresh plastic of a new shower curtain.

"*Shit!*"

Martin froze, hearing flesh and bone slam against wood. He quick-stepped backward, into the bathtub, up against the farthest wall, where he pulled the shower curtain across and held his breath. There was nowhere else to go, and as he crouched there in the old plastic tub, Martin again understood the clumsiness of his life, of all lives. A hard padding of feet turned, heading directly toward him. The light clicked, shining on the bright colors of bath salts and decorative soaps. Martin stared, at the stained green wall tiles, the thick black shower curtain, and, in the silence that followed, seemed to almost hear the pounding of his own heartbeat.

How could he have been so unprofessional? So reckless? His head jerked, at a startling crack that might have been a gunshot—but was actually the plunk of the toilet seat. For more than a minute, urine gushed into the toilet water and a woman, not three feet away from him, mumbled obscenities.

The toilet flushed. Martin exhaled, and then held his breath again as the woman's voice rose to a violent shout: "You said you weren't going to do it again! Right? *Didn't* you? So why'd you let him do it? Why'd you fuck up, fuckhead!?"

She ran water in the sink. Martin felt the urge to scratch, up and down his arms and legs.

"Damn you! *Shit!* Stupid motherfucker!" she said, still standing there, and one of her feet stamped the floor twice.

The light snapped off.

Around an edge of the shower curtain Martin saw her walking back to the bedroom, a slender woman with kinky, fire-colored hair, wearing white underpants and nothing else. The bedroom door closed partway. Martin let his breath out again, in a long slow stream, like air from a balloon. He stepped from the tub and into the hallway, but the squeak of the floorboards made him stop.

Outside, a car door slammed.

Martin, wondering which way to go, stood still. A thunder of sound rolled up from the bedroom, became crashing guitars and drums that he recognized as Garth Brooks. He hurried out the back, running into the woods, leaving the screen window leaning against the house. Wayne would notice that, probably. And maybe the phantoms would come even closer. Maybe it was time to go to the police, he thought, leaping the stream, though his instincts told him not to, to find this story himself, to not trust anyone else with it. As he came up Sharktooth Lane again, along the sidewalk, Martin saw Wayne's Blazer back in the drive. It was 11:23 as he pulled his wagon out of the Publix lot, headed into the wind.

**37**

SHADOWS LENGTHENED, shapes grew together. As certain as he now felt that Wayne Vaughn was responsible for killing Rudolph Reed, Martin wondered how it could be proved. Police had found no blood at the scene other than Reed's. There had been no skin under the victim's fingernails, as there often is in physical altercations. A vacuum of the body turned up no hairs other than Reed's, and although there were several foreign fibers, they most likely came from clothes Wayne Vaughn had long since thrown away. The flashlight contained no fingerprints, no clues other than traces of Reed's own blood.

So how close was he, really?

Back at the office, Martin was buoyed by the sight of China's Mustang. There was a note on his desk: "See me. China." He looked at Hobart P. Lanahan's office, where Q. V. Robertson was arguing robustly, stabbing her finger toward him. Hobart squinted uncomfortably, as if she were a temporary blaze of sunlight. Thomas Persons had a miniature television on his desk and was listening through an earphone to an old movie Martin recognized as *High Noon*.

In Advertising, China greeted him with dark, wary eyes, and for a moment Martin saw the thing he craved, and sensed that he was becoming addicted again—to something he might never be able to control or understand. As she began to whisper, the other two advertising reps, seated in adjoining cubicles, seemed to be holding their breaths.

"Just a friendly warning," she said. "I overheard Little

Napoleon talking to Elmer this morning. He said he's afraid that you're, quote, spending too much time on too little story."

"Ah."

It wasn't surprising, somehow, that as he got closer to understanding things, he'd be pulled away. Martin signed out for two hours and he drove east, with the wind, down Avenue of the Royal Palms toward the city limits. Crossing the bridge into East Bananaville, the road suddenly dipped, and the air tasted dirty again. Middle-aged men sat on stoops with bottles in paper bags. Reformed dreamers. He drove past pawnshops, pool halls, windowless bars, boarded-up buildings. A block north of the Treasure Chest, he circled around and parked in a metered space across the street.

There was an unpleasant oniony smell in the air, which made Martin long for the citrus-scented breeze on the other side. A homeless man, huddled under a blanket in a doorway, watched him closely, from some part of the soul that would never be filled. Martin felt the sidewalk vibrate with rock music as he approached the club. Its name—Treasure Chest—was stenciled in black on a faded piece of red plywood, along with the figure of a naked woman, holding a highball glass and standing in what Martin assumed was a pirate's treasure chest. A long spring squeaked as he pulled the door.

It was dark inside, smelling of beer and perfume. A disco ball showered light across the room, on velvet drapes, plush red chairs and tables, stanchions, brass rails, wall mirrors: much posher than Martin would have imagined. When his eyes adjusted, the shapes at the tables became men, dressed in suits and ties mostly, with beer bottles or drink glasses in front of them. A statuesque woman with thick reddish blond hair was dancing naked onstage to a slow song by Bruce Springsteen, moving with easy sensuality. Her pubic hair was shaved into the shape of an exclamation mark.

Martin took a table against the wall, and watched. A black woman wearing pink hot pants and a halter came up the aisle with an urgent rhythm in her arms as if she were dancing. He ordered 7UP, and watched as she went back, buttocks bouncing, arms swinging side to side. In the darkness he began to see other people's eyes glancing sideways at him from the other tables as the dancer gyrated suggestively.

The waitress returned with his drink. Four dollars for a splash of 7UP, in a tiny hard-plastic cup packed with ice. As he tipped, Martin asked, as casually as he could, "Is Wayne in today?"

"No, honey, he'll be in tonight."

He waited appropriately, while she added his tip to the roll of bills she had in a pouch around her waist.

"How about Ginny?"

The bloodshot eyes widened, then squinched up. She tilted her huge head and made a scary face.

"Who do you think you're looking at?" she said.

Martin stared blankly.

She nodded, then, toward the stage, and slitted her eyes.

The dancer was taller, with thicker hair and a more muscular build, than the other Reeds. But as he watched, he saw something in the stubborn, downward set of the mouth that he recognized—though on her it seemed sultry whereas on the others it was sullen.

He sipped 7UP and melted ice, seeing her face like a hologram, which became a Reed only at certain angles, but then perfectly, for a few seconds. Eventually Ginny's eyes found Martin's, and she turned and danced, briefly, just for him, her periwinkle blue eyes sparkling, as she moved rhythmically to music by Snoop Doggy Dog. At one point she licked her lips lasciviously, and Martin tried to smile. She had wide, inviting eyes, he thought—it was not a stripper's face at all, though, more of a TV newscaster's. Turning away, she glanced at Martin over her shoulder—a practiced, meretricious move. Most of the men, including Martin, applauded boisterously as soon as the song ended.

AFTER HER SET, Ginny pulled a chair and sat with a table of four gray-haired businessmen, while the next dancer began her set.

This one was wide-hipped and small-breasted. She wore a leather fringe vest, holster, and toy pistol. Her smile, as she tried to stir some reaction, was oddly inappropriate. Most of the men seemed more interested in Ginny, as she made her way around the room, moving with a sexy swagger, a high-heeled confidence, mingling with the men as if this were the second part of her act.

When she reached Martin's table, Ginny pulled out a chair and sat, giving him an easy smile.

"Buy me a drink?"

"Sure."

"I haven't seen you here before," she said. "Do you work in town?"

Martin nodded.

"What sort of business?"

"Oh, publications. Printing and distribution of periodicals, primarily."

"Yeah?" She sniffed, her eyes creased. She seemed to be digesting what Martin had said, as the waitress came dance-walking up the aisle again.

"Flo," Ginny said, "just let me have a glass of Chardonnay."

"My name's Ginny," she said with a husky voice, so close that he felt her breath on the side of his face, smelled her perfume each time he breathed. "What's yours?"

"Martin."

"That's nice. Like Martin Sheen?"

"Similar, yeah."

They both looked for a moment at the woman onstage, Martin feeling the illusion of space in all the mirrors. The moving sign above the bar told which dancers were working this afternoon: Tiffany, Monica, Ginny, and FiFi.

"You're a very good dancer," Martin said, to make conversation.

"Yeah?" This seemed to amuse her. She took out a pack of Marlboros and set them on the table, smiling. "I enjoy it."

Martin nodded.

"Well. I like people." She slid out a cigarette and, sniffing, held it ready for Martin to light. As the match struck on a Treasure Chest matchbook and lifted toward her face, Martin saw the pores in her skin beneath the heavy makeup. "And, I guess, I like being the center of attention occasionally," she added, looking off reflectively, as if she were being interviewed. "I don't like it in the afternoon so much, working this shift. I'm just filling in today. But you get a charge out of it Friday and Saturday and stuff." She sniffed again. "Everybody's clapping, cheering you on, and the guys are giving you, like, ten- and twenty-dollar bills sometimes in their teeth—you know, you got to reach down through your crotch to get it, give 'em a good look." She grinned, her eyes moving with a quick, nervous energy, and took a sip of wine.

Another dancer came out of the velour-draped doorway behind them and walked past, trailing a harsh cloud of perfume. It was the flame-haired woman Martin had seen leaving Wayne Vaughn's bathroom.

Between songs he heard the hiss of the cigarette disintegrating as Ginny inhaled. Joan Osborne's "One of Us" was replaced by AC/DC's "Highway to Hell." Most of the men stared blankly toward the stage, as though watching a war documentary.

Martin was trying to think of something else to say, some means of keeping her here at the table, so that he could ask the questions he needed answered.

"That was my last set," she said, getting up. "Any interest in giving me a lift home?"

"Oh."

Martin shrugged, looking at his watch.

"I don't see why not."

 HE WAITED ON the street in front, blinking at the wild sky above the brick buildings. Ginny came out dressed in black jean cutoffs, a pink short top, and combat boots, carrying a matching pink gym bag. As they drove to her place in Martin's wagon, she told him, with an accent part pseudo-British, part hillbilly, that her name was Ginny Dean and that she had been brought up in California.

"I don't know. I had to get out, though, eventually."

"Is that right?"

"I mean—I'd like to be an actress, I suppose, ultimately. I did some acting out there, but it wasn't what I wanted. It can be a real trap, anyway," she said, sniffing. "If you're not getting the right kind of work."

Past shuttered stores and brick apartment houses, Martin glanced quickly, saw a played-out look in her eyes, and had to remind himself Ginny was only twenty-three years old. "The thing I like about dancing? Is the people you meet. Supposably, it's exploitive to the women and whatnot. I don't see anything exploitive about it. I think it's an opportunity to meet people and to make some money."

"Sure."

"You know, a lot of the men that come in will come in as groups, like the lawyers who come in after work sometimes? But in the daytime especially, this is like their secret world. A lot of them are very successful in town, have a wife and family and whatnot. And I just give them an extra little fantasy. I don't see anything wrong with that."

"Yeah."

Hispanic girls whizzed by on Rollerblades, cutting right in front of the wagon so Martin had to slam his brakes. Ginny didn't blink. She looked at him wet-eyed, and he sensed in that moment some distant, intangible glow, a fire that could only be fanned by other people. Palm trees whistled in the wind. The sidewalk stoops were becoming crowded as people emerged from the brightening rooms behind these brick facades, to taste the gathering energy of evening.

SHE LIVED IN a colonial-style apartment development called The Pelican, set behind clusters of palm trees. Across the street was a row of cheap, open-front eateries. The sky was silver and charcoal. Martin pulled to the curb and took a deep breath, again trying to figure some way to hold on to her.

As if his thoughts were word balloons, Ginny said, "You can come in if you'd like. Just for a bit." Martin cut the engine.

Three old black men sat on rusted metal chairs by the sidewalk, holding brown bags shaped around the necks of quart beer bottles. They nodded distantly at Martin and Ginny, more an acknowledgment that they were all sharing space on the planet than a real greeting.

The apartment was a small one-bedroom, cluttered with expensive-looking antiques and a hodgepodge of furniture—in the living room were bamboo chairs and glass tables, an early American–style sofa, another with a flowered chintz pattern, a butcher-block table, numerous blue and white porcelain objects, Oriental vases and Japanese screen paintings, bric-a-brac, four Tiffany-shaded lamps.

"Make yourself at home," Ginny said, stepping into the bedroom. "Relax."

"Sure. Thanks."

Martin sat on the sofa, smelling the cool, exhaust-tinged breeze through jalousied windows. A moment later, he smelled marijuana.

"Here."

Ginny came in, holding out a joint, keeping her eyes on him after he shook his head.

"No?" Ginny inhaled once more and then she strolled and she strutted, back and forth in front of Martin, cupping her breasts seductively as if she were still onstage, until she had smoked the joint down to a roach.

"Martin," she said, mashing it out in a Treasure Chest ashtray. Her wide eyes watched him—eyes that had seen too much, he sensed, that had no secret places to go. Martin looked down, and noticed that a green serpent was tattooed on her left ankle. "I'm going to go in here now and change for a minute. Okay? Why don't you try to relax, and loosen up a little bit?"

Martin looked at the clock: almost six-thirty. Her pocketbook was on the glass coffee table, and he slid across to open it: a string of four condoms, Tampax, hairbrush, a wad of something wrapped in tin foil, cigarettes, pack of Wrigley's, a wallet. He unsnapped the wallet, and riffled quickly through it, seeing a photo of Ginny in a bikini on a boat. Another of her in a golf cart, sitting on Bob Hope's lap. And one of Joshua Reed.

"We having fun yet?"

Ginny returned dressed in a mini baby blue terry cloth robe that almost matched the carpet. Without smiling, she sat next to Martin on the sofa, in Tiffany lamplight, and sniffed. Her right leg pressed against his left. The robe fell open slightly. He smelled fresh perfume.

"What's your pleasure?"

"Pardon?"

For a moment, Martin felt caught in the great disorder of her apartment—the expensive collection of things that seemed somehow put together wrong.

"Straight massage for thirty," she said. "Anything else, you have to suggest, and it's extra."

"I'm not—"

Her eyes seemed sad, reminding Martin for some reason of the Samuel Barber quartets Katie used to play on their living room stereo as she watched, drunkenly, rain in the cornfields. Instructively, Ginny placed her hand on Martin's, pulled it inside the robe, and rubbed over the soft flesh of her breasts. Martin let it go lifeless, not sure how to change course. He understood exactly how people drifted, how they got caught on currents of bad habits and were carried to places from which they couldn't get back.

"What's wrong?"

"Ginny." Martin cleared his throat. "What I really want to know is what went on between your father and Wayne Vaughn."

She stood, and with a disarming calmness strode across the room.

"And what is this?" she said, leaning against a huge Oriental vase, and tapping out a Marlboro. "Are you a cop or something?"

"No, I'm with the newspaper. My name's Martin Grant. I talked to you yesterday on the telephone."

She seemed uncertain now, her initial reaction transforming into something else; after a moment she sat back on the sofa, softening the lamplight a notch.

"I told you I don't do interviews, didn't I?" The blue eyes seemed to be thinking.

"Off the record," Martin said. "Nothing you say comes back to you, nothing goes in the paper. It's all background. An exchange between you and me, to help figure out what happened to your father."

Ginny thought about it, the mouth tugging downward in a Reed-like gesture, the eyes blinking. Finally she said, "This your massage?"

"Okay."

"Okay."

Martin sensed himself crossing another line; he wondered if he'd become addicted to this story the way he had been to alcohol. There were good addictions and bad ones, and some that seemed to fall in between. He thought of China Rinaldi, the way her taut muscles felt outside in the wind beside the swimming pool, and he wanted to leave this room, this apartment full of objects culled from a haphazard life, and not come back.

Martin reached into his pockets and pulled out what he had, counting the bills on the sofa.

"I've only got twenty-three dollars."

"Then we make it a quickie," she said, humorlessly. He saw a tamed hunger in the way she handled his money, turning the bills the same way, like a clerk in a convenience store. "Nothing I say leaves this room."

"Right."

Ginny Reed tucked the bills into her robe pocket, and a new self-assurance lit her eyes. There were freckles on the tops of her thighs. "I decide what questions I want to answer and which ones I don't?"

"Sure."

"And I decide when we stop."

"Any way you want it."

She sat back, again the guest on Martin's interview show, and began: She explained, without a trace of self-consciousness, how she had been dancing here for two months, but had been turning tricks for five years, mostly in the Los Angeles area. Turning tricks wasn't as much fun as dancing, she said, but it wasn't bad. Ninety percent of her customers were decent, lonely men. She enjoyed providing them with a fantasy.

"And so what's it like working for Wayne Vaughn?" Martin asked.

"Oh, it's all right." She seemed unsurprised by the question. "I don't really have much to do with him, actually. I just met him two months ago. He leaves me alone."

"What's he do?"

"Wayne? He's like the—I guess, the manager, or whatnot."

"The manager of the club."

"Yeah, supposably. Like—the night manager, weekend manager. Or whatever you want to call it."

"What did he have against your father?"

"Who? Wayne?" Her eyes narrowed uncertainly. "Nothing," she said, sniffing.

191

"No?"

"No, I mean—he told me once him and dad used to be friends and whatnot. In the church or something."

"And what happened?"

"What do you mean?"

"Between Wayne and your father?"

"I don't know. We didn't get into it."

"You don't see any reason Wayne might have been involved with his death."

"His death?" Her face seemed to register an emotion: genuine surprise. She reached for her purse, unwrapped a stick of gum, and folded it into her mouth. "No, uh-uh. Supposably, they were friends. I mean, I think I know who killed my father," she said, chewing loudly. "But I'm not ever going to say it. Because, I mean, I just know it could never be proved, right? So there's no sense in getting into anything." Martin looked away. He was starting to dislike Ginny, the grating affectedness of her voice, the mistaken arrogance in her eyes, the sloppy gum chewing, the way she said "supposably" instead of "supposedly." Yet he had to remain steady, had to keep the interview flowing.

"Do you know if Wayne ever drives a white pickup truck?"

Ginny nodded. "It's a company vehicle, or whatever. It's parked right out back behind the club. I mean, yeah, he drives that sometimes."

"I see." Martin crossed his legs casually, saw the red neon of the clam bar across the street: FRESH SEAFOOD. BEER. "Ginny, you went away four years ago, didn't you? You were pregnant when you left."

He saw the heat rise in her face.

"I'm not getting into that."

"The father of the child paid you to leave, I assume. It was someone here in town, wasn't it?" He added, "Someone prominent."

"Where'd you hear that?"

Martin shrugged. Car headlights swept the room. Sometimes interviewing was a sport; you faked and parried, took chances.

192

Ginny nervously pulled out a Marlboro. As Martin lit it, a distracted look crossed her face. Martin shook out the match.

"I mean—I was given some money, yeah. To have it taken care of. And told to make sure he didn't ever hear from me again." She smiled crookedly at something, lifted her head and elegantly exhaled the smoke. "That was the end of it. It was, like, I mean, decent money. But that's it. It's over with."

"How'd you meet this person?"

"How do I meet anybody? I was an escort for him. For about two weeks, you know, that's all. Ten days of it in Honolulu. On business, supposably."

"A convention?"

"Maybe."

Martin watched her smoking, comfortable inside herself again.

"A Realtors' convention," he guessed.

"Maybe." She watched his eyes as she smoked, her jaw tightening. There was something inaccessible about Ginny Reed; he couldn't imagine her having close friends. "He never knew who I really was and I didn't see any reason to tell him. I told him a story. It was just between me and him and it was all very discreet. I provide people with fantasies."

Martin let her smoke.

"You didn't get the abortion, though, did you?" he asked.

"I'm not getting into it."

"Was the businessman Joey Keen?"

"I'm not getting into it." She tried to remain expressionless, but for a brief moment the lips curled, as if she were about to cry.

Martin watched as she slowly tapped ashes into a large glass ashtray.

"I guess I'm surprised," he said, "that you didn't get the abortion."

"Yeah, well, don't be," she said, and sniffed. Her eyes moistened, studying the cigarette at the end of her outstretched arm. And then Martin sensed something begin to slowly—and then much more quickly—break apart inside her. "I don't know. It was like. For the first time, I had something, or whatever. That's what I thought. It felt like success was inside me, you know? This thing my father'd dreamed about for all his life but never knew how to get. Well, I felt I had it and I was only eighteen years old." An unpleasantly self-satisfied look soaked her eyes.

"Is that what your father dreamed about?" he asked skeptically.

"Oh, who knows? Who knows anything? All I know is I'm okay. I like my life right now. I do the same thing the town does, in a manner of speaking, I provide a fantasy for people."

Martin looked out at the lights of traffic as Ginny began the lengthy procedure of mashing out her three-quarter-smoked cigarette.

"So, off the record, what'd you tell your parents?"

She shook her head once, still pushing at the dead cigarette. "Nothing. I mean—I came back and my mother took me in. End of story. I just told them it was someone I met in a bar. Which is true. I came back and we had the baby up in Coconut. My father was a fucking wreck, as you can imagine, but he always threw himself into his work, you know. Trying to save the world."

"So Keen never knew he had a son living under the same roof as Rudolph Reed?"

"I'm not getting into that." Ginny stood, pulling the cord on her bathrobe. "I'm going to have to cut this off. I really don't care to talk about it anymore." She looked uncertainly toward the kitchen, and added, "You want a beer or anything?"

Martin almost said yes. He watched her open the refrigerator, pull out a Budweiser, and twist off the top. He knew exactly how the bubbles felt in her nose, how the foam tasted on her tongue.

"Here's the thing," she said, stepping around a bronze Buddha and porcelain vase. "About a week before my dad died—this is ironic, I admit, and I felt sort of bad, because he was a good person, or whatever—I did lose my cool with him. He was telling me he wanted me to come back and be part of the family and all this crap, he was going to get out of politics, not run again, and be a better father. And I thought, well, okay, but isn't it just a little bit late? So we were arguing, and I came out and told him who the father was. Which maybe I shouldn't have." She took a long drink of beer, looking uncomfortably for a moment at what she had done. "I mean—I didn't mention it to anyone in four years. And so, of course, he freaked. And I think he wanted to confront this person who was the father."

"I see." Martin tried to frown sympathetically. So the thing Reed had found out had nothing to do with Bananaland Park, as Cora Carlson implied. The thing he'd found out had to do with his daughter's illegitimate son. Gazing out, he saw a new sharpness in the neon, the colored lights on the palms, the beams of headlights.

"Why did you leave Joshua there, then?"

"I just wasn't ready, I don't know." She sniffed, pulling the bathrobe tight around her as if she were cold. "I've had some screwed-up periods in my life where I, like, OD'd and different stuff or whatever. I'm okay now, more or less." She smiled, sadly, her eyes no longer able to meet his. "I legally changed my name to Dean, you know, when I was in California."

"Is that right?"

"Oh, yeah. Yeah," she said, and slowly drank Budweiser. Her self-absorption, the lack of accountability, made Martin want, for just a moment, to slap her. "Yeah, I used it as a stage name. I just wanted to be someone other than 'one of the Reeds' or 'the Reed girl' or whatever. Joshua's the only reason I came back."

"Sammy does an admirable job keeping things together over there," Martin said. "She sure could use some help."

Ginny seemed not to have heard. "Someday," she said, "I hope very soon, I'm going to get it together and take Joshua and do my own thing. That's why I came back the last time. I just don't know that I can pull it off at the moment. But he's mine, wherever he lives." She looked to the window, and her big eyes seemed to brighten briefly with tears.

"Why don't you confront Joey Keen?" Martin said. "God knows he's got enough to pay child support."

"I don't want that. I mean—I'm not interested in the whole thing, him denying it, doing blood tests, being in the newspapers."

"Of course, he wouldn't do that," Martin said sharply. "How could he afford to? With the elections coming up, Lodge McCloud grooming him to be mayor. He'd more likely just pay you off."

Martin's words didn't seem to register. "No. Joshua's mine," she said, her face settling into an exasperating stubbornness. "The father's gone, it's not even an issue who the father is. I know what happened, and I know he's mine. Someday I'm going to take him somewhere."

Martin sighed, nodding, looking at all the disconnected things she'd collected in five years as an adult, as she reached complacently for the pack of Marlboros again.

It didn't feel right, somehow, to just walk away, leaving her there. A part of him wanted to help, to show her a pathway, to give her something that would lead her out. He knew, though, that people were glued together, however delicately, by their own quirky senses of who they were, and that there was only so much anyone else could do to really change another person.

He shook her hand and walked into a strange misty darkness, tasting steamed seafood in the wind as traffic whisked back and forth and the tops of the palms whipped invisibly overhead. As Martin climbed into his car, the phantoms seemed right with him, it was as if he had come too close to this Big Story, and now couldn't get home. As he drove over the tree-lined bridge back into Bananaville, the town's dark, tree-shrouded, narrow lanes seemed to be tunnels, lonely passageways to private places. He couldn't taste promise in the wind anymore.

CHINA SURPRISED him with two homemade pizzas—one piled with pineapple, peppers, onions, and anchovies, the other plain, as the munchkins preferred. The four of them ate off of tray tables on the patio in the wind, trying to decide what China would

196

do once she left the paper. Jody favored a move to Africa, which was where her grandmother lived. Jamie wanted her to work at Disney World.

Enjoying the thick Sicilian crust, the hot crunch of cheese and onions as he chewed, Martin stopped thinking about Ginny Reed. He thought instead of China Rinaldi, and her interesting problem, the fact that she hadn't planned her future and didn't believe much in plans, anyway. Where she was going, Martin might go, too. He felt this new craving, the place in China's eyes that took him in, and kept him there.

They talked about it until after one o'clock, then fell asleep with the windows open, the lifted shade-pulls knocking on the frames in the wind. He woke once and, turning over, heard a distant foghorn, tasted the bittersweet night flowers in a cooler air, and realized that he knew—almost—everything he needed to know about what had happened to Rudolph Reed. Through the window he stared at the moon's glow, the shaking tree branches, and distant lightning, as China snored softly beside him. He saw, later, a flash through another window, and peaceful white flames burning in the night. Martin pulled his thoughts, his consciousness, up through the windows of sleep and dream and saw—sitting in the bed, staring through a clear pane—what had happened: The first floor of the house he was renting from Pete Fudd had blown up.

**39** FIREFIGHTERS WEARING yellow coats with phosphorescent orange-red stripes, and gray helmets, moved in a surrealistic sweep of flashing red light outside the old Fudd place, carrying hoses and axes and fire extinguishers. The flames had been doused with foam and dry chemicals, but smoke still billowed from downstairs doors and windows, drifting in the wind like a thin gauze into the trees and across the moon. Martin stood in the street, with China and the munchkins, staring numbly at where the wall had come apart, exposing splintered two-by-four beams and plasterboard.

"Smell that gas?" one of the firemen said, coming over, smelling of smoke and rubber and chewing gum. "You got a gas line explosion. Blew up your heater. Must not have had an inspector here in a while. Anyway, it's a hell of a lucky thing no one was in the house."

"It is."

Martin nodded, knowing. Knowing that it hadn't been an accidental explosion; that Wayne Vaughn was somehow responsible. And knowing that China and her children were now a part of his life and he had just taken them this close to being killed. Neighbors from nearby streets were gathered out front, many dressed in slippers and robes, witnesses to this event, this piece of news at the end of Coconut Lane. The scene seemed slightly unreal to Martin, like a life-sized movie. He looked up at the stars, night-lights of his childhood, the constellations he'd pondered through the panes of an Iowa window long, long ago.

Peter Fudd parked his long black Cadillac in the center of the street and jogged over. He was dressed in loose-fitting Hawaiian-print pajamas, a safari hat, and huarache sandals.

"Martin, thank God you're okay!" he said, grabbing him and roughly patting his back, as if Martin were his young son. "My God! Look at that! I had my scanner turned off and just got the call from the fire chief or I'd have been here sooner. My God, will you look at that. That damn fire inspector! I had him in the house not four weeks ago! Checked everything. Pressure regulators, relay transformers, everything checked out."

"It's a hell of a mess, isn't it?"

"My God."

The breeze was cool and dewy and mixed unpleasantly with the smoke. There was nothing, really, to see, just a ruined house. Eventually people returned to their own homes, and a clear silver light began to replace the darkness, to shape the trees.

Martin walked into the house with Pete Fudd and one of the fire investigators, to assess the damage. As they stood in the foamy, still-smoldering charred wood and ashes—some of which had once been Martin's books and bookcase—he saw pieces of the exploded gas heater.

"Joseph, Mary, and Jesus!" Pete Fudd said, looking at both of them, his jowly cheeks reddening.

Martin couldn't tell if his reaction was fully genuine; he had never seen, or imagined, Peter Fudd angry.

"That's a new heater, too! believe it or not. What type of products are we dealing with? My God! I can't believe this."

Martin noticed among the debris a molten piece of a Pepsi bottle. And he suspected then just what had happened. A gas heater, he knew, could easily be rigged to blow up: If someone cut the line from the safety control switch to the thermostat, the gas valve would open when the pilot light went out, and a small spark could cause an explosion. The spark—the start of this fire—probably came from a tossed Pepsi bottle filled with gasoline and a wick. Martin didn't drink Pepsi.

**40** IN THE MORNING, a thick smell of scorched wood carried on the breezes through China's bedroom window, and pieces of ash hung like stray snowflakes in the air as Martin stepped outside. In the full glare of day, the charred house had taken on an eerie presence, silhouetted against the blue sky with sunlight streaming through pieces of roof and rafters, falling on blackened furniture, while wind creaked and whistled in the ghostly spaces.

There was a fire inspector's car in front, but no sign of anyone inside. Martin ducked under the tape to have another look, stepping through the soot and broken glass, not sure what he might find. The explosion had blown away the southeast corner of the house, including the bedroom, directly overhead. Parts of the kitchen, though, in the northwest corner, were still nearly intact: The box of Cherrios on the counter appeared ready for a cereal bowl and sprinkling of milk. Would Wayne Vaughn actually have done something like this? Was he so worried about Martin's story that he would have tried to kill him? Something about it just didn't ring true.

On his way back up the gravel drive, Martin absently opened his mailbox, and was surprised to find a letter inside, with a return address from Hamlet, Iowa. The schoolgirl-style scrawl was unmistakable. More good news: a copy of Katie's divorce papers. Martin looked into the woods, up at the sky, and didn't recognize anything. The charred house whistled. Even though he had been trying to accept what had happened, Katie's easy way about the breakup stung like a deep wound. He had grown comfortable with her on the plains of Iowa during all those years—with the rhythms of their life, the pitch of her voice, and the peculiar grace of her body; her schedules, her smells, and, later, their evenings of drinking in front of the TV, until both had passed out. Her life had become mixed with his, intricately and intimately, and he felt sometimes as if a large piece of himself were missing now. There was something romantic about starting over again, but it could never fill the space of someone you lived with for fourteen years.

He was still thinking about it at noontime, staring at Spanish moss in the live oaks along the river, when his telephone rang and a vaguely familiar voice said, "Grant. What were you doing sniffing around the harbor for?"

"Pardon?"

"I understand you were looking at my boat. Down to the harbor. Something I can do for you?"

"Excuse me?" Martin meaninglessly switched the telephone to his other ear. "Who is this?" he added, realizing it could only be one person.

"Archie Duval. What were you expecting to find down there?"

"Nothing. No, I just wanted to talk with you."

"Yeah?"

Martin listened as he breathed heavily into the phone several times.

"About the Reed case."

"Okay. What about it?"

"Your being brought in for questioning. Uh. The flashlight in your truck?"

There was a long pause during which Archie's breathing sounded nearly like snoring. "Okay. So. What—are you trying to do some kind of exposé or something?"

"Not really. Just trying to tie up loose ends."

"Okay." He coughed once into the phone. "You going to be there at two o'clock?"

"Here? I expect to."

"Okay. Feel like going for a drive?"

"Pardon me?"

"What I said."

"Going for a drive?"

As much as Martin wanted to talk with Archie Duval, the idea of "going for a drive" had an ominous ring to it.

"I would like to talk with you."

"Okay. You free at two o'clock?"

"I expect to be."

"Okay. Walk up Riverside to that rise in the road. Where the clearing is? I'll pick you up there at two o'clock, sharp. Just make sure you don't tell nobody what you're doing, okay? Don't mention me to nobody. All right? See you then."

Martin replaced the receiver and looked at Hobart in his office, with all the framed pictures of his blond family. He watched the copy desk editors laughing about something on television, saw Thomas Persons carefully applying black polish to one of his shoes. The newsroom seemed so safe, compared to what really went on in the world.

MARTIN SAT ON the back deck with China, beneath Spanish moss and the purple, star-shaped flowers of banana magnolias. Her dark eyes came closer, speaking to him; China was all he felt connected to anymore, and her stare held him, kept him interested, though it still contained languages he didn't understand.

"You don't think it was an accident," she said, her fingers twisting among his.

"No. It wasn't. It's a long, involved story, and I want to tell it to you. I want to tell you everything I know," he said. "I want you to know everything I do."

"Okay."

Martin watched her eyes, saw the brown-green sparkles, the places her thoughts went. He pointed, as an anhinga spread its wings above the water. At five minutes to two, he asked her, "What do you know about Archie Duval? Anything?"

"Archie?" She seemed amused.

"Do you know him?"

"Sure. Who doesn't know him? He's a good old boy. A little overbearing at times, but harmless."

"Is he?"

"Oh, sure. You know." It was her turn now to watch Martin. "I think he feels like he—like it's his responsibility to in some way police the fricking town. You know, looking out for his late uncle's interests and all that."

"His late uncle."

"Was the mayor here. Long time ago. He sees himself as part of that old guard, I think, and has a pretty inflated sense of what his role is. He considers himself a—what's the word? There's a word for it."

Martin guessed, wildly. "Vigilante?"

"Vigilante. He's not polished enough to get into politics himself, but all the politicians know him and sort of put up with him. A few people—like the state attorney?—can't stand the sight of him. But most people don't take him all that seriously. They let him do his thing."

Martin and China both looked into the warm, darkening currents of the approaching storm, feeling comfortable out there, waiting for things. Martin saw a flash of heat lightning in the western sky, tasted sulfur in the wind.

AT TWELVE MINUTES PAST TWO, a black Rolls-Royce Silver Cloud with mirrored windows pulled to a stop at the rise on Riverside Drive. The passenger door came open and Martin saw the bulky figure of Archie Duval behind the wheel, dressed in loose-fitting jeans, a wrinkled T-shirt, and fedora hat. The car was at least fifteen years old, Martin guessed, as he got in, and needed a tune-up.

Archie tipped his hat, then pressed down on the accelerator. There were dozens of what seemed to be tiny spaghetti sauce spots on his T-shirt.

"I understand you had a close call last night." He grinned.

"Yeah. I did."

"What do you think happened?"

"Gas leak, one of the firefighters said."

"Yeah? That what you think?"

"Not really."

Archie smiled a long, ambiguous smile and the flesh around his eyes and cheeks molded into waxlike creases. When at last it faded, his face seemed like two slabs, lifeless pieces of pale meat. They drove on in near silence, deep into the swamplands of Coconut Creek Preserve, past long hammocks of pine and cypress and miles of swaying saw grass. Archie whistled occasionally—always the same tune, which Martin finally recognized as Roger Miller's "King of the Road"—but only grunted at each of Martin's attempts to make conversation. He seemed at ease with the silence, with his own private thoughts, as many people are who live alone for a long time. At length, he turned onto an incredibly narrow gravel road, and the car rocked over potholes for several minutes toward its end.

"This here," he said, stopping among the pines and cypress. "They call this Duval Creek. It was named for my family." He lowered his window and took a deep, satisfied breath. "I used to come down here all the time as a kid, hunt and fish. I still come back here every once in a while. Just to be by myself."

He hawked and then spit into the swamp apple trees. "You said you had some questions you wanted to ask. What about?"

"I'm curious—you were taken in for questioning about the flashlight, and then released. How do you feel about that?"

He was grinning again, with a confidence that reminded Martin for a moment of early Marlon Brando.

"How am I supposed to feel? They were doing their job. They felt obligated to follow up on a tip they got. How can I be angry about that? But, see, here's the thing: I got a thorn in my side right now, Martin. I got a certain weakness that a few people are very aware of. This guy—this state attorney—he's been trying to get something on me for quite some time." His eyes scanned the swamps with an animal-like steeliness. "He's kind of a pretty boy, from up north. You ever met him?"

"Who?"

"The state attorney. He's convinced that because I don't have a nine-to-five job, well, I must be doing some sort of nasty business out here. I make him nervous, that's all it is, and he's been dying to get a case on me. A lot of people know that, see."

Martin remembered the brief exchange between Nellie and Archie Duval at the Paradise Club. *He needs to know anything, just have him give me a call.*

"So that puts me in a sort of vulnerable position. Which is one of the reasons the flashlight ended up in my truck."

"What are the others?"

"The others?" Archie's face squinted, as if the sun had suddenly flared up through the cypress trees. "Well, I mean, it would also neatly wrap up this Rudolph Reed case. And see, I'm not one of those who thinks it's all going to blow over. I *did* think that. But I'm not so sure anymore."

Martin studied his pale, lifeless features, waiting for him to say more. He was a simple man, Martin sensed, who liked to figure things out on his own.

"Do you know who put the flashlight in your truck?" Martin asked.

"Sure. I know who put it there." A smile warily edged his lips.

"Why can't you go to the police with it?"

The dark eyes slipped away. It was sunless but humid and the wind blew a taste of tree bark and swamp water. "I'll tell you— what the thing is, Martin: I follow these guys, I try to make it my business to know what's going on in this town. And I had a pretty good idea what was going down with Reed. Okay? Before it happened, after it happened. I knew where the players were, and it was—everything seemed to be going one way, okay? And then out of the blue this flashlight turns up in my truck." He was shaking his head, frowning again, his face becoming shiny with sweat. "That was another way. And this fire last night? That's another way, too. So, what I'm starting to think is this: Something's coming unraveled somewhere, somebody's getting nervous. And I just want to make sure you know everything that's going down before you get into any more trouble by looking at the wrong things."

"Wrong things."

"Yeah."

He was smiling vaguely. Martin felt the energies of the story swelling up again, out here in this thick tangle of cypress and mangrove and pond pines.

"You know there may have been a witness last night?" Archie said, speaking suddenly in a low, conspiratorial tone.

"A witness."

"Saw our boy in the vicinity of that fire? You heard that yet?"

"No."

"Well, check it out. That's what I'm hearing."

"Wayne Vaughn."

Archie's expression changed, the way a car shifts gears. "And see—that's where this thing started to get unraveled, Martin. Someone decided to get Wayne involved. Wayne's a guy—he'll never talk, he's perfect in a lot of ways. Loyal, hard worker, no scruples. But he's got one problem. He's got a big problem. A problem that makes him a liability."

"To who?"

Martin stared at the unrevealing slabs of Archie's face, as his eyes scanned the swamp.

"How did Wayne get involved in the first place?" he asked. "Who hired him?"

"See, that's the thing. That's the one part of this that you'd probably never get to on your own. And, of course, I'd never tell you—if it hadn't been for that flashlight." Martin waited, watching the trees. "That flashlight changed things a little bit for me."

"Wayne planted the flashlight to divert suspicion from him—was that the idea?"

"No. Uh-uh." Archie was staring somberly at the windshield. "No, it wasn't Wayne," he said quietly. "Wayne didn't have anything to do with planting that flashlight."

"He didn't."

"No." Archie turned his head to take the wind that gusted through the open window. "Here's the deal, Martin—and this is the part you can't repeat to no one, can't say where you heard it. Okay? It can't come back to me, and if it does, we're both going to be sorry."

"All right."

"All right?" Archie frowned through the windshield, as if he wasn't sure now if he wanted to say anything. "Every few weeks," he began, "Lodge McCloud comes into town and holds court— that's what they call it, holds court—at that big deck table down at the Paradise. Okay? I've sat at the table myself a couple times," he added, his voice seeming to choke with pride. "I was there beginning of December, last time he come down, and they were all talking about Rudolph Reed."

"Who is they?"

"That's something you got to figure out on your own. But— like I say, the topic that day was Reed, and what another four years would mean. Was there any way around it? That kind of thing. Just off-the-cuff type stuff, while they were eating enchiladas and hamburgers and drinking Coronas."

"How many were—"

"All right? And then they got to talking about what could be done to keep him from running. Was there anything that might be said that would persuade him not to run? You know, concerns about the kids, that kind of thing. So they kicked that around for a while. And then one of them at the table said something like, hell, he knew someone who could fix the problem for six or seven grand. And everybody sort of laughed. Or. No, I think the quote was something like, 'Hell, I could get Jersey to take care of it for six or seven grand.' "

"Which—"

"Okay? Now, here's the thing: Nothing went down that night, okay? But the next day—this is what I learned—the next day an envelope appeared in this individual's office or vehicle, I'm not sure which. It had the word 'Jersey' written on the outside and seven grand in cash inside."

Martin felt a shiver of recognition as wind shook the car and a blurred image slipped, for a moment, into perfect focus.

**41**

"It made for an interesting problem," Archie Duval continued. "Because there were five other people at
the table the night this conversation
took place. He knew the money had to
come from one of them. But he didn't
know which, so he had no way of giving it back. And he knew
he couldn't pocket it, because some of the people at that table—
they were important people in this town, okay? So the man was
in a dilemma."

"So what'd he do?"

"See, that's the thing."

Archie started the car, backing out through the tunnel of
trees.

"Maybe one day," he said, "you and I can come out here fishing."

Martin mmm-hmmm'd.

"Which of the people—?"

"See, the thing is. Watch it," he said, pushing Martin's head
so he could see where he was steering. "The thing is: Normally
none of this would really be my business." Back on the main road,
he shifted into drive. "But like I say, something's starting to come
unraveled. That flashlight was the first thing. And then that fire.
It tells me we got a desperate player out there."

"Wayne Vaughn."

"No. That's the thing: It's not Wayne Vaughn."

"Who?"

"The rest you got to figure, Martin," he said, his cheeks creas-
ing into a smile. "That's all I can say."

And then, as if all the trees within fifteen miles of Bananaville were filled with high-tech listening devices, Archie didn't say another word, only whistled into the wind, the same several notes—"Trailers for sale or rent . . ." Staring through the mirrored glass, Martin felt as if they were driving directly toward the Big Story now; he could see it becoming clearer in the distance as the road twisted among scrub pines and cypress and gray swamp waters. He suddenly felt that he understood what had happened, how Rudolph Reed had been killed. But he was missing one key puzzle piece.

AT THE RISE on Riverside Drive, Archie stopped and Martin stepped out. "Okay," he said, in the tone of a taxi cab driver. "Oh, and remember, Martin. What I said: If any of this ever comes back to me." Archie tugged down on the brim of his hat and pointed a pistol finger. Martin stared at his own reflection for a moment in the mirrored glass, and then Archie was gone.

As he walked down the hill, thinking things through, Martin was surprised to see Dale Bunch on the edge of the street. A cutting board of Brie cheese and apple slices rested on his lap.

"Archie Duval?" he said, nodding toward the pines.

"Yep."

How he knew, Martin couldn't guess. He watched as Dale Bunch sliced a piece of cheese from the wedge and ate half of it. "His uncle was once the mayor here, you know."

"Yes."

"Not a bad guy. I've had a few good talks with him."

They both stared up the road, as if Archie Duval were still there.

"It's interesting. Everybody in the Duval family—which goes way back, of course; in fact, they were one of the founding families, in a way, along with the Folsoms and McClouds—made a mark on this town, except for Archie. And I suspect, in some way, he's still trying to do that." His milky eyes found Martin's, as he pushed the other half of the cheese slice into his mouth. "What's up, my friend?"

"I don't know, actually."

Dale nodded, as if it were the answer he had expected. "We're all motivated by similar impulses, aren't we, Grant? The essential difference, then, becomes one of value. What is the value of being twenty-two years old, let's say. Of the mystical chemistry of love—which can never be adequately explained or gained through an act of the will. Of being able to walk." Slowly he cut and ate two slivers of cheese. Martin forced a smile when he looked again; as much as he had come to respect Dale Bunch, he felt tugged now by the story, by more immediate mysteries than those concerning the religion editor.

"I suppose we ought to fess up, though," Dale said, his tone lifting pleasantly.

"How's that?"

"One of our problems, you see, is this business we're in. No longer are we—as a country, I mean, now, as a people—much interested in the language of the spirit, other than in its most temporal, superficial manifestations. No, we're far more interested now in the news of the day, aren't we? And that's the business we perpetuate, Martin. As soon as what we do is digested, it is not news anymore, it's discarded, as unnecessary as an empty soda pop can. That's what we do here all week: We produce soda pop. And I suppose it's time we ought to fess up to it."

He pushed a piece of apple in his mouth and smiled, seeming to sense Martin's preoccupation, his edginess.

"Adopt the pace of nature, Emerson said. Her secret is patience."

Dale Bunch rolled himself back toward the building and his dark, book-filled office.


FROM A PAY PHONE on his way back to China's house, Martin called Nellie, surprised that she answered on the first ring. She had left a message at work about the fire, offering to help in any way she could. But this evening she seemed more interested in setting Martin up with Jocelyn.

"Who is it?" he asked.

"The gal in Records I told you about. We could probably even do something tonight, if you want."

"Tonight's not good."

"Cuz? I really, really think you ought to meet her. She's dark-haired, cute, sort of intellectual. I've got very good vibes about it."

"What have you heard about the murder?"

"Which murder?"

"Reed."

"Nothing." Her tone downshifted. "Why? What about it?"

"Hear anything about Wayne Vaughn?"

"Oh. Well. Yeah," she said. "He was brought in this afternoon."

"Was he?"

"Nothing to do with the murder, though. He was brought in on drug possession, distribution. And I hear there may be other charges pending."

"Like . . ."

"Well, I mean there's speculation. What the hell happened to you last night, anyway? Where were you when the house burned down?"

"Out."

"Yeah?"

"Listen," he said, turning toward the thick night traffic. "I'm curious. You go to the Paradise Club a lot, don't you?"

Nellie waited.

"You ever seen Lodge McCloud there?"

"Yes," she said, drawing out the word into two syllables.

"You've seen him there?"

"The Big Man?"

"Is that what they call him?"

"It's what I call him. He comes down once in a blue moon to

meet the movers and shakers. Has his own table."

"Have you seen him there recently?"

"Months ago, I guess. Or I don't know; maybe a few weeks."

"Who was with him?"

"Well." Nellie sighed deeply, with a hint of exasperation. "Joey Keen. He's always there. And, oh, I guess Jack Messer-smith—he's tight with them. My pal Archie, occasionally, just because he's old family."

"Who else?"

"Well." She exhaled dramatically. "I've seen Antonio DeRosse there once. And Cora Carlson. Not recently, but—"

"Okay."

"Why?"

"I don't know."

He saw a pair of women runners struggling against the wind, and realized that's what he wanted right now—to get the sweat pumping, the hormones flowing, to find his rhythm again.

"Let's have lunch."

"Sure."

"Good, I'll invite Jocelyn."

"I don't know."

"I tell you. I've got some really good vibes about this."

**42**

To Martin's surprise, nothing else happened that night. He woke several times in China's bed and stared at the stars, the outlines of trees, wondering who had planted the flashlight in Archie's truck and why. The winds faded with the new day, and in the bright afternoon, Martin went on a good, hard five-mile run. When he returned to the office to check his messages, there was a letter in his mailbox addressed to "M. Grant, Reporter." The name and newspaper address had been typed out on a manual typewriter with a weak ribbon—the kind Martin had used when he started in journalism. It was postmarked Coconut, although there was no return address.

He opened it in the parking lot beneath the swaying moss of a live oak: a message spelled in letters cut from magazines and glued to a sheet of paper. The sinister sort of message Martin hadn't seen since he was in grade school.

> FYI. SEVEN THOUSAND WAS PAID BY J.M. TO A. ON 12/10. CHECK BANK RECORDS.

J.M.
Jack Messersmith.
A.
Archie Duval.
Martin sat there, listening to the sound of palms clicking up high in the warm breeze. Something about it just wasn't right. Something about the letter was designed to steer him a certain way, to manipulate him. As he thought about it more and more,

the outlines of the story became clearer, like shapes in the dark after your eyes begin to adjust. For Martin, the path to the center of a mystery wasn't paved just by assembled details; it was also made by deciphering motivations. As he sat there, thinking about the old-fashioned cutout-style message, Martin began to sense there was only one person who would have done it. Or planted the flashlight in Archie's truck.

Martin parked down the road from Olive Avenue in a beach lot, and stared for several minutes at moonlight on the Gulf, breathing the bracing salt breezes. He locked the wagon and began to walk toward the city, wondering if anyone was following, watching him from the shuttered windows. Most of the shops and offices were closed at this hour, and the street had a disquieting emptiness.

Half a block past Olive, he turned in to a narrow brick alleyway. Along the east side of the alley were the backs of shops, all closed, and an old apartment building; on the west side a real estate office and Mario's Family Restaurant. Antonio DeRosse's office, he saw, was dark.

As he walked past a row of metal trash cans, Martin sensed that there was someone in the darkness; someone breathing, watching him from behind a window screen on the east side of the alleyway.

He circled back and walked past again—and this time he was certain. A pair of eyes, looking from one of the darkened apartments, as he went by. Martin kept walking, checking his watch as he came out to the front of the restaurant: 7:42.

One more line to cross.


Inside, a huge metal fan blew the greasy pizza air. There were several people at the counter, eating slices off of paper plates, their hair and napkins fluttering. They seemed, to Martin, as forlorn as the characters in Edward Hopper's *Nighthawks*. An elderly couple, dressed up as if returning from church, sat at a booth by the window, diligently twisting spaghetti around their forks. Pearl Jam played quietly through ceiling speakers.

Martin walked quickly down the side hallway toward the rest rooms, unnoticed by the teenage girls who were working the counter.

He reached into his pocket, seeing the hollow-wood door marked OFFICE at the end of the hallway. He extracted the "cheap lock" pick he'd bought years ago in Iowa and inserted it. Not strictly legal, of course, but Martin had established his own rules over the years. This was one: When he was certain a truth lay behind locked doors—figuratively or literally—and when there was no other way of getting inside, he allowed himself to pick the locks. So far, it hadn't gotten him in trouble.

Inside Antonio DeRosse's office, Martin closed and secured the door, then switched on the fluorescent ceiling light. He scanned the room, his heart beginning to thump with the urgency of what he was doing. There was a small stack of unopened mail on the desk, several soda cans in the trash. Otherwise the room looked the same as he remembered it. Martin reached toward the top wall shelf and found what he had come for: The envelope marked "Jersey" was still there. The envelope someone—Jack Messersmith? Cora Carlson? Archie Duval? Lodge McCloud?— had stuffed with seven thousand dollars shortly before Reed was killed.

Feeling something else, Martin reached up once more, and found a second envelope on the shelf. Similar straight-line Magic Marker lettering spelled out a different word.

A name.

Five letters.

"Grant."

A story he didn't know. As he stood there, staring at the envelope, Martin felt a shiver run through him. He had come too close—and would never get back to where he had been, to who he was. The doorknob jiggled. A key scratched the lock. Martin scrambled across the room, unlocked and opened the door to the alley. He slammed it shut and began to run—to sprint as fast as he could in the blowing night air, away from Antonio DeRosse, cutting west to the next alley and then continuing south, not looking back—sprinting through the dark narrow alleys as if all of the demons were right there at last, half a stride behind him— sprinting until he came to the sheltering darkness of the beach and collapsed in the sand, gasping at the sea breeze as surf scuffed over the sand and shells. He had come too close. And now Martin would have to live with what that meant. Try to.

MARTIN SLEPT FITFULLY beside China, waking and watching the wild treetops. He heard sounds in the woods and imagined they were footsteps, saw tree branches shift and sensed the wispy forces that controlled this town repositioning again. Trying to fall asleep, he held on to her as if otherwise what they had might escape and disappear before daylight returned. She was a good person, China Rinaldi, still searching for the right answers—better answers, perhaps, than he was chasing.

Dawn gave definition to the branches; 6:25, his clock said. It was the time that Rudolph Reed had left his house on Pineapple Lane, started up his station wagon, and driven to the beach to be killed. Martin fell back into sleep, into delicious dreams about paddling to Sicily with China and the munchkins, about racing wild horses on a remote African beach. When he woke again, sunlight glared high in the oaks and there was a surreal stillness along Coconut Lane. It suddenly fit together: *Antonio DeRosse*. He had been the one at the table who could "get Jersey." It not only sounded like him, it made political sense—DeRosse needed the blessing of the powers that be. But they wanted it done cleanly, and it hadn't been. "Jersey" was a fiction, DeRosse's fantasy. Instead of going there, he had gone to Wayne Vaughn, an ex-con who had helped DeRosse get elected four years earlier, placing his campaign signs around town and removing those of the other candidates.

Somehow, the flashlight had come into DeRosse's possession and he had planted it in Archie's truck as a diversion. DeRosse had become nervous, worried that he might be found out. Which was also why he sent Martin the letter—trying to steer him toward Archie Duval and Jack Messersmith. To muddy the trail.

If the plan was "coming unraveled," as Archie said, it was because DeRosse had started to run scared.

Still, there was one other question he couldn't yet answer, one piece he didn't have: Who was ultimately responsible for what had happened? Who had delivered the envelopes?

IN THE NEWSROOM that morning, the only sound was clicking keyboards. There was a message on Martin's desk: "Antow Ross" had called.

Thomas Persons was eating a bowl of Froot Loops, staring intently at the back of the cereal box. Martin dialed, instantly recognizing the gruff voice that said, "Mario's."

"Antonio? This is Martin Grant."

"Grant? Hold on." He listened as DeRosse turned down a radio and told someone, "Just tell 'em we're not in'erested, would'ja? What do they think, we're fuckin' caterers?" He cleared his throat conspicuously. "Grant? Hold on a second." He heard a door close. "How you been, Martin? Listen. Martin? Is there anything dat you and me need to talk about?"

"Excuse me?"

"After d'deal last night: Is there anything you think we need to talk about?"

"I don't know what you mean."

"Okay." He cleared his throat again. Martin heard him scooting forward in his chair. "Martin? I have very good reason to believe dat you might've been here in my office last night, you follow?"

"Your office?"

"Yeah. Got anything to say about dat?" He waited, and Martin thought he heard a faint trembling in his breath, as if he were holding back some great reservoir of anger. "Okay? I'm calling out of—whaddaya call it?—a courtesy call, you follow? My wife says she walked in on someone last night. I have reason to believe it was you." He waited again; both men breathed into their receivers. "You seem a little tongue-tied dere, Martin. You want to think about it? You think about it. You have something to say, give me a call in d'next hour, you follow? I don't hear from you, I'm going down to police headquarters dis afternoon, you follow me? I intend to press charges. And—" his voice burst suddenly with a guttural anger "—I'll see that you never write another story in this town again. *Ever.* You follow?"

DeRosse hung up, and something in the abruptness of it joggled Martin's memory again. What he had seen as he emerged in a panic from DeRosse's office into the alleyway the night before: Dark eyes. Old eyes. A white-haired man, watching him through a window screen.


THE BANANAVILLE City Council that afternoon took a tour of an endangered mangrove forest—right by the stretch of beach where Rudolph Reed had been beaten to death. Martin used the opportunity to return to the alley behind Olive Avenue—to hunt the thing that was haunting him.

Walking through the alley's warm shadows, Martin felt a growing uneasiness; as he approached DeRosse's office, he remembered the sound of the doorknob jiggling, the key in the lock, his frantic run to the beach, fearing that DeRosse had seen him. But it was his wife: Had she actually seen him, or just heard the door close? Something in DeRosse's tone indicated he wasn't sure. Sunlight gleamed above the phone lines, fans spun in second-story windows, breeze rattled the loose tops of trash cans. Passing the old stucco apartments, Martin stopped, hearing it again: a heavy sound of breathing, coming from behind a dirty screen window. He moved closer, toward it, until he was right by the window, looking in at an unlit, dusty apartment: an old sagging bed, an antique chest of drawers, a coffee table. He twisted his head and saw them again: ancient-looking dark eyes, staring at him from an old bony face.

"Hi," Martin said.

222

The man didn't blink. He was seated in an armchair beside the window, dressed in a sleeveless T-shirt and suspenders, dark trousers. If not for the steady rasp of his breathing, he might have been dead.

Martin walked to the front of the apartment house, trying to think of how he would explain himself. Nothing good came to mind. He knocked several times on the door and waited. He put his ear against unit six. A chubby mailman wearing short pants frowned suspiciously at Martin as he crossed the street into the sunshine. Before turning to go, Martin rested his right hand on the knob. He twisted; to his surprise, the door opened.

The dark eyes by the window turned toward him. He was a very small man with thin white hair and a pink scalp, a narrow face. Settled features indicated to Martin that he had lived a life of contemplation and observation, not confrontation. Martin guessed he was eighty years old.

"I'm sorry," Martin said, standing there. "I didn't mean to walk in. I'm just . . ." He tried to think of a good story, but couldn't. The two men stared at one other, neither knowing what to say. "I just wanted to talk with you for a minute. I'm Martin Grant, a reporter. And—I just wondered if I could ask you a couple of questions."

As the man continued staring, Martin took a glance at the room: A box of Ritz crackers was on the dresser, along with a Bible and a book of food stamps; a dirty glass rested on a tray table beside the armchair, and a stack of *Reader's Digests* on the floor next to it. The air had a foul smell of old clothes. Martin fished a business card from his wallet, and tried to hand it to him, but the old man wouldn't take it.

"I'm working on a story," he said. "I only really need a couple of minutes."

As Martin continued to bumble through his explanation, the man's eyes softened slightly, and his lips began to move, as if he were warming them up to speak. At last, a small smile appeared.

"You say you want to ask me some questions."

"Yes."

"Why?"

"I guess I just have a sense that you could help me. That you might know some things that could help me."

"You do?" He looked at the dirty window, through which Martin had seen those dark eyes the night before, watching him. "I was about to go and get myself some dinner, though."

"I see," Martin said, not seeing. He rubbed his hands together, trying to think of what to say next.

"Unless you would like to pick up something. Bring it back. Then you could ask me your questions."

The man had a high creaky voice, which Martin suspected he didn't use much.

"I could do that," Martin said.

The man nodded once and smiled thinly, looking away. "You were the one who was in there last night, weren't you?" he said, and his eyes glowed uneasily with a remembered image. Martin could almost see what he was thinking: He was wondering if Martin had come here to hurt him.

"Listen," he said. "Whatever you want, I'll go out and get. If you'll just take a couple of minutes to talk with me."

"Do you want me to make a list?"

"A list?"

He nodded toward the dresser. "There's paper in the top drawer. And should be a pen. My name is Franklin Clearwater."

Franklin wrote his list in what seemed to be slow motion. Several times he stopped and looked up, as if hearing an interesting sound outside. At last he folded the paper in half and handed it to Martin. He watched attentively as Martin read it.

"One (1) bottle Old Grand-Dad bourbon. One (1) Domino's Pizza with everything."

As HE ENTERED the liquor store, Martin imagined it was a hardware store. The product he emerged with was a hammer, a tool. It was not the key to his dark rooms, the source of negative happiness he had lived in for years. It was a product.

Forty minutes later, he was back at the apartment. Franklin had opened a second tray table and had set both with Dixie cups, paper plates, and neatly folded stretches of toilet paper.

Martin sat on an edge of the bed and watched as Franklin, with trembling hands, filled his Dixie cup with bourbon and took a slow, satisfied sip. He was a talkative man, it turned out, once he got started. As they ate, Martin learned that Franklin had worked most of his life in a textile mill, and had come down from Ohio a year ago after his daughter tried to move him to a retirement home.

"I placed an ad in the paper. Said I needed a ride south." He sipped his bourbon and smiled. "Yep. I get by fine being by myself. Just fine." His hands shook badly as he lifted the pizza to his mouth, spilling anchovies and black olives onto the floor. "Yep. Don't need anybody. Do just fine here by myself. It suits me just fine."

He had an endearing way of pushing out his lower lip when he said things like this, and Martin was beginning to like Franklin Clearwater. "It's sort of funny, though. You say you want to ask me questions." He was pouring more Old Grand-Dad into his cup. The booze seemed to give a warmth to his eyes, which were finally beginning to connect with Martin's; it seemed to add color to his face. "I've seen a lot of things," he said. "Yep. No one's ever thought to ask me about any of them. No one's asked me much of anything for years," he said, chuckling. "So I don't feel obligated to say anything."

"But you've seen things," Martin said, casually.

"Course. All my life."

Martin sipped tap water. The sky had clouded over and he realized there was no lamp in Franklin's room. The ceiling fixture, he saw, had no bulbs.

"Yep. Spend my time right here by the window mostly, reading, or just thinking about things. Suits me just fine. Picked a pretty interesting place to live, it turns out."

"Is it?" Martin looked out the window, saw the doorway to Antonio DeRosse's office. "What sorts of things have you seen?"

"Oh. Just a lot of things. Want that last one?"

"Go ahead."

Franklin's trembling hands reached for the final piece of pizza. He had already eaten five of the eight slices.

"Yep. That man over there, for instance," he said, nodding in the wrong direction.

"Antonio DeRosse?"

"Man who owns the restaurant, yep. Before I say anything about him, though, I'm going to want to ask you to do me a favor."

"What?"

"I'm going to have to ask you to close that window. Because I've heard him say some things in his office that he probably didn't want anyone to hear. There's just something about how sound carries in an alleyway."

Martin got up and pulled down the window, seeing that the lights were off in DeRosse's office.

Without a breeze, the smell of bourbon seemed to soak the air. Martin tasted it with each breath. "That's interesting," he said, sitting back on the bed. "What sorts of things have you heard him say?"

"Oh, he talks about many different things. With many different people. Yep." The toppings continued to dribble down his shirt and onto the floor. He finished eating and reached again for the bourbon bottle. "Of course, I can't tell you exactly what he's done. But I don't think it's all been—well, I guess you'd say—legal. You want to get me some more toilet paper?"

"Oh, sure."

Martin unrolled several yards of toilet paper from the bathroom spool. Franklin Clearwater messily wiped his hands with it.

"Yep. For instance, he had a number of arguments with a little man—man named Wayne. Wayne was over there once, I've seen him. Most of the time, I've only heard him talking to Wayne. On the telephone. Yep." His gaze settled easily on Martin; the lower lip pushed out. "I could tell you some stories about him, if you're interested. Here. Can you pour me another drink?"

Martin did. The deep smell of the bourbon stung his eyes, lifted deep into his nostrils.

"Like this one night. Yep. This one night, I heard him saying, 'Wayne, I can't talk about it on the telephone!' He must've said that five or six times that night. Each time his voice getting louder and louder." Franklin smiled. A shaky hand tipped more bourbon into his mouth. "And then another night. Another night, he lowers his voice—of course, I can still hear him—and he says, 'It's got to be done differently, Wayne. It's got to be an accident.'"

Martin pictured the gregarious Italian man saying it, and imagined what he must have meant. "Another night, I heard him saying, 'But the deal's not done, you follow?' He kept saying that."

The man seemed to be studying Martin all of a sudden, looking at him with knowing eyes. Martin checked his watch: 3:45.

"Listen, it so happens I have an appointment this afternoon. But I wonder if it would be okay for me to come back again for a few minutes this evening."

"Alone?"

"Alone."

Franklin picked at pieces of pepper and olive and anchovies. "Well. Yep. I don't see why not. You might want to bring another small bottle, though, if you do. This one we could share."

The pint of bourbon was nearly half finished, Martin saw as he got up. Outside, there seemed to be a dangerous excitement in the wind.

MARTIN SAT AT his terminal, staring through oaks at the rush of the river water, and wondering how he would prove this story. If he hadn't been so startled, if he had kept his wits, he might have taken the two envelopes from DeRosse's office. But that was evidence that was now surely gone. He had left both of them there on the desk.

Hobart P. Lanahan, talking on the telephone, whinnied loudly and repeatedly in his glass-enclosed office, a sound so similar to a horse it could have been one of Pete Fudd's sound effects tapes. Martin had never heard him make the sound before.

Q. V. Robertson put down her telephone receiver and stood. "Latest from NWS: The storm's breaking up offshore. Heavy winds and rains tonight, but no damage expected."

Martin nodded, though she wasn't speaking to—or looking at—anyone in particular. Thomas Persons whistled, looking up from the *Field & Stream* he had been reading.

An especially shrill neigh came from Hobart's office, and Q. V. looked sharply and disgustedly at Martin—as if she had just heard a deliberate sound of flatulence.

"Say," Martin said, holding the stare. "Q. V.? If I wanted to find Joey Keen. Right now. Where would I go?"

"Right now?" Q. V. moistened her lips; the eyes went somewhere else for a moment. "I guess at the downtown office. He's got the whole third floor there, and that's where he usually is in the afternoon if he isn't at home or doing one of his human potential tapes." She added, "But unless you're the mayor or Lodge

McCloud, his secretary's going to say he isn't in."

"He! He! He! He!" came the sound from Hobart's office. Martin realized, as he walked back outside, that it was Mayor "Gator" Gorman Hobart was talking with, speaking in a tone Martin had never heard him use with anyone else.

PIECES OF PALM fronds gusted across Banana Boulevard as Martin drove into the darkening air of downtown. At a crest in the road, he saw the whitecapped waters of the Gulf—and a ribbon of low rainclouds across the horizon.

Martin parked in a metered space across the street from the Keen Enterprises main office. He looked up at the smiling yellow and black bas-relief face on the marquee and sensed for the first time that Keen wasn't smiling so much as he was laughing— at all he'd achieved in the names of human potential and positive thinking.

Martin studied the mirrored-glass-front building. There was an exit in back, which might get him to Keen's office on the third floor. But he tried the door, and it was locked.

So Martin went in the front, stepping into a plush reception area that smelled of polished wood but reminded him of a bank lobby.

"Joey Keen, please," he said to the coquettish receptionist.

She smiled, displaying beautiful teeth, but looked at his trousers; something about Martin's tone seemed to disagree with her.

"I'm sorry, sir," she said. "Mr. Keen is not in the building right now. May I ask who's calling?"

"Oh, no. That's okay." Martin whistled five notes and glanced about the room—dark paneling, burgundy carpet, Italian chairs, a gilt table with silver ewers, wrought-iron lamps. "No, I was wondering if you have any listings, uh, in Banana Estates. I saw Mr. Keen's commercial for it—where he says, 'Stop by today and see me.' "

"Oh." Her face brightened with a practiced congeniality. "Of course. One moment. Let me see if one of our sales associates is available to talk to you."

"Thank you." Martin checked his watch as she got up: 4:45. He pointed vaguely down the hallway. "I'm just going to use the rest room."

Martin walked past the rest rooms, though, found a stairway door at the end of the hall, and quickly climbed the two flights. He came out in another dark hallway, on the third floor.



KEEN'S PRIVATE secretary looked up as though Martin had a gun pointed at her.

HOPE GARRITY, her nameplate said.

"I'm here to see Joey Keen."

"I'm sorry, Mr. Keen isn't in the office today. Do you have an appointment?"

Just as she said it, though, Keen's voice rose from the next room. "Did you see in the paper today, this jackass Hennessey's whining again about the density? He's the one that wanted to open it up for Hayes and the town houses in the first place!"

Hope Garrity's efficient blue eyes never left Martin's. She continued looking as though she hadn't heard a thing. Martin, matching her stare, digested what he'd heard: Herbert Hennessey was president of Bananaville's largest citizens group, a retired steelworker from Pennsylvania. In Q. V.'s story this morning, he had spoken out against further high-rise development along the beach.

Keen came out, with a relaxed but supercilious strut, and set some papers on Hope Garrity's desk. His stance—and, it seemed, his personality—changed the instant he saw Martin.

"Well, hey!"

"Hey! Do you have a minute?"

"That's about all I do have," he said, widening his eyes. "Actually, we're closing a deal in the north end of the county in about—" he looked at his Rolex "—twenty-one minutes."

230

"Mind if I come in for just one minute, then?"

Martin rose and walked in without waiting for an answer, knowing that the only way to get close to Keen was to push past his check stations. His office overlooking Banana Boulevard had a hardwood floor and Chinese rug, an enormous Oriental desk flanked by Balinese teakwood chairs. As the two men sat, Martin imagined that everything successful about this town, its confidence and energies, seemed to be contained in Joey Keen.

"So. What can I do for you?" Joey Keen asked, with an edgy friendliness.

Martin leaned forward. "I'm just curious about a couple of things," he said, wanting mostly to see Keen's reaction when he posed his questions. "Off the record, of course. For example: I'm curious why you fired Wayne Vaughn from the property management arm of your business four years ago. This would have been two years, I guess, after the Coleman properties burned down."

"Fire who?"

"Wayne Vaughn."

He licked his lips once and checked his watch. "I'm not even sure who that is."

"That's not what I'm told."

Keen leaned back, sighing, the white Armani shirt opened two buttons to reveal dark tufts of chest hair. He stared for a moment at the chandelier above his desk, and a look of benevolence transformed the rugged features, as if he had slipped on a mask. The easy way his face worked seemed to Martin both fulsome and fascinating, a kind of magic.

"Look," he said, softly. "I know precisely what you're doing, Martin. I know what you're after. But you must remember: This is a very painful chapter for the town. And, I daresay, for the Reed family."

Martin felt his chest tighten for an instant. Keen's surface positively glittered, concealing the beasts that lived underneath.

"We've got elections here in five weeks. A lot of important issues are going to be out on the table, issues that in many ways will determine the future of this town." He looked to Martin, lids heavy, as if he were giving a speech and it was time to make eye contact. "And by all rights, it will be a good future. You know why? Because of the commitment this town has made to the freedom of opportunity." He carefully enunciated these last three words. "The freedom to do and be whoever you want.

"And at this point. There's been, what? Six weeks now of innuendo and speculation? I think we need to put this tragedy behind us and move on. We have to."

He stared with a confidence, a clarity, that seemed all-consuming, a utilitarian man, Martin thought, who made his living peddling illusions, whose blue, unblinking eyes saw the here and now with a lucidity the rest of us couldn't afford.

"In fact, at our Council work session yesterday—you didn't happen to be there, but Q. V. was and she reported on it quite accurately in the paper today—I made the suggestion that we name the bridge into town the Rudolph Reed Memorial Bridge." He touched his chin delicately. "The point is, what can we do to turn this horrible negative into a positive? That's what the town's about. And that's why it works."

"The town."

"Damn right, the town."

There was something in his voice—some faint, provincial quavering that made these platitudes sound sincere, a quality that Martin suspected could only come from self-persuasion.

"Did you know Wayne Vaughn was paid six thousand dollars several days before Rudolph Reed was killed?"

Keen laughed heartily—a buoyant, happy sound that made Martin want to join in.

"Lookit," he said, punching his index finger once on the desk. "I don't even know this boy, Wayne Vaughn. Are you talking about Cora's second husband? There's nothing whatsoever between us, never has been, never will be. Nothing." Smiling, he closed a folder on the desk, as if he'd just finished his business with Martin.

"What's interesting," Martin said, "is that six thousand or

seven thousand dollars—whatever it was—as I understand it, wasn't supposed to go to Wayne at all. It was actually supposed to go to 'Jersey,' " Martin said. "Right?"

Joey Keen's expression seemed to cave in for a second—it was as if Martin had transformed before his eyes from a man into a llama. But just as quickly, the metamorphosis seemed the first stage of some elaborate magic trick; a new grin lifted the corners of his mouth.

"The interesting thing—to me, now," Martin added, "is that the evidence is sitting right there in the man's office, right there out in the open. There's one envelope marked 'Jersey,' another marked 'Grant.' It really surprised me."

"Now you've lost me," he said, with retreating eyes and a guarded tone. "You care to explain that?"

"Actually, maybe I ought to be going," Martin said, checking his watch. He began to stand and then, as if remembering something, sat back down. "Oh, one other thing. I almost forgot." He gazed at Joey Keen, who was hunched over his desk now, watching Martin, seeing him, perhaps, for the first time. "One other question: I wonder what you can tell me about Ginny Dean. Or Ginny Reed—whichever you prefer."

All the life seemed to drain from Joey Keen's face. His eyes became blue marbles. He blinked several times before finally trying a smile.

"I don't know the name."

"My understanding," Martin said, "is Reed was going to confront you about it on the day he died."

"Look, pal." He leaned across the desk, shaking a threatening finger at Martin. "I don't know what you're fishing for, or what you've heard. But you're way off base, Jack. Way off. And what I think is that you better get your goddamn facts straight in a hurry, because you're about to go off the tracks. And I'm no fan of train wrecks." He suppressed his vituperative anger by looking at the Rolex. A pleasant, almost serene look came briefly into his face as he gazed out the window. "The minute's up, anyway."

234

"Yes, it is." Martin, standing, had his answer. As he walked back out, past a nervous receptionist in the front lobby, he felt certain that Joey Keen knew exactly what had happened to Rudolph Reed. And suspected that the reason for his elusiveness was that in real life Joey Keen wasn't quite as slick as he seemed to be, and didn't want anyone to know that. He was like the mirrored windows on Archie's Rolls-Royce: reflecting the town as he moved through it, but never allowing others to see who was really driving.

4 8

MARTIN STOOD ON the sidewalk below the laughing likeness of Joey Keen, seeing that thunderclouds had come closer in the past twenty minutes. The air smelled pleasantly of baked bread. Martin had made some mistakes, perhaps, letting his instincts take him too close to things that weren't part of the story Peter Fudd wanted, and he now felt profoundly vulnerable. Yet Joey Keen had revealed to him in those disoriented moments something essential, a piece of the Big Story Martin had been chasing most of his life.

The voice telling him this, though, didn't sound like his own. Martin recognized it later, caught in traffic a mile from the office. What he heard seemed more an echo—his father's voice, perhaps. His own was saying something else, as clearly as the look in Joey Keen's blue eyes: to quit, to stop moving against the currents of this self-willed town, before it was too late.

Instead, Martin pulled into an ABC liquor store. He came out with a pint of Old Grand-Dad.

THERE WAS A meeting that evening of the East Bananaville Liaison Drug Task Force. As chairman of the committee, Antonio DeRosse would be in East Bananaville for the seven-thirty meeting. As he drove back toward Olive Avenue, Martin wondered what it would be like to sit in the dark with Franklin Clearwater, drinking bourbon with him and watching the alleyway.

But when he reached the apartment house, there was no answer to his knocks. Martin called his name several times and listened at the door, but Franklin didn't seem to be home. He tried the knob: locked.

Martin was walking back to his car when he heard a sound behind him and turned.

Franklin's old eyes seemed disoriented, staring at him from the doorway.

"Is that Martin?"

"Yes. Are you okay?"

"Come on in, Martin," he said, and shuffled across the room to his chair. His voice was different, husky and slurred. "Sorry. I must've taken a nap."

Before closing the door, Martin saw that there were two empty pint bottles on the floor by his bed—Old Grand-Dad and something else, a cheap whiskey. The impression of the bedspread was still on the side of his face and there was a trail of drool down his chin. Martin had forgotten what alcohol could do to you when you weren't able to stop. As he set the bottle of bourbon on Franklin's tray table, and watched him reach for the Dixie cup, Martin disliked who he was and what he was doing. He wanted to go back out into the gathering evening, to travel somewhere with China and her children, to let this story go.

"You're a good man," Franklin said, pouring with trembling hands. His face changed with the first several sips; his lips glistened, his features became oiled. "Yep. I'd offer to beat you in checkers. Only I don't think we have enough light left to finish a game."

"Why don't you have a light in here?"

"Never saw the need for one. Get by just fine without one. Yep. Mostly I enjoy sitting here looking out the window."

"You might fall some night and hurt yourself."

"Don't see how I would. Nope. Never seen the need for one."

Darkness began to fill the air. Lightning bugs blinked in the sky. Franklin Clearwater didn't seem interested in talking tonight. He seemed content to stare out the window, sipping bourbon. As nighttime settled in his room, the sound of the electric clock motor became louder, the smells of dirty clothes and whiskey grew stronger. Periodically there was a sound of bourbon splashing in his Dixie cup, and the smack of Franklin's lips as he drank. "Yep," he said, several times. The whiskey smell permeated Martin's spirit, reached to places he hadn't been for months, places he shouldn't be.

He saw Franklin's dark eyes watching him and realized that there was no exit from this room other than the one he'd come in through. For a while Martin wondered if this might be part of some trap. He had begun to understand how conspiracies worked, how wide their nets could stretch. Across the room, Franklin's thin lips seemed to be smiling.

At 7:27 headlights glared bouncily up the alley. A van stopped directly behind Mario's Family Restaurant. The motor died, the lights went out.

"That'd be Cora," Franklin said.

"Cora?"

"Yep."

"Cora Carlson?"

"Don't know her last name. Gonzalez, it might be. She delivers fresh vegetables, odd hours of the day. Peppers and tomatoes. What you get on your pizzas come from Cora. Yep," he said.

They didn't talk again. The van's headlights burned on Franklin's narrow face as it pulled away. Several inches of bourbon were already gone. Martin heard footsteps in the alley, but they didn't sound as if they were coming closer; they stayed the same distance and then stopped. A few minutes later, Martin heard the doorknob jiggle. His heart skipped in the darkness until he realized it was the apartment next door. His imagination became as active as a child's in the cool bourbon-scented breeze.

A vertical bar of light suddenly appeared in Antonio DeRosse's office. It spread quickly over the desk and across the room. A figure stood briefly framed by the inside doorway. Then the door closed.

"Who was that?" Martin whispered.

"Hmm? What—didn't get a look," Franklin said, slurring his words again.

"Someone in the office."

"Nope. Didn't get a look."

But the man apparently hadn't gone in the office—there was no further sign of light or movement. More than an hour passed. Martin felt his mouth dry up. He thought about China's eyes, wondered about her husband, why he had abused her.

"There," said Franklin.

"What?"

"There," he said, nodding. "Yep. There comes someone." Martin leaned forward as Franklin reached again for the bourbon bottle. A figure was moving up the alleyway toward them, dressed in dark clothes. As the shadows cast by the moon and streetlights overlapped, it became several people—a woman, then a man. He stopped before the alley-side door, reached in his pocket, and inserted a key. DeRosse? No, this was someone smaller.

The door opened and the man stepped in. There was a sudden flash, an explosion. Martin saw a familiar figure rise to full height in the doorway, standing over the crumpled man. It took him a long time to say anything. But when he did speak, Antonio DeRosse's voice seemed to be filled with terror and disbelief.

"Joey!?" he said.

**49** THE RAIN FINALLY began after midnight, first as a soundless spattering in the oak leaves outside China's bedroom. Then, as wind misted through the screen, there was a sudden drumming and Martin pulled the window down, propped his elbow, and watched, as sheets of rain swirled in the streetlights. China slept, but Martin couldn't stop his thoughts long enough to join her, couldn't stop the scenes, as regular as rainwater in the drains, replaying like newsreel loops: Joey Keen's limp form being lifted into an ambulance, as Antonio DeRosse sobbed over and over, "I'm sorry, Joey, I had no idea it was you."

No—he had expected someone else. He had shot him twice in the chest, to kill, not to wound, because he had expected someone else. He had expected Martin Grant, not Joey Keen. And although Martin had traveled to the heart of a Big Story now, it wasn't a place he wanted to be, or to go again. Justice has a strange way of playing itself out, and Martin knew that what had happened this night in the alley behind Mario's Family Restaurant meant Bananaville would be different in the morning. It would never again be the same, and maybe that was good. But whatever happened, he was a part of it; he had caused something to occur that he hadn't expected.

Martin was still watching as the sky lightened in drizzle, the trees took form again through the squares of window screen, glittering wetly with stray spiderwebs.

The still windy air smelled of earth and dew and wet gutters, but became a green mist with the sunshine, a clean beauty that returned on schedule each morning, oblivious to what happened overnight.

THE AFTERNOON WAS warm and sunny. As the four of them drove through a flood of violet and golden light along the coast road, the Big Story seemed to evaporate like a mirage. Martin steered inland, between thickets of thatch palm and mangrove and swamp hardwoods, to Highway 428, a road once called the Shangri-La Expressway. It was flanked now by the vestiges of old ambitions: A boarded-up "Sam's Luncheonette." Part of a brick building that might have once been a souvenir shop. The outlines of a miniature golf course in gravel and weeds. "Seashell City," a cinder-block building with broken-out windows. They were going to try again, Nellie had said, the two-lane would be widened to four, and there would follow shopping centers and housing developments, Burger Kings and Wendy's, 7-Elevens and Wal-Marts.

Uncle Otis's tiny pink building stood alone in a distant patch of swamp. It was like coming upon a childhood dream many years later and realizing the absurd size it had once assumed in his imagination. Martin turned in to the overgrown gravel lot and parked, staring at paint-chipped letters that spelled PARADISE GIFTS in one window. Beyond it, he was struck by the beauty of the sunlight dancing on the swampland. All that land left to develop, land the Spanish explorers had tromped through expecting to find gold and riches; in a sense, Martin thought, it was an illusion that survived. He felt China's hair in a soft breeze against his arm, and knew that he had something valuable again.

"That was my uncle Otis's shop," he said, feeling almost ashamed. "It's the reason, I suppose, that I'm down here."

China squinched up her face, not getting it. The munchkins hung over the front seat, both with deepening, disappointed frowns; their little mouths chewed gum.

"What happened to him?" Jamie said.

"No one knows." Martin sighed, and China turned to see his eyes, to be with him.

"What is it?" she said.

It wasn't the building that made Martin frown, it was the sign in front. FOR SALE OR LEASE, it read. COMMERCIAL PROPERTY. GREAT START-UP OPPORTUNITY. CALL JOEY KEEN.

# EPILOGUE

THE STORM PASSED and the story settled. In the March elections, Joey Keen was the top vote-getter, even though he remained in critical condition at Coconut County Community Hospital. Antonio DeRosse withdrew from the race "for personal reasons." Second place in the election was Jack Messersmith, followed by Rudolph Reed Jr., whose victory party drew hundreds to Newt's Sunoco.

Martin and China moved outside the city limits, to a house on the coast, a mile down the road from where Reed was killed.

Franklin Clearwater, Joyce Jasper, and several others gave testimony linking the death of Rudolph Reed to Wayne Vaughn and DeRosse. In April both were charged with first-degree murder. Rumors circulated—and still circulate—about the crime, but no evidence has ever come forth to implicate Joey Keen or Lodge McCloud.

One week after the election, the City Council acted on Keen's suggestion and named the bridge into town the Rudolph Reed Memorial Bridge.

Bananaville continued to prosper. And as he drove home each night, crossing the border back into soberer climates, Martin Grant came to know that what people had tried to tell him when he first came down was, in a sense, true: It was the town that had killed Rudolph Reed.